THE GATHERING
AT GETHSEMANE

THE GATHERING
AT GETHSEMANE

EDWARD ALEXANDER MULRAINE

E. A. Raine Publishing
White Plains, New York

© 2009 by Edward Mulraine

Published in the United States by E.A. Raine Publishing

www.earainepublishing.com

Library of Congress Cataloging-in-Publication Data

Mulraine, Edward.

The gathering at gethsemane.

This book is a work of fiction. Names, characters, places and incidents either are products of the author's imagination or are used fictitiously. Any resemblance to actual events or locales or persons living or dead is entirely coincidental.

Book Design by Randy Williams

Scripture taken from the Holy Bible, New International Version, Copyright 1973, 1978, 1984 International Bible Society. Used by permission of Zondervan Bible Publishers.

"Beat Street Breakdown" by Reggie Griffin and Melvin Glover, Published by Hargreen Music (BMI), Administered by Next Decade Entertainment, Inc., All Rights reserved. Used by Permission.

"One Mic" by Nas and Chucky Thompson, © 2001 Universal Music – Z Tunes Llc., Ill Will Music, Inc., and Sony/ATV Songs Llc. All Rights for Ill Will Music, Inc. Administered by Universal Music – Z Tunes Llc., (ASCAP), Used by Permission. All Rights Reserved.

"U Saved Me" by R. Kelly © 2004 Universal Music – Z Songs and R. Kelly Publ., Inc.

All rights administered by Universal Music – Z Songs (BMI), Used By Permission. All Rights Reserved.

"Paid In Full" by Eric B. And Rakim © 1987 Universal – Songs of PolyGram Int., Inc. and Robert Hill, All rights administered by Universal – Songs of PolyGram Int., Inc. (BMI), Used by Permission. All Rights Reserved.

Song Lyrics Cleared By:
The Law Office of Hakim Mulraine, LLC
33 William Street, Suite 3E
Mount Vernon, NY 105552
Phone: 914-548-4630
Fax: 914-371-7259
hmulrainelaw@gmail.com

ISBN 978-0-578-00375-7

Dedicated to my wife, the love of my life, Monifa,
My children who bring me life—Shandira,
Adia, Malachi—
And to all those who struggle with the Word of life, most
sincere Christians

Additional Thanks:
Dr. W. Franklyn Richardson, Pastor
Prof. Jimmy Jones, Manhattanville College
Dr. Cornel West, Princeton University
Dr. Derrick Bell, Visiting Professor, NYU School
of Law
Rodney J. Reynolds, Publisher, American
Legacy Magazine

The loving support of Unity Baptist Tabernacle

"When I want to do good, evil is right there with me."
Romans 7:21 (NIV)

Contents

Author's Note

The War Within

Although this book is appropriately and artistically considered a novel, it does not shy away from confronting serious political and cultural issues in our society and the personal issues of those in the ministry.

The Gathering at Gethsemane is a story of the battle between flesh and spirit. The spirit seeks to do God's will, while the flesh desires the will of the world, which many times is contrary to the kingdom of God. This battle is scripturally referenced with Jesus at Gethsemane and the war he encounters as a result of having to die for humanity. In his agony, Jesus asked the Father to "take this cup away from me," a strong indication that the flesh did not want to bear the punishment that came with death. However, Jesus shows victory in the spirit when he pronounces, "Not my will but thou will be done." Once the spirit overthrows the flesh, then God's glory is realized.

If Jesus struggled with the flesh, who are we to escape it? We are all walking around with some type of war within that interferes with our sincere relationship to God. The battle within can be described as moral versus immoral, good opposing evil, or simply as right rejecting wrong. *The Gathering at Gethsemane* shows how preachers can be so brilliant at executing the word of

God, confronting the complex matters in the world and strengthening the souls of the weak, yet suffer from personal issues within. The war between flesh and spirit can create multiple personalities that lead to deviant behavior and mental instability. Jesus warned the disciples at Gethsemane that the "spirit is willing but the flesh is weak."

All political and cultural issues raised in this book are examined from a biblical perspective. While some of the issues are global, such as the war in Iraq, some are national, such as the death penalty in the United States and the devastation of Hurricane Katrina. Other issues—responsibility, reparations, racism, discrimination, black-on-black violence, male-female relations, for example—directly impact the African American community, yet ultimately affect all people.

The actions of this book's characters reveal the inner conflicts created by these issues as they wrestle their lust, hate, arrogance, depression, desperation, guilt, homosexuality, confusion, fear, and lying.

The book is referenced with quotes from writers such as William Shakespeare, John Calvin, Dietrich Bonhoeffer, John Adams, Henry David Thoreau, Frederick Douglass, James Cone, Howard Thurman, and Ralph Ellison.

Although the book focuses on the clergy, there is no doubt that politicians, business executives, professors, and every man and woman, whether Christian, Jew, Muslim or other, can relate to: *the war within.*

1

A Chosen People

1 Peter 2:9

I was part of the chosen before I knew it myself
It was all part of God's plan, before I took my first breath
For what I didn't know until I came of my age
To start my life's journey somewhat with a rage
Outraged at the cage of the condition I'm in
Poverty, no money, just livin' in sin
So I worked my way out just to look at my life
Better than presidents who had shut out the light
I climbed out the barrel, through rhyming and such
Never knew, such a talent, until God gave me his touch
But it wasn't only me I was concerned about
I turned around, looked down, and my peeps were drowning in
    doubt
So the life line I had, I threw it out to others
So hopefully, through mercy, we'll find promise together
I guess being part of the chosen that's what you do
Spread love, help others, like God helped you

Dear Rev. James G. Parks:
Congratulations!

The word shocked me with a current stronger than electricity. In my delirious state I found enough awareness to read the next sentence in the letter: *You have been selected to participate in our annual Gathering at Gethsemane conference.*

I paused, shocked again. The unexpectedness of such a blessing startled me to the point of incapacitation. I could not finish reading the letter before pausing and absorbing its impact. How had I been chosen? I didn't quite know, but the letter I had in my hand confirmed my acceptance to one of the most highly respected, spiritually connected and intellectually referenced conferences in the nation.

The conference's history read like a *Who's Who* of religious genius in the publishing, preaching, and academic circles in the country, if not the world. Its main objective was to examine the ability of the clergy to deal with the cultural, political, and spiritual issues of humanity amid their own personal issues. In other words, it tested whether clergy could bear the cross of the world and their own cross at the same time. And this is why it was called Gathering at Gethsemane, because Jesus had to make a decision to endure his pains and the sins of the world at a place called Gethsemane.

At Gethsemane, Jesus' personality seemed a dichotomy, shifting from agony and fear to courage and confrontation. The war between flesh and spirit was pronounced. Jesus told the disciples at Gethsemane, "The spirit is willing but the flesh is weak." When the flesh is weak, we fall to temptation and can't handle life's confrontations. When the spirit is willing, we overcome both temptation and life's tribulations. Jesus, filled with agony at Gethsemane, begged the Father to "take this cup away from me." The cup referred to Jesus' dying a brutal death for humanity, to reconcile us back to the Father in eternity. The spirit that Jesus was given, however, was willing to overcome agony and confront the enemy so that life could be given impunity. After prayerful consideration, Jesus rendered to God a show of victory over agony and a spirit willingness over flesh weakness by stating, "Not my will but thy will be done." Jesus was able to both prevail over his agony and fight for the life of humanity. And just as Jesus battled with the body, so too are we subjected to the same dichotomy, particularly the clergy. As German theologian Dietrich Bonhoeffer wrote, "Discipleship costs."

Being asked to participate in the conference was no small feat, for even to be considered required an excellence not only in academics but in character. The conference board mandated references, from past vocations to present occupations. A highly respected colleague of mine at the university had suggested I apply to the conference. He even wrote a great recommendation for me. After the eleventh interview, the board told me it not only was impressed with my intellectual and pastoral abilities but also with my intriguing personality.

I had decided to go on sabbatical after suffering a number of breakdowns due to the overwhelming pressure of the pastorship at the church and professorship at the university. Being in the clergy and academic field for fifteen years, I had begun to swallow the problems of the world and the personalities of the people I was assisting. My colleagues in ministry, my family, and even my physician agreed it would be a good break from ministry and the university to apply to this exclusive conference while on sabbatical—especially since this year the Gethsemane Board was focusing on the intellectual and emotional state of the African American clergy and community.

In previous years it had focused on other faith communities. Last year it received a lot of attention by examining the lives of Catholic priests. It found that being celibate led some priests to an inner conflict that unconsciously transformed them from priests to pedophiles. The year before that, the board had focused on Jewish rabbis. The awesome demands of their religious laws in opposition to the American culture drove some of them to deviant behavior, causing them to live double lives— rabbi by day and sexual pariah by night. So now the African

American community, with its various issues, had to be confronted, and I, along with others, had been chosen to take up that task.

But still I couldn't figure out why I had been chosen. Many who applied were easily the most competent in their fields, as well as confident in their souls. They're acknowledged as scholars, full of velocity and wisdom. Their epistemology is profound, their theology is world renowned, and their presence is revered. Many had been in the ministry and academics much longer than I. I was sure their minds were ready and their souls eager for a conference such as this to break away from the stress and the strain of their jobs. For such people not to be chosen must have been a blow to their egos and careers.

As for me, I had not even thought of being accepted, I just submitted my application, believing that there is a God, and waited upon the Lord. And I guess, to a large extent, my belief in God and willingness to wait upon the Lord were the reasons I was chosen.

I think it was John Calvin who set forth the notion of predestination, the belief that God in his sovereignty has already chosen a few to be favored in God's kingdom, while others are predestined to damnation. Such a theological perspective of the selection process has always baffled me, for it has, in its doctrine, made God out to be prejudiced and capricious, rather than loving and merciful. The doctrine has debased the fullness of God as Lord and savior. For if he is Lord and savior, how can he predestine some to damnation and others to salvation when he is Lord and savior of *all*?

As 1 Timothy 2:4 states, God "wants all men to be saved and to come to a knowledge of the truth." Or as 2 Peter 3:9 says, God "is patient with you, not wanting anyone to perish, but everyone to come to repentance." Or my favorite, which sums it up best in Romans 5:12–20: As in Adam all died but in Christ all shall be made alive. The word "all" is a significant factor in all three books because it shows God's unbiased love and mercy for all his creation. God is a savior of all, not a few. For a few to be chosen in advance takes away from the merits of grace and diminishes the worth of faith that God has given to all. Paul makes this distinction by stating in Ephesians 1:4, "For he chose us in him before the creation of the world to be holy and blameless in his sight."

Even the faithful are excluded from the Calvinistic theological equation. And that—complete faithfulness—is the key to entering heaven and every earthly blessing. I believe the reason many are not accepted is because of their incomplete application of faithfulness, not because of predestination calculations as set forth by Calvinistic reasoning. Many, I suspect, did not complete the application. To complete the application, one must confess and believe.

Romans 10:9 says, "that if you confess with your mouth, 'Jesus is Lord,' and believe in your heart that God raised him from the dead, you will be saved." Many confess with their mouths but don't believe in their hearts. It's an incomplete submission of the application, so therefore one is chosen but not accepted. God does not accept incomplete applications; he wants full submission. In order to truly submit the application, confession and believing must unite. Mouth and heart must engage. Then, "You will be saved."

To refute such a limited notion as John Calvin's, I can justly acknowledge by faith that God had already given me the position, and the conference was catching up with God's giving—just as God had already chosen me, but I had to accept his calling. Like the fourth-century monk and theologian Pelagius said, predestination can be interpreted as a foreknowledge of God's knowing who will accept and who will reject, rather than a plan by God that many will be rejected and not accepted.

To be chosen is to accept the offer that God has given—to enter the doors that God has opened—which means that we are all chosen; we're just not all accepting the calling.

A lot of people believe those in the ministry choose their path, as if it was a career rather than a calling. And although there are many false prophets among us, those of us who have struggled with this ministry know that we don't choose this path; the path chooses us. We either accept or reject the calling. And sometimes, no matter how hard we try, we can't run or hide. Jonah tried to run and hide from God, but God trapped him and held him in a big fish until he accepted his calling. If we in the clergy had known what we were getting ourselves into, many of us would have run—or at least hidden a little longer. After all, who wants the burden of God as your boss, people as your responsibility, and the devil as your number one adversary? Who *wouldn't* break down? But who can run or hide from God? As the psalmist David puts it, "If I go up to the heavens, you are there; if I make my bed in the depths, you are there." When God calls, you must answer, regardless of your flaws and apprehensions, which is what I and many others—gratefully yet fearfully, like Jesus at Gethsemane—did.

After my analytical debate with myself, I found strength to continue reading the letter, but I could not keep the tears from my eyes.

As you know, this is one of the nation's most exclusive and premier conferences. Its selection process is unusually rigorous, and its membership is highly restricted. Many applied but only a few were accepted. It is the combination of thought-provoking cerebral erudition on the theological questioning of the American experience, coupled with analytical pragmatics, which qualifies recipients as incomparably competent and proficient prognosticators for this session. One must possess the finest in theological thematics, academic schematics, scholarly credentials, intellectual diversity, clear articulation, doctrinal discourse, exceptional pastoral or professional leadership and, of course, charitable contribution to and unquestioning love for humanity.

There also must be a reverberating distinction in the style and voice of the members we select to participate. No two personalities are ever the same. Most of all, the testimonial and personal weaving of the biblical, sociopolitical, and cultural issues of the day give the conference participant uninterrupted access to the table.

Each session is recorded for analysis and future publication.

The conference is about engaging in dialogue and examining multiple national and personal issues as they pertain to the secular community in relation to the general biblical society. The goal is to determine, through questioning and examining, whether those in the faith community can successfully lift and carry the concerns of the world in the midst of their own issues. For this is Jesus at Gethsemane, wrestling with his body to bring divinity to humanity and humanity to victory.

The conference will be at the Princeton Research Center. Upon your arrival that evening, dinner will be served in your room, as will be breakfast the next morning. This is to prevent any premature introductions and discussions prior to our session. You will be escorted at 10 a.m. to the research center for official greetings and introduction before our discussions begin.

Again, congratulations on being one of the chosen!
Yours in truth and power,
Rev. Dr. Edward Brent King, PhD
Coordinator and Moderator

I put the letter down, then picked it back up. With fear and trembling but also with great excitement and anticipation, I ran to my wife and said, "I've been chosen!"

She looked me up and down, gave me a cup, and said, "So have I."

2

From History to Testimony

Acts 22:1–10

But now I learned to earn 'cause I'm righteous
I feel great, so maybe I might just
Search for a nine to five,
And if I thrive, then maybe I'll stay alive

—"Paid in Full" by Erik B. and Rakim

G ood morning. I hope you all had a wonderful sleep and breakfast." The voice was a familiar one—Rev. Dr. Edward Brent King, known to many as "Rev. Ed," had been a fixture on the conference scene for the past ten years. Although highly studious and well educated, he was a naturally gifted man. He was young in body and spirit, and his energy complemented his image. One might assume he was in his mid-forties, but he looked like a kid out of college. Many older, more rigid scholars dismissed him, based on his appearance, and he would humble himself to their foolish and uninformed assumptions and bow to their authority. But as soon as he spoke, they fell prey to his dominion. He possessed the resonant, clarion voice of reason. He pronounced each syllable, and his words sang like those of a young Martin Luther King Jr. The words slid from his tongue like a river flows to a lake, an undisturbed flow from mind to mouth. And the air received it with joy. He made speaking look easy. The transmission of his words was flawless. Listening was like hearing a jazz tune with an awesome blend of instruments. But greater than his speech was his mind. The knowledge and logic he possessed could make others envious, even covetous. The way he worked words, glazed sentences, and recited stories made him renowned in literary and theological circles.

I had been escorted to the conference room before the others and had set up a place card by each seat around the conference table. I intentionally positioned myself across from Rev. Ed and in view of every participant. The chairs were positioned around a long rectangular table; all faced the moderator at the head. The research center had placed us in one of its smaller yet architecturally grand rooms. It was on the top floor, which was why it was called the "upper room." Quite a coincidence to the conference. All doors were sealed to prevent interruption and interference. The two guards which had escorted me stood outside the room and were able to look in through a small window in the door. Their presence assured no one entered in without permission. And because these were ministers—black ministers—we were given a soundproof room to ensure the conference did not interrupt other guests. The soundproofing also kept unauthorized people from listening to the dialogue, which was to be published, so the recording and handling of the information had to be protected.

When Rev. Ed saw that everyone was seated, he abruptly started the meeting. "I see that most of us are present, but two of our scheduled conference participants will not be on time due to unexpected conflicts with a funeral and a wedding. And we all know that those are two events you cannot miss in the church."

"Ain't that right," said a man with a deep voice who was seated to the left of Rev. Ed. Everyone's gaze immediately gravitated toward him, and some people nodded their heads in agreement.

"However," Rev. Ed continued, "they will be joining us later today. I hope sooner than later. What I would like to do first is introduce myself. I'm Edward Brent King—"

"We already know who you are, for Christsakes!" the same man scoffed. "The whole world knows who you are." The place card in front of the man read Rev. Dr. William Taylor. Everyone smirked in response to his remark.

Rev. Ed, always witty but humble, quickly responded, "They know *of* me, Rev. Taylor, just as I know of you, but I want you to know *about* me from me. My goal for the end of this session is that we will all know more about each other." The old man with his huge almost bubble like face, quickly turned his head in the other direction. Rev. Ed continued as if determined not to waste any time. "I'm also known as Rev. Ed for short. After I give a little synopsis of my professional and personal vitae, I will briefly introduce each of you, based upon the information you sent and my personal connection with those whom I've met before."

"Why don't you allow us to introduce ourselves?" Rev. Taylor asked, and I wondered if he was intentionally trying to disrupt the outlined order. The man I knew as Bishop Samuel, with his smooth baritone voice, tried to hush Rev. Taylor, but Rev. Taylor persisted.

Rev. Ed nodded but looked annoyed as he said, "Let's see how that works," probably to avoid unnecessary commotion. "As you know and I know, we don't really get to know each other from what is written about us but rather by what is hidden. So I will leave most of the introduction and persuasion to your revelations of yourselves during the conference. By the end of the session, I hope we will get to the hidden intelligence and feelings of each conference attendee."

"Sounds good," a woman said, nodding as if she were ready to begin.

"My format for introduction will be historical and testimonial," Rev. Ed said. "The historical will be a biographical detailing of my educational, residential, and familial background." He had rhythm. "And the testimonial will be my spiritual conversion, ministerial calling, and ecclesiastical mission. Paul gives us a good example of how we are to tell our story."

Rev. Ed gave us his understanding first in connection with Paul the Apostle. Everyone was glued to his interpretation of the text. His format presented a theme that each of our presentations would reflect: that nothing should be without reference to the biblical text. That the way we would prove our theological and epistemological worth—and our faith, if we said we were people of faith— is by supporting our words with the word of God. And so Rev. Ed first shared his life with us, but he was also showing us his biblical knowledge. This was to set the tone for the rest of the conference.

"In the book of Acts," Rev. Ed continued with an easy flow, "the Bible speaks of Paul, who entered into Jerusalem and was seized by the Jews because of his rebellious actions, illegal teachings, and defilement of the holy city. Such disgrace to the Jews provoked their anger and their attempted assassination of Paul. The story goes that his arrival in Jerusalem aroused the whole city, whose inhabitants exacted revenge by beating Paul. News of the uprising and commotion reached the ear of the commander of the Roman troops, who quickly assembled soldiers to calm the crowd. Upon seeing the soldiers, the Jews and crowd immediately ceased their beating of Paul. The commander inquired of the purpose for flogging Paul, but because of the crowd's loud uproar, he couldn't hear a satisfactory answer. So the commander quickly summoned Paul to the barracks. But in the midst of the uproar, Paul made an abrupt request to the commander to speak to the crowd. The authorities permit Paul's request. Paul spoke to his tormentors in their language, which quickly quieted the crowd." The story flowed from Rev. Ed's mouth without pause or interruption. It was like he had memorized a script; he was poetic and knowledgeable. His voice was an escalating tenor that was waiting to hit its peak. I caught his essence and upon my introduction I was ready to propose a similar course.

"Paul offered the crowd a brief biographical sketch," Rev. Ed continued. "Paul stated, 'I am a Jew, born in Tarsus of Cilicia but brought up in this city, Jerusalem.' Then Paul said, 'I was thoroughly trained in the law of our fathers by Gamaliel.' Paul told the crowd how zealous he was for God, just as they were. He detailed his background, noting his past activities, including how he had persecuted the followers of Jesus, the Way. He told them how he had arrested Jesus' supporters and had thrown them in prison and exacted the greatest punishment upon their bodies. But suddenly, he shifted from history to testimony."

"I like the way you talk it, Doctor," Rev. Taylor's strong bass voice again interrupted. His face looking huger and more bubblier every time he spoke like he was hungry to get in on the conversation.

Rev. Ed just continued, without much acknowledgement. "Paul said it was about noon as he was nearing Damascus on his way to persecute and imprison Christ's followers. Suddenly, a bright light from heaven flashed around him. He fell to the ground and heard a voice call to him, using his former name, 'Saul, Saul! Why do you persecute me?' He then asked the question and answered it, all in one voice: 'Who are you, Lord?'

"The voice came back, 'I am Jesus of Nazareth, whom you are persecuting.' Those who were with Paul saw the light but did not understand the voice.

"In a quick response to the call and a surrender to the voice, Paul asked, 'What shall I do, Lord?' And the voice of Jesus said, 'Get up and go into the same place you were going in Damascus. And there you will be told what your assignment is.' After he met Jesus, Paul changed from being a persecutor to being a prognosticator."

"I like the way you broke that down," The compliment came from Bishop Samuel, whose baritone voice seem to give a pleasant interruption to the conference. "Thank you," replied Rev. Ed. "But my point is that I believe, just like Paul, that we all have a history that gives our ministry authenticity. It is the hermeneutical response to our pilgrimage. We should be willing to tell our history to validate our testimony. For it is our past that has brought us into our present relationship with crisis and Christ. Paul absorbed the legal lessons and practiced the persecutions with vigor and venom—until he met Jesus!"

Amens were blurted out and smiles were seen on most faces. Rev. Ed was now preaching our language.

"He was a persecutor—until he met Jesus," Rev. Ed repeated. "He was a murderer—until he met Jesus." Rev. Ed paused for dramatic effect. His voice singing and his hands slightly waving. We all automatically paused with his vibe. Then he said, "Or should I say, until Jesus met him. Jesus met him and accosted him on the road. Hit him with a blinding light! Knocked him off his high horse! Rerouted his destructive destination and evil intentions into a new direction with instructions to fulfill the work of his calling! That's Paul's testimony.

"As I stated, my name is Edward Brent King, also known as Rev. Ed. I am the pastor of the Unifying Spirit Church in Arlington, Virginia. I have been preaching for approximately twenty years and pastoring for about fifteen years ... since I was two." laughter was heard. "I graduated from Howard University in Washington DC in ... well, let's just say I graduated.

"I went on to Yale Law before being diverted into the ministry. During my second year, I was transitioned from Yale Law to Yale Divinity, where I earned my master's degree in divinity and eventually a PhD in religious ethics and psychology. I have taught at the university for five years on the subjects of psychology, theology, and the black community. I have written several books on race, religion, and psychology. I was chosen by the university to facilitate this conference this year because of the inclusion of race in the discussion of religion, politics, and culture. I am married with three children; my wife is a college lecturer. I enjoy mountain climbing and good discussion."

From my limited courses on psychology I could determine that Rev. Ed was mixing psychology with theology. He was tapping into Sigmund Freud's theory of psychoanalysis, gathering information and associations from the past to come to current mental conclusions. But because of his theological understanding, he used a much more profound connection in order to get our attention.

He continued with ease. "My call was not like Paul's, not with light flashing, but I did experience heavy hitting to aid in my conversion. I would liken it to Amos', who said, 'I was minding my own business and suddenly the Lord came to me and gave me a word and I had to speak it.' I was indeed minding my own business when I stumbled into the ministry and felt compelled to pursue it. My grades in law school were exceptionally good—until I met Jesus." He was awesome at making the connection. "I had been looking forward to becoming a great lawyer—until I met Jesus. My family wanted a lawyer in the family, not a broke, chicken-eating, jive-talking, overweight preacher." Those present laughed and agreed. "That is, until I met Jesus," continued Rev. Ed, showing the genius of his homiletic style. "I met Jesus in a car accident.

"While I was driving home from the library one day, a car slammed into my driver-side door. Although I escaped without a scrape, the accident left me thanking and praising and feeling indebted to God. So I pursued my study in divinity, regardless of my unsupportive cast of family members, and ultimately, my call to ministry."

"You didn't see a light flashing when the car hit you?" a voice demanded to know.

"No," responded Rev. Ed. "I felt a shock that was more like a hand-hit to redirect my path. The collision was symbolic of my going in the wrong direction, so in order to get me going right, God hit me—hard and clear. And I got the message. The spiritual conversion was real, for I had never felt such a compassion and strangling at the same time.

"To say where and how it came, I don't know. I grew up in the church but never had an urge to preach the gospel until I went by Rev. Richardson's church in Mount Vernon, New York, two weeks prior to my accident. There, the freedom of speech and the power and focus on the issues touched my soul. So I leaned on the Lord.

"I live by the verse, 'Trust in the Lord with all your heart and lean not on your own understanding; in all your ways acknowledge him, and he will make your paths straight.' Because, as I said, sometimes I really don't know how I got here. Thank you."

"That was indeed a history and testimony combined, but I'm sure you're not a poor preacher," suggested Rev. Taylor, who seemed unable to resist a comment.

Rev. Ed just smiled as he said, "Rev. Dr. William Taylor, since you gave us our first laugh, why don't you give us the brief biographical sketch of your history to ministry?"

Rev. Taylor's was a brown-skinned man with a salt-and-pepper Afro from the sixties. His face was huge and he wore thick black glasses. His moderate dress was old school: black suit, black tie against a white shirt, and shiny black shoes that I was sure he'd polished himself. His stomach pushed his jacket open and his shirt out of his pants. As he spoke, he faced everyone as if they were members of his congregation rather than conference members.

"As Rev. Ed just mentioned, my name is Rev. Dr. William Taylor, son of Herman Taylor and Alice Taylor. In my parents' day, the woman just took on the man's name, no hyphen. She knew she was becoming one with him, and he with her, so a hyphenation meant a separation not only of name but of spirit."

"Whoa!" Rev. Ed interrupted, quickly seeing that Rev. Taylor was heading off the path. "Let's stick with the introduction and bio. We'll get to the issues later."

"That *was* the introduction," Rev. Taylor insisted. "Now I'll get to the bio."

I decided immediately that Rev. Taylor was obnoxious and arrogant. His overconfident character made me believe he was going to be a problem throughout the conference. He finally fell into the parameters of introduction.

"I grew up in Nashville, Tennessee, and graduated from the local college in Nashville before getting my bachelor's at Tennessee State University. I went on to Candler Theological Seminary at Emory University in Atlanta, where I earned my master of divinity and doctorate of ministry degrees." Rev. Taylor's bass voice was strong and clear. He hummed after each sentence, as if the preaching in him was a natural part of him.

"My call to ministry occurred with lightning flashing, and to tell you the truth, it's still flashing; I don't know if it's my eyes going bad or God trying to tell me something—again." Everyone laughed, including Rev. Taylor; he wasn't afraid to laugh at himself. "I am seventy-two years young and still have all my mental and physical faculties. No Viagra needed. You don't believe me, ask my wife." Again, all laughed, although the women present looked embarrassed. "I've been married for fifty-two years because she's the only one who can put up with me."

"Yeah, you seem like a set one," A beautiful woman on the right of him commented.

Rev. Taylor looked as though he was ready to respond, but Rev. Ed who saw the venom in his eyes, kept him on the path of righteousness by interjecting, "So, about your call to ministry?" Rev. Taylor shot an exasperated look at the woman, then began again. "My call to ministry came in 1952 at the National Baptist Convention in Chicago. There, I was listening to the preaching of my pastor, Rev. J.B. Moody, when I looked up, and it seemed the windows of heaven shone upon me and the clouds parted, and I heard the voice of Jesus saying, 'Speak my word to the nations.'" Rev. Taylor spoke as if he was giving a moving testimony. He made eye contact with everyone as he continued with the same expression and humming tone. "After the call, I pursued my studies and prepared myself for ministry. While an undergraduate in Tennessee, I was called to pastor a local church in Nashville. I stayed there four years until I finished my undergraduate studies. In 1956, while still in seminary, I was called to the New Found Faith United Church of Christ, which had four hundred members when I arrived. I will have served for forty years this November." Everyone applauded, which Rev. Taylor seemed to love. "And I ain't thinking about retiring!"

Many seemed amused by Rev. Taylor, but Rev. Ed spoke up in a polite yet direct tone. "Rev. Taylor is also a member of the national board of the NAACP and a former vice president of the Southern Christian Leadership Conference." He thanked Rev. Taylor, and then, in obvious attempt to move the session along, said, "It is necessary that we be as brief as possible in our introduction. We want the real introduction to be in our engagement of the upcoming discussions."

Bishop Samuel, who was just as well known as Rev. Taylor, said, "Brief! If you wanted brief, you should have invited Catholics, not Protestants!"

Everyone laughed, including Rev. Ed, who shot back, "Your friend Rev. Taylor has really had an affect on you." Rev. Ed pulled out a folder. "In the interest of saving time, I'd like to go back to my original agenda and introduce each of you." Everyone seemed agreeable. "Bishop Preston Holden Samuel is the former pastor of the Allen Temple African Methodist Episcopal Church in New York City. After being elected bishop in 1996, he left his church of twenty-seven years and has been the bishop of the Eastern District for the past twelve years. His call to ministry came early in his life, and he has pursued it with vigor and earnestness. He has been written up in *Ebony* magazine as one of the nation's top ten preachers in America and has been cited in *The New Yorker* magazine as one of the most influential twenty-five people in the country today." Although the folder was in his hand, Rev. Ed spoke without looking at it, as if he knew Bishop Samuel's history very well. "Bishop Samuel once said, 'My call to ministry is my call to life.' Prior to ministry, his life was filled with sadness and sorrow, many times unexplained. He lost his parents at a very early age and was raised by his eldest sister and her husband. His call to the ministry came in the darkness of night, while he was sleeping. He likens his call to the biblical prophet Samuel's, whom the Lord called in the middle of the night three times before Samuel got it right. But Bishop Samuel could not go back to sleep. Since his call to the ministry, his life has been dedicated to the uplifting of his people— morally, spiritually, and politically. His books have caught the attention of a critical nation, and although he has been praised by many, he has also been accused of being unsympathetic and unpatriotic for his recent publication of *Our Nation, Our Soul*. His sermons can be heard every Sunday around the nation on National Public Radio, and he attracts a broad audience. He is a graduate of Morehouse University in Atlanta. He credits Rev. Dr. Benjamin Elijah Mays, former president of Morehouse College, for being his mentor and inspiration in the ministry. Bishop Samuel received his master of divinity and doctorate of ministry degrees from Union Theological Seminary in New York City. He is the father of four and has been the husband of Mary Jane Samuel for the past thirty-eight years."

Rev. Ed seemed to say it all in one breath, which saved us at least an hour from Bishop Samuel, who sat with humbleness. His appearance was impeccable in every way, from his smooth black skin and shiny bald head to his evenly groomed gray beard that slid across the sides of his face, down his chin, and around his mouth. His dress was immaculate, right down to the cut of his sleeves that showed off his monogrammed French cuffs fastened with gold cufflinks. He looked like he was in his early seventies or late sixties but since black don't crack it was hard to tell. As Rev. Ed introduced him, he sat there like a humble servant, chewing gum with mouth closed, looking directly at Rev. Ed.

"Let us welcome Bishop Preston Holden Samuel," Rev. Ed concluded. Everyone applauded. Rev. Ed quickly pulled out another sheet of paper from his folder and pronounced a name: "Rev. Dr. Gwendolyn Smith aka Dr. Smith." He glanced around the table, and a beautiful older woman raised her hand. I had heard about Rev. Smith but couldn't remember when or where.

She had the look of a grandmother who rocked you to sleep when you got tired. A heavyset woman, she wore all black clothes, as if trying to make herself appear slimmer. Her face was smooth and her eyes bright. Her salt-and-pepper hair was tied into a ponytail that trailed down her back, giving a touch of youth to her look. She smiled as Rev. Ed spoke about her.

"Rev. Dr. Gwendolyn Smith is the pastor of the Wesleyan United Methodist Church in Baton Rouge, Louisiana, where she has served for the last twelve years. She is also an adjunct professor of African American history and literature at Dillard University in New Orleans, which is still recovering from Hurricane Katrina. She has written many historical and literary novels, her latest being *I Shall Fear No Man*, which was at the top of the *New York Times* best-seller list in 2005 for two weeks. Oprah Winfrey applauded her work as the ground-breaking novel of the year. Her call to the ministry, she says, has been in motion. Dr. Smith believes the trials of life are what constantly call one closer to Jesus. She lives by the understanding that there is not one call, but that each obstacle we encounter, every battle we endure, every heartache we handle, and every fear we confront is a call closer to Jesus. She recognized her first call when she became ill in her early twenties. While in the hospital, she promised the Lord that if he kept her alive, she would serve him forever. Her favorite verse is Psalm 23:4: "Even though I walk through the valley of the shadow of death, I will fear no evil, for you are with me." She is a graduate of Vanderbilt University in Louisiana where she earned her bachelor's degree in literature and of Harvard Divinity in Boston, where she earned her master of divinity degree. She is the mother of thee children and grandmother of eight. Let's welcome Rev. Dr. Gwendolyn Smith."

"Hey! I didn't get a welcome." Rev. Taylor blurted out. Laughing but ignoring him at the same time, everyone looked at Dr. Smith and applauded.

Rev. Ed quickly went to the next introduction. I could see he was eager to get into the discussion. "Rev. Malik-Haj Bryant …"

"Yow," Rev. Bryant acknowledged.

"… is a young, up-and-coming star in the ministry. For the past five years he has served as the pastor of the historic New Way Baptist Church in Philadelphia, Pennsylvania."

"Oh, Rev. Wells pastored that church for thirty-two years. He was a great friend of mine," Rev. Taylor interrupted. Rev. Bryant nodded his head at Rev. Taylor's statement.

Rev. Ed quickly continued, "Rev. Bryant has been known for his involvement in the hip-hop community and in the church. Prior to becoming pastor, he recorded two rap tracks that received a lot of attention in Philadelphia. Rev. Bryant says his call to the ministry came after a shoot-out that left his best friend dead and him in jail. The death of his friend was a wake-up call to get back to Jesus. And he did. Leaving the streets, he earned his GED and went on to Temple University, graduated at the top of his class with a bachelor of arts in religion, then went on to Pittsburgh Theological Seminary, from where he recently graduated. Rev. Bryant has been applauded for infusing rap with preaching and says it is a way to communicate with the young and bring them to Jesus.

"However, his church, because of its historical roots, serves the whole community, and Rev. Bryant believes that churches should encourage economic development in the minds of people through theology. He says we need a gospel of prosperity to lift us out of spiritual and moral poverty."

Rev. Taylor groaned at that last statement. Rev. Ed paused, looked at Rev. Taylor, and then continued. "He is the father of two boys and husband of Margarita Lopez Bryant. Let us welcome Rev. Malik-Haj Bryant to our session."

Rev. Bryant bellowed, "What up," the standard greeting of his generation, as applause welcomed him. His deadpan expression was disengaging and the scars on his face made me wonder if he had just recently made the conversion from hoodlum to Christian. He kept a low-cut wavy fade that went well with his dark black, rough skin. From the look of him, I pegged him to be in his early thirties—still very young to be around all these deep scholars and experienced lecturers.

His attire seemed to rebel against the suit and tie adopted by most preachers. He wore a casual brown cotton jacket and matching pants, with a black T-shirt that had Sean John printed all over it. I figured he probably lifted weights—he had the build of a football player or ex-prisoner, as well as a look of readiness, as if he was more at home fighting on the streets than battling with minds. He kept punching one hand into the other as he was introduced. No one seemed impressed by him, and he seemed slightly ill at ease, as if he was certain that everyone was judging him because of his past.

Rev. Ed ruffled his papers and then called out the name Rev. Zora Minor. A woman quickly raised her hand and softly called out, "Present."

Rev. Ed smiled at her as he began: "Rev. Minor is the senior pastor of the First Presbyterian Church in St. Louis, Missouri. She is one of the first women in the last ten years to ascend to such a height. In 1998 she founded the Healing Thy Soul ministries within her congregation. This ministry has been responsible for healing the pains and hurts of thousands of women all over the nation. She has written extensively on various issues of healing. She is a much sought-after preacher and teacher for women's conferences. She boasts one of the largest congregations of the Presbyterian denomination in the nation.

"Rev. Minor received her calling to the ministry in 1972 in her senior year at Spelman College in Atlanta. Her call to ministry, as she described it, was 'to get up out of her blood and accept the blood of Christ.'" Everyone appeared as baffled by that description as I was. But we would have to wait for an explanation. "She has been recognized for her achievements in political writing and her challenges to injustice and ineptness as well. Rev. Minor is a graduate of Princeton Theological Seminary in Princeton, New Jersey. She is the wife of General

George Mason and mother of two. Let us welcome Rev. Zora Minor."

Everyone welcomed her. She again smiled and waved both her hands, a gesture that spoke louder than her voice. She was a petite woman, but her résumé made her look large. She represented her naturalness with a short-cut Afro and dressed in African attire. She had a proper and attentive manner. Her dark skin was immaculate, and she had a naturally beautiful clearness to her face. Her smile showed gleaming gums and teeth. She brought to my mind the moon on the backdrop of a dark night. She wore her glasses tilted halfway down her nose, making her look studious.

Rev. Ed, perhaps sensing a comment from Rev. Taylor, hurriedly went on to the next introduction. "Rev. Michelle Mellowin." He paused, then looked up. There was no response. "Oh, that's right, she'll be joining us later." Rev. Ed called out the name of Rev. Bobby Terrence Charles. A man—so fair-skinned, he could have been white—acknowledged hearing his name with a salute. I couldn't help staring at him. He did have black features—flat nose and curly hair, but it was so fine that I had to look closely to see the waves. He wore a military outfit.

"Rev. Charles—also Sergeant Charles—is the former pastor of the historic First Street Baptist Church in Richmond, Virginia. He served there for twelve years before becoming pastor of Greenfield Baptist Church in Chicago, where he has served for the last three years. Prior to becoming a pastor, he was a military man, serving in the Army for ten years. His call to ministry came while in the Gulf War. He says that in the middle of the night when a bomb hit his brigade and tore off one of his legs, his revelation was quick and certain. Upon departure from the military he joined the Lord's army and has been learning to walk right with one good foot. The experience of a tarnished nation helps him to speak justice through God with authority. Since his departure from the service and his call to ministry, he has—poignantly and unapologetically and militaristically— challenged the nation to do more for its citizens, particularly

African American men. Rev. Charles' ministry is largely built upon African American men who have turned their lives around for the purpose of love and justice. He is a graduate of Virginia Union College and Union Theological Seminary, both in Richmond, Virginia. He is not married and has three children, all in college."

Everyone looked at Rev. Charles, perhaps wondering about the marital history of a man with three children. He looked back, seeming to push their eyes off him. His military demeanor commanded attention and respect. I could see from the look of him, with his thick hands and squinted eyes, that he didn't play games. I imagined it was hard for him to crack a smile to acknowledge his introduction.

"Let us welcome Rev. Bobby T. Charles." Without pause, Rev. Ed swung into an introduction of Rev. Curtis Franklyn, who quickly raised his hand and whispered, "Here."

"Rev. Franklyn is the pastor of Greater Hope Church in San Francisco, California. He is the author of numerous articles in the *San Francisco Chronicle* and is a sought-after revivalist. Rev. Franklyn received his call to ministry in the suburbs of Detroit, where he grew up. He says he was a shy child but the ministry brought him courage. He says his call was like Jeremiah's: he didn't know what to say. But God put the words in his mouth, and he went out and began to speak. He says he just wishes God would have added bass to his voice." What did that mean? Perhaps no one knew except Rev. Ed and Rev. Franklyn. I felt we would soon find out.

"Rev. Franklyn has also been credited with engaging the gay community in church services and fighting alongside them against discrimination and for civil rights. He also works within the hip-hop community. Rev. Franklyn says he was educated by the word of God, taught by the Holy Spirit, and learned from Jesus. He is the father of two and husband of Erica Franklyn, the gospel singer."

"Oh, that's your wife." Dr. Smith slipped in the comment, as if she knew his wife well. Almost stepping on her words, Rev.

Taylor slyly remarked, "So you didn't attend college or seminary?"

Rev. Ed quickly jumped. "That means he was reared with education from on high. We'll get to the rest of it later. Let us welcome Rev. Curtis Franklyn."

Rev. Franklyn didn't look like anyone who wanted to fight. He was a very thin man, and his smooth, caramel-colored skin and curly hair gave him a pretty rather than handsome look. His brown suit coordinated with his skin tone. He sat with his head down and the tip of one finger in his mouth as he was introduced.

Again, Rev. Ed moved on quickly. "We have the wonderful, beautiful, and intellectual Rev. Stacy Lee Johnson, a.k.a. Lady Johnson. She is assistant pastor of the Abundantly Blessed Tabernacle in Houston, Texas, where her husband, Rev. Dr. Jeremiah E. Johnson, is pastor."

"Oh, he's your husband?" Dr. Smith chimed in again, clearly impressed. Lady Johnson answered with a terse yes. She was beautiful—Halle Berry had nothing on her. She appeared to be in her late forties to early fifties. Her brown eyes seemed to blend into her brown skin. Her dark black hair was highlighted with stripes of golden-blond hair. She was the kind of woman who caught the eye of everyone, male and female, as soon as she stepped into a room. Her dress was classy yet sexy, complete with a Sunday-morning hat that matched her attire. She looked like a model or movie star, and she carried herself like one, complete with sunglasses, although she had removed them as Rev. Ed introduced her.

Rev. Ed continued with enthusiasm. "Lady Johnson is preacher, teacher, and organizer. She has been noted as one of the top fifty female preachers in the nation. She has a testimony that brings tears of sorrow and, ultimately, of joy. She travels around the nation, teaching men and women how to be better Christians for Christ. Her calling came some fifteen years ago while, she says, she was down-and-out, and God picked her up. Prior to the ministry she was intently sinful in her works, but now she is intently serving the Lord. In 2000 she founded the First Ladies Affair. It gathers several hundred wives of ministers together, and they work to support and befriend each other. She says First Ladies Affair has helped her and so many others to deal with the difficulty of being in the ministry while married to a pastor and mothering children. She is a graduate of Texas A&M University and currently completing her studies at Chicago Theological Seminary. In addition to being a wife, she is a mother of four. Let us welcome Rev. Stacy Lee Johnson."

She waved her hand and smiled without speaking, leaving Rev. Ed an opening for my introduction.

"Last but not least is the Rev. Dr. James G. Parks, who is the pastor of Garry Street Baptist Church in Baltimore, Maryland, and professor of politics and religion at the University of Maryland."

I quietly yet confidently confirmed my presence with a wave.

"He has been pastoring for fifteen years and teaching for eight years. Rev. Parks graduated from the University of Pennsylvania with a BA in political science and went on to Drew University to receive his master's degree and doctorate in politics and religion. He has written many articles on politics and religion and several books, the latest being *The Emotional Struggle and Condemnation at a Cost*.

"He describes his call to ministry like God speaking to Abraham and telling him to go, but he didn't know where he was going. But he had been used to moving from one place to another because of his family's poverty, history of drug use, and instability. At the age of seventeen—after graduating from high school at the top of his class—he went to Philadelphia, where he walked into the dean's office at University of Pennsylvania, about which he knew nothing, presented his transcript, and told the dean of his family's instability. The dean was impressed with the report card and moved by his testimony, so he pulled strings to get Rev. Parks into the school. Rev. Parks graduated at the top of the class and has been excelling ever since."

Everyone applauded as I sat there with a weak smile. I had worn my blazer, dress slacks, and loafers to feel at ease. I was older than some but younger than others. Because I began getting gray in my early twenties, people always thought I was older. By the time I hit thirty I had a full head of silver hair. I looked like a black mountain with snow at the top. My height, which was six-three, gave me more of a mountain look. I've always been able to maintain a somewhat slim fit, not slim, like Rev. Franklyn, but a healthy look.

"Well, thank you all for your patience," Rev. Ed said. "I'll introduce the other two when they arrive."

3

Spiritual Renewal

Nehemiah 2:17–18

It's time to rise up
Get up – Stand up
We've had enough
Stand up for your rights
We're burning our bridges
And killing our kids
Our ancestors are crying
Because of how we live
We live with the madness, disgrace and shame
We've got to get our family back in Jesus name

Rev. Ed immediately dove into the discussion, as if the silence in the room was a sea of calm water waiting to be disturbed. His eyes focused first on Bishop Samuel—I suspected that Bishop Samuel could spark the flames of spiritual intellectualism and mix them with emotion and wisdom.

"Bishop Samuel…" Rev. Ed began.

Bishop Samuel looked up out of the corner of his eye, as if he anticipated that Rev. Ed would address him first.

"Bishop Samuel, at the beginning of your most recent book, you exercised real emotions, some might say too much emotion for a man of your stature and sophistication."

Bishop Samuel just looked at him, like a boxer before the bell rings. His smooth black skin and silver beard while he was chewing his gum made him look even more like a fighter. Rev. Ed continued, meeting Bishop Samuel's stare and egging him on.

"It caught many off guard because they know you to be a cool yet no-nonsense preacher, highly concerned with heralding the truth and speaking courageously yet diplomatically. Here is an excerpt of what you said ..."

"I know what I said," Bishop Samuel retorted in a smooth deep baritone.

"But others may not know," Rev. Ed said easily.

"Yes, what did he say?" Dr. Smith chimed in.

Book in hand, Rev. Ed read: "'Cry with me, because as I write this story I am crying. Tears are falling and my countenance is one of utter dismay. I will convey these emotions and others throughout this book because my story is not disconnected from a people, a people's condition that demands that the eyes water and the face shatter. I don't know if you've ever been there—the place where you're not only crying for yourself but also for your world. It's like when I was watching the news the other night and saw how a man lost his mother, wife, and daughter in a fire. Three generations perished—gone just like that. It hurt my heart, and I cried. And this crying is not always tears in my eyes; my soul cries, and it is displayed in my emotions and countenance, leaving one to realize there is sadness.'"

When Rev. Ed finished, everyone looked compassionately at Bishop Samuel. Rev. Ed motioned to the bishop, but Bishop Samuel kept his eyes to the floor. Then, in a low tone, like quiet thunder, he spoke. "It is not that I haven't been crying." He looked up to meet our collective gaze. "I chose this book to reveal my emotions, and I knew I would catch people off guard because of the character and personality I present. But as the song goes, 'Trouble in my way, I have to cry sometimes.' I'm getting older, and there is no need to hold it in any longer—not because I don't want to but because I can't."

"I agree—" Rev. Ed began.

"Please. I'm not finished, Rev. Ed," Bishop Samuel steering directly at Rev. Ed with even more deepness to his voice. Rev. Ed stopped in his tracks with his mouth wide open. "When a people are in a sad state of affairs, it is hard to ignore their pain. Black people are in a sad state of affairs. Poor people are in a sad state of affairs. Religious people are in a sad state of affairs. This nation is in a sad state of affairs. We are in a state of emergency, and our community is in a state of urgency, and our response time is slow in dealing with it."

Bishop Samuel's voice was direct and authoritative, yet humble and open. His observations of the nation's condition justified his emotions, it was clear that he was conveying his true feelings. "This is Gethsemane!" he blurted out. "The fight for humanity makes one cry. Jesus' agony was a fight for humanity. I can't help but connect my emotions to the struggle, for it is, as Rev. Parks wrote, an emotional struggle. And I am not alone in my sorrow for my people. Let me justify it like this. ..."

With all eyes glued to him, Bishop Samuel took a deep breath and then said calmly, "I am reminded of Nehemiah, who displayed his concern for his people and community with the same melancholy as mine. Nehemiah was internally broken over the external condition of the fallen walls of Jerusalem. The Bible says that the walls of Jerusalem were broken down, and its gates burned with fire. Upon hearing of this, Nehemiah began to cry. The Bible places emphasis on the fact that Nehemiah cried for many days. Some might say that sort of reaction was extreme, ridiculous, insane, or highly emotional." He looked pointedly at Rev. Ed before he continued. "But in order to understand Nehemiah's lamenting, you have to understand the historical connection. This wasn't just any city; it was Jerusalem. Jerusalem had historical as well as ancestral significance for the Hebrews. Jerusalem was regarded as the royal city, the capital city.

"But what really exercised its existence and amplified Nehemiah's emotions was that Jerusalem was celebrated as the city of David. David was renowned as the unifier of a divided and scattered nation. David brought Judah and Israel together— two of God's chosen scattered vessels—and fostered a sense of pride, strength, power, privilege, life, and ownership. Never had so much authority been obtained or unity realized for Israel. King David brought dissidents together and established his capital within the walls of greatness in the city of Jerusalem.

"The walls were sanctioned and sealed with divine authority—this is body and spirit working in harmony, rather than disunity—that was the result of Gethsemane. God approved the conquest and establishment of the city. The Bible says that after Israel 'came together to David,' the Lord said to him, 'You will become their ruler.'"

The bishop's discourse was brilliant; each point seemed to take his passion and perspective up a notch. As far as I could see no one took their eyes off of him, and because of his passionate appeal no one interrupted him not even Rev. Taylor. He continued, his next revelations becoming even more earthshaking. "God gave the Israelites unity, authenticity, authority, and territory. When Nehemiah began to reflect on all the ancestral history and divine authority that had been ruined by the fallen walls, his eyes began to weep and his heart began to bleed.

"So, you ask me why I revealed my weeping emotions: it is because, I, like Nehemiah, feel for my history, family, and community." He stared at Rev. Ed with almost a deadly gaze. "When I think about our present community, in comparison to our royal history and divine authority, how can I not lament?" His question seemed to shake the walls. "How can I not mourn! How can others not weep with me? And my weeping is not a sign of weakness or surrender; it is a sign of sorrow and shame. I must say that it shames me externally, saddens me profoundly, and disturbs me spiritually to know that in churches, every week, people are jumping and shouting and not paying attention to the horrific condition of our community. Many of our preachers are praising and ignoring, rather than praising and acknowledging."

Rev. Ed shuffled in his seat. "That's deep," he said, seeming unsure of whether he should interrupt. "Elaborate on that."

Bishop Samuel shot Rev. Ed another withering look; clearly he'd intended to elaborate without Rev. Ed's encouragement. He sat erect—the bishop had impeccable posture—and it seemed that the only part of him that moved as he spoke was his lips. His hands and legs remained folded as he continued, the timbre of his voice slightly deeper. "When you praise and ignore, you keep your head up like you're above everyone, and you disregard the condition of the community. Such people are what I call 'paralyzed praisers for the purpose of posturing.'" We all chuckled appreciatively at his terminology, but Bishop Samuel persisted as if he wasn't joking. "They truly live by the old pie-in-the-sky theory—that when we get to heaven, everything will be better. Their greatest words are repeated every week: 'The Lord will make a way somehow. If he did it for me, he'll do it for you. Weeping may endure for a night but joy cometh in the morning.'"

The gathering erupted in applause, and Rev. Ed shouted, "Those are the words!"

Bishop Samuel held up his hand to silence us. "But let me not preach; let me speak."

"Yeah, because I was getting ready to pass the collection plate," Rev. Taylor sniped. "Nobody told me we were coming to a church service."

"Oh, you must know that anytime you're around preachers, you're coming to a church service," Rev. Ed joked to hand claps.

"As I was saying," Bishop Samuel continued, commanding our attention with his intense tone. "Churches are ignoring the overcrowded and broken-down schools. Ignoring the gangs and the misogynistic music. Ignoring the substandard school curriculum. Ignoring the elections that would give us leverage and input in decision making. Praise is not what they do—praise is *all* they do."

"Hey, I know that song by Shakanah Glory," Lady Johnson jumped in.

But Bishop Samuel ignored her and kept moving with his point. "There is somehow the promotion of a religious cover-up which hides the reality of a broken people and a busted community. They hide and disguise the reality of pain and trouble in an effort to gain followers. Because in order to get people to Jesus these days, you have to tell them or sell them something they want to hear, rather than something that's real."

Bishop Samuel was just getting started. He had warmed up and seemed ready to take his argument to the next level. And no one dared interrupt him. Rev. Ed had started the fight, but Bishop Samuel was determined to finish it. He continued, as if accusing every preacher in the room of substandard sermons and ministry malpractice. "What they want to hear is that there will be no more heartaches and disasters when you come to Jesus Christ. Preachers distort and fabricate the word, turning it into Mickey Mouse theory rather than a serious theology. Jesus faced heartaches and threats and difficulties at Gethsemane. But we've reduced the gospel to fantasy because people prefer dreams over reality. Pay a dollar and get a praise."

"Ooh." The utterance seemed universal.

"Church folks want a place to praise all day. So now when churches advertise Jesus, they give folks the roses without the thorns. The sunshine without the clouds. The mountain without the valley. The money without the problems. Life without death. Gain without loss. Cake without extra calories. And Bush without bombs."

"I hear you, Doctor," Rev. Taylor verified. Everyone clapped at the phrases that slid smoothly from his mouth, like a sleigh on snow. He kept going as if he was caught up in the spirit.

"They want people to be disillusioned into discipleship rather than truthfully obtained into Christian citizenship. When Jesus spoke, he told it like it was. He didn't tell half the story to gain followers. Jesus told them the truth and nothing but the truth. He said, 'I am sending you out like sheep amongst wolves.' That's not rosy talk. He said, 'On my account you will be arrested and brought to court.' 'Men will hate you because of me.' 'A man's enemies will be members of his own family.' 'You will be blessed but you will be persecuted for righteousness' sake.' 'You will be blessed but men shall revile you and say all manner of evil against you falsely, for my sake.'"

Amens rang out as Bishop Samuel continued to speak.

"That's Jesus at Gethsemane, facing the truth about his life. He will be beaten before he is risen. He faced the truth. You can't ignore the fact that some people are just not going to like you."

A loud amen rang out from Dr. Smith. She was listening intently, like a student to a professor. Her grandmotherly look was now like a youthful cheerleader encouraging a football player. She jumped at times almost out of her seat at Bishop Samuel's phrasing.

"Face the truth!" Bishop Samuel shouted, now unfolding his hands.

"Yes. But what about the other part—praising and acknowledging?" Rev. Ed apparently felt compelled to intercede in order to redirect Bishop Samuel toward his conclusion.

Bishop Samuel nodded, and his voice again became calm and collected. "When one praises and acknowledges, he sees the pain and hears the cries of people who hurt. He praises and fights for restoration and restitution. He knows that the Lord will make a way somehow, but he uses himself as the vessel by which God will operate. The Bible says, 'His praises will continuously be in my mouth.' While I'm fighting, I'm praising. When I'm crying, I'm praising. When I'm working, I'm praising. When I'm cussing, I'm praising. Because some folks understand only cussing."

"Okay, now," Lady Johnson spoke up. Her beautiful smile almost taking my attention off of Bishop Samuel's discourse and on to her looks.

"That's why I prefer to be like Nehemiah rather than like Mike—Michael Jordan," Bishop Samuel went on. "I can't feel good when my people are in shackles and my community is in ruins. My soul is disturbed. My heart hurts. Many may say they've gotten used to bad news and are either numb or dumb to the situation. But like Nehemiah, I get teary-eyed for days sometimes—especially when an eight-year-old dies from gun violence or our sisters get raped. I can't feel anything but emotional distress."

"Yes!" said Rev. Minor. Her voice rising to seemingly unexpected heights for her size. She quickly repositioned herself and looked down rather than at Bishop Samuel.

"That's my people. That's my community. Those are my children. Call me a baby, if you will, but I'm glad I still have the emotional innocence of a child to keep me near the pain of the people."

"That's deep," Rev. Ed came in.

"Such a feeling can prompt either rejection or action, but as I said, I'm like Nehemiah."

Rev. Ed made another attempt to bring the bishop to a conclusion. "Well, what do we do about it? How do we address and prompt action?"

Bishop Samuel responded eagerly. "Well, the first thing I do—and call this a lesson on Nehemiah, if you will—is go to the Lord in prayer." He looked around the room expectantly, and then directed, "Somebody say amen." Amens rang out like a chorus. "Nehemiah went to the Lord in prayer. Before we make any moves on restoration, it is important to talk to God first. I've seen a lot of people take action to restore a broken situation but they ended up doing more harm than good. Nehemiah realized that in order to truly fix what's broken, you have to go to the master craftsman first. To the potter's house."

"Preach!" Dr. Smith yelled out. Everyone turned to look at her.

"As a preacher and man of God, I must emphasize this," Bishop Samuel went on. "Nehemiah talked to God. He did what Jesus requested of his disciples at Gethsemane: he prayed to God. In prayer, Nehemiah uttered truth and confession. Nehemiah admitted that the truth of the matter was that the walls were down not because of enemies but because of actions. Nehemiah confessed and realized that the disobedience of the Israelites caused the demolition of the walls. The annihilation was because of arrogance. The falling walls were because of falling to temptation. We are guilty of the broken walls. The scattered people. The exile. The breakdown. The loss of hope, pride, and privilege. *We* did it, Nehemiah says. We, including himself, too.

"When I look at our communities, from New York City to Los Angeles, Chicago to St. Louis, Atlanta to Washington DC, and every urban and suburban platform where we reside, I can't help but hold us partially responsible for much of the pain and breakdown."

I felt his point had more truth than assault. As Bishop Samuel scanned the room. His eyes touched everyone, as if to confirm that we, too, were responsible. After his survey, he continued.

"We fell away from God. We allowed the walls to fall and the devil to rise. We allowed crack in our communities and poverty in our neighborhoods. We allowed others to make our clothes and cook our chicken and do our nails and raise our children."

"Cook our chicken?" someone blurted out and laughed.

"Yes," Bishop Samuel shot back solemnly. "Our mothers cook the best fried chicken and collard greens and mac-and-cheese in this land. But we're allowing Kennedy Fried and Kentucky Fried and Boston Market to make our food. We should own those restaurants. But we let others take over. We could have had the money circulating three or four times in our neighborhoods. But when you leave a hole, someone is going to fill it! We left God and allowed drugs and guns and gangs to love our children. We allowed pimps and prostitutes to influence our young. We allowed children to run the home and kick us out the house."

Dr. Smith yelled out, "True!"

"That's pretty harsh and victim-blaming, don't you think, Bishop Samuel?" Lady Johnson jumped in with her pretty smooth yet emotionally filled voice.

"Yes!" Bishop Samuel thundered. "But until we acknowledge this part of it, we will never rise! In order for an alcoholic to be free from alcohol, he must first confess and realize that he has a drinking problem. *We* have a drinking problem. And it's not the living water of Jesus."

"He is right," Dr. Smith cut in, as if Bishop Samuel needed backup.

Then Rev. Charles jumped in. "I remember the Million Man March organized by Louis Farrakhan—it was the same understanding of confession. A million men came together to confess that they had fallen short and caused a lot of the destruction in our community, in our women, in our families. And it was up to them to reverse conditions in their lives in order to make the community and our family better." His voice was hard and direct. Each word punctuated to convey the point but also the power of his tenor.

"Thanks, Rev. Charles," Bishop Samuel stated. "That's exactly what I'm saying. It is the same in our own lives: we can't ask God to fix the problem without recognizing how we contributed to the predicament. Nothing will be fixed until we confess our role in it. We've all fallen short, missed the boat, did the wrong, hurt the faith.

"Many of our kids go wrong because the mothers did wrong. Many kids aren't just on the corner. Just selling crack. Just doing wrong. Children went wrong when mothers ignored them, didn't properly enforce principles and values. Feared them when they were three years old and now can't control them at ten!"

"It's not only the mother," Lady Johnson insisted.

But Bishop Samuel would not be interrupted—his frustration was too high. He straightened his shoulders and continued. "I remember hearing T.D. Jakes say, 'Somebody fell asleep on the job.' I believe that to be true: somebody in the house was overworked and overslept, and while we were working and sleeping, the enemy was creeping."

"Speak on!" a voice rang out, giving Bishop Samuel more momentum to go on.

"When Nehemiah found out that the enemy was attempting to break down the walls that he had come to restore, he strategized. He assigned men to work by day and watch by night. If anyone fell asleep, the enemy would creep up and destroy the wall. Jesus had the same problem at Gethsemane. The disciples slept and the enemy crept. As soon as they got up, the enemy was standing there, ready to take Jesus.

"We're sleeping and the enemy is creeping to take and destroy everything we own. From our community and our church. Taking our Jesus of the poor and turning him into a conservative compassionate—some weird creation not mentioned by Jesus or sanctioned by God. But when people are sleeping, you can feed them anything. We have to work and watch so that there will be twenty-four hours of surveillance around our community.

"I remember reading about a young girl in our community who left her boyfriend of three months home with her nine-year-old daughter. He raped the girl each time he was left home with her."

"Oh, Christ, help us!" Lady Johnson cried out, not realizing how loud she was.

The bishop continued. "Finally, after two months, the mother realized that something was wrong. She fell asleep, believing that she could trust someone after three months with her most prized gift from God. How stupid!" The words bellowed out of his mouth, saliva spewing. "Should I not be crying when I hear stuff like this? Should we not all be in tears?" He asked plaintively. His hands shook and his voice cracked as he spoke, like the earth splitting in two. "We've lost a lot over our own stupidity and foolishness. Over our own disobedience. So many of our young girls are on the street because of what a stepfather or boyfriend did to the girl while the mother was out of the house—or in the house, for that matter. Somebody left the young girl home with the boyfriend. He gave her money and took her virginity, now she's on the street corner making money with her body.

"We have to pray first. Nothing will be fixed up until we 'fess up. The next thing we must do is go to work."

I'd heard that Bishop Samuel was a point preacher, and now I was seeing this in action—he laid out the proposition, gave it substance with synthesis, and then came to a conclusion at least three or four times before he got to his celebration.

"Faith without work is dead," he went on. "Nehemiah literally went to work. His day job was cup-bearer to the king. While Nehemiah was at work, the king noticed his countenance—when something is on your heart, it can show up on your face. The king immediately inquired about Nehemiah's sadness. Nehemiah answered the king with a question: 'How can I be happy when the city where my fathers are buried lies in ruin? Its walls are down and its gates are destroyed.'

"The king said, 'What do you want?' All it took was a burning heart and a poignant expression for the king to ask the question. Nehemiah gave his demands, humbly yet plainly, as if he had already planned it. He said, 'I need time off to rebuild the walls. I need visas to give to the governors so that I can get to my destination safely. I need subsidy money for the gates and the residence I will occupy. I need my men to come with me to observe the ruins. I need an architect. I need brick and mortar, and skilled and enthusiastic laborers. I need a historian to restore the history.'"

Everyone at the table appeared to be amazed by his knowledge and his connection. I was too fascinated to say anything but "Amen."

"Nehemiah was the man," Bishop Samuel continued. "He was ready for action. He had his list of demands in place. He knew what it would take to restore the walls and the city as well as the history and divinity.

"You can't expect to get things fixed if you don't have a plan in place. Jesus at Gethsemane had a plan in place. He knew what it would take to restore us to God. It would take giving up himself for our lives. Nehemiah was not afraid to engage in politics. God had already worked out the spiritual to make way for the political, and Nehemiah used his lowly cup-bearing position to make all of this possible."

His voice shifted along with his head away from Rev. Ed to the rest of us.

"Within the White House there are African Americans who have not urged adequately or clearly the demands of the black community. The poor community. It is said that everyone who is our color is not necessarily our kin."

"Speak!" A heavy voice demanded. When I looked for the source, I saw that it was Rev. Charles. His light face grew red as if he not only heard the fire coming from Bishop Samuel but felt it. He looked as though he wanted to jump into the discourse but Bishop Samuel took his suggestion and continued. "This is true for many who walk side by side with the president. Although they are in the White House, their countenance does not reflect the demands of the community. Their facial expressions do not lead to inquiry. Their talk is not directed toward the sad condition of the poor. No one in the White House is hurt enough nor torn enough for the president to ask what the problem is. Everyone is looking for a deal for himself. As a result, the black and poor and disconsolate suffer."

"That's highly political, don't you think, Bishop Samuel?" Rev. Ed asked.

"No, I don't," Bishop Samuel responded firmly.

"Well, some might say the church has gotten too political and that it needs to go back to its spiritual base," Rev. Ed suggested. "I mean, too much politics seems to be eroding the goal of the church and the focus of the people. Most politicians know that they can just stand up in your church, even though some of them have never been to church in their lives, and they decide to get religion during their campaign." Rev. Ed paused as he got a couple of amens out of that statement. Then with his own tenor voice and singing articulation he continued. "They speak in sound bites at the pulpit to appeal to the people. And many of us, in our naïveté, applaud their limited appeal with great enthusiasm, as if it were Jesus himself speaking. Some of these politicians, black and white, you will never see again until the next election."

"True," Rev. Charles asserted.

"In addition," Rev. Ed urgently pressed on, "some might say too much political talk is not biblical. Jesus came to inspire the inner hope of the hopeless. To bring healing, to restore dignity, but most of all to offer charity. Where is the love for ourselves and the love for one another?" He looked at Bishop Samuel and pointed a finger at him. "As you said, Bishop Samuel, we dropped the ball, we fell asleep, but restoration is going to come foremost through charity, not political expediency. When we begin to love ourselves and others, that's when we'll see a change. I do believe if our young people were taught to love themselves and others, there would be less homicide and suicide. The old saying goes, 'Charity begins at home.' We're not teaching charity in the home. First Corinthians 13:1–2 says, 'If I speak in the tongues of men and of angels but have not love, I am only a resounding gong or a clanging cymbal. If I have the gift of prophecy and can fathom all mysteries and all knowledge, and if I have a faith that can move mountains but have not love, I am nothing.' And here is where that scripture passage relates to your premise of supporting the people: 'If I give all I possess to the poor and surrender my body to the flames but have not love, I gain nothing.' Jesus at Gethsemane loved us enough to sacrifice his life for us. Don't you think so, Bishop?"

Bishop Samuel pursed his lips, seeming annoyed that his words and meaning had been taken out of context. Still, he addressed Rev. Ed's question with confidence. "The reason I cry is because I love my people," he responded sorrowfully yet deeply. "This idea of love should not subtract from political involvement; it should propel it. Was it not John Calvin who declared that we are under two governments, one spiritual and the other political? The spiritual has its piety with God, and the political its purpose with civility. Calvin exercised the epistemological reasoning that the spiritual government pertains to the life of the soul, while the political government pertains to laws of regulating a man's life amongst his neighbors with holiness, integrity, and sobriety. As Calvin stated and as Jesus related, people are under two worlds, capable of being governed by various rulers and various laws. The two are inseparable and interrelated; give unto Caesar that which is Caesar's and unto God what is God's."

"Very good!" Rev. Ed applauded him, as did everyone else.

Bishop Samuel wasn't finished. "Do we not give our tithes and pay our taxes? Our tithes are our obedience to God. Our taxes are our obligation to the nation in support of protection and services. We are blessed by the grace of God with liberty but at the same time restricted by the laws of the land because of civility. The nation is obligated to support us because we pay taxes, but when we find the nation lacking in fulfilling its duties—when we're paying our taxes but not receiving the protection and the services that we are entitled to—is it not our moral, loving, and civic obligation to demand our rights? Frederick Douglass said, 'Power concedes nothing without demand.'"

"Amen," said Rev. Charles.

"Apostle Paul asserted and Calvin confirmed that we should obey government not only to avoid punishment but also for the sake of our conscience. Thus conscience is bound by political law. When we do wrong, it weighs upon our mind. As Thomas Hobbes once said, 'The conscience is a thousand witnesses.' It is the tribunal of the soul. So the conscience of conviction submits us to the law. When we do wrong by God, it is the conscience that convicts us. When we don't love our neighbor, it is our conscience that reprimands us. When we don't do right by the law it is our conscience that challenges us. As a matter of conscience, do we not find it expedient to condemn ourselves when wrong is done? Also as a matter of conscience, do we also not find it just as expedient to condemn the wrong that is done to us, whether it be man or government?" He paused briefly, giving everyone time to soak up that last statement. "For the conscience not only corrects the wrong in us but the wrong done to us. The conscience we have for our sin is the same conscious we have for our society, because our society is God's property. So I believe the conscience that convinces us to do right by law is the same conscience that is disturbed when the law is not doing right by us."

"Oh, he's taking us on a roller-coaster ride now. You shouldn't have brought out the philosophical in him!" Rev. Taylor roared.

"Conscience convicts and so does love. Conscience does not have to fear if it is doing right, but the government has to fear the conscience of a just person if the government is doing wrong. A just person will fight and die to follow his conscience."

Everyone erupted in a cheer, but Bishop Samuel pressed on above the roar of our voices.

"The poet Claude McKay wrote' If We Must Die,' which in part says:

> Though far outnumbered let us show us brave,
> And for their thousand blows deal one death-blow!
> What though before us lies the open grave?
> Like men we'll face the murderous, cowardly pack,
> Pressed to the wall, dying, but fighting back!"

Everyone jumped up from their chairs and applauded, including Rev. Ed. It seemed to me that although Rev. Ed had boxed the bishop into a corner, Bishop Samuel had fought back into the middle of the ring and delivered the knockout punch.

But Bishop Samuel apparently decided to keep hitting his opponent while he was down—he came back with a right hook. "Let me get back to Nehemiah. Nehemiah did it for the love of God but also for the love of community and ancestry. The political was a means to an end, not an end that determined his means. Love is the centerpiece and cornerstone of our movement. Charity is the place of conscience, while politics is an act of charity."

"Very good!" Rev. Ed yelled out.

Bishop Samuel persisted, as if his reasoning needed a proper conclusion. "Nehemiah prayed, went to work, and finally got his people to see the devastation and the need for revitalization. Nehemiah said to the men, 'Do you see the trouble that we are in? Jerusalem lies in ruins and its gates have been burned with fire.' The ruins represented not only physical destruction but an emotional disturbance and spiritual separation from God.

"I ask the same question today of us who love our communities. Do you see the trouble we are in? Look at our cities. Their walls of greatness are in shambles. Their streets are filled with liquor bottles. Their corners are packed with gangs. Do you see the trouble we are in? Our dropout rate is the highest in the nation; our graduation rate is low. The music is lustful and unloving. The videos are vixenish and poisonous to the young. HIV and AIDS are infecting and killing our community.

"I ask again, do you see the trouble we are in as a community, a nation, a church, a people?"

"Yeah, I see it clearly. Even Stevie Wonder could see it," Rev. Taylor joked.

"But let me just end with this from Nehemiah," Bishop Samuel urged. "The reason for seeing it was not just to witness but to fix it. Sometimes things break down so that you can do them over again. I had a friend whose house caught on fire, and it was burned pretty bad. Fortunately, no one was home at the time. I ran over to the house, all frantic and hysterical, but when I got there she was at ease and calm. She said, 'I have insurance, and the good thing is I can do it over again. Make it better than the first time.'

"When we look at the ruins, when we look at the disgrace, when we look at the demise, when we look at the desolation and destruction, the good news is that because of Jesus, we can do it over again. We have insurance. His death gave us insurance."

"Oh, you preaching now!" Rev. Charles yelled.

"We get an opportunity to do it over again. Make it new. Restore our lives. Make it right. Sometimes things go wrong so we can get them right." Bishop Samuel rolled on with force, his hands gesturing wildly. "Things break down so we can fix them. Our communities have gone wrong but because of redemption, we have a chance to do it over again. We have a chance to build it again. We have a chance to make it work again. It's time for community renewal through the spirit of God! God bless!" With that, he pulled a piece of gum from his pocket, slipped it into his mouth, crossed his legs, and sat back in his chair like a king on his throne.

4

Second Chance

John 8:3–11

And the doctor said i'm sorry but u got cancer
I could not believe it so
I call my mama to calm my nerves
(mama) she got down on her knees
(mama) she said a prayer for me
(mama) just keep on thanking Jesus
(mama) he'll give you what you need
(thank you Jesus)....
Gave me a second chance

—"U Saved Me" by R. Kelly

E xcuse me, Rev. Ed," Rev. Taylor interrupted, "I don't mean to get ahead of the agenda, but that point reminds me of a message I preached some years ago called Second Chance." Rev. Taylor clearly had grabbed the baton and intended to run with it. "I took my text from the story of the adulteress woman."

"Oh, yes!" Lady Johnson called out.

"I believe from this story we see God using our sin for a second chance at life. With salvation come second chances. In fact, when we look at our communities and our people and our ruined condition as a result of our disobedience, we become perfect candidates for a second chance."

"Amen," Lady Johnson came in again.

"Second chance is that opportunity we get from God to do things differently. Walk differently. It is our turning from our sinful humanity toward our glorious divinity, as Jesus did at Gethsemane. And what makes salvation necessary are sin and temptation. If it were not for the sin, there would be no salvation—there would be nothing from which to be saved. It is through redemption that we come to the salvation that we receive—as a people, as a nation, a second chance."

"Take your time, Doctor," Rev. Ed said, clearly loving every minute of it.

Rev. Taylor was a seasoned preacher. He was more adamant and forceful and less sophisticated in his style than Bishop Samuel, but he was just as perfected in his biblical exegesis. His gestures conveyed his every word and emotion, as if he were in a sword fight, cutting down everyone in his path. His voice bass was intrusive, rambunctious and rude but easily understood.

"Although the story of the adulterous woman bases its text on testing Jesus' theological approach to sin, there is a subtext that speaks to the notion of sin in connection with salvation and second chances. The subtext highlights a distinction between the ruthlessness and condemnation of the world and the love and salvation of Christ. The Pharisee takes the woman while in the midst of sex and drags her to Jesus and tells Jesus that her sin should result in her being stoned to death, because that's what the law of Moses requires. No second chances. According to the law, she should be stoned to death for sleeping with someone else's husband.

"And I do believe that's a big problem in our society; it seems as though only *our* people are dragged out and publicly disgraced before the people because of their sins. No one makes better and bigger news than we do when it comes to our alleged wrongs—whether it is O.J., Michael Jackson, Kobe Bryant, or Mike Vic for his dog episode."

"Oh, but they're sure making big news off those white girls," Rev. Bryant interrupted with a rough sore throat sounding voice. "That Hilton girl, and let's not forget Britney, who the media has driven crazy with their constant attention."

"But soon, they'll be out and we'll be back in as usual," Rev. Taylor insisted nastily. "We've always been the focus of their scorn. Britney is white trash and just as good to the media as our black ass!"

Heads quickly snapped in his direction, seemingly shocked by his language. Rev. Ed looked shocked, too, but nodded at Rev. Taylor to continue.

"We are constantly dragged out and brought before the judge. Someone is always watching to see what we're doing, and when we fall, it's all over the news. The Pharisees represent the thinking of most people—that once a crime or an offense has been committed, we're ready to take the necessary actions to condemn and crucify. There are no second chances. But let's not totally sidestep the Pharisees' thesis and dissertation on the correlation of sin and death."

Rev. Taylor, a master philosopher, used reason and synthesis but otherwise demonstrated no formal structure to his speaking style. I found it rather stream-of-consciousness—he seemed to say whatever was on his mind to make his point and get his message across—but nonetheless riveting.

"The Pharisees were right in that sin can lead to death. Because as the Bible states, the wages of sin is death. And the relationship to the law and the theological authenticity of their epistemology were not disputable. Jesus wasn't going to argue with their legally binding reference and footnote of sin's relationship to death, which is why Jesus took so long in answering the question. The Bible says he stooped down and began writing on the ground, not yet answering their question. If anything, Jesus supported their argument; he just wanted to add a clause to it."

"Oh, you developing something, Doctor," Rev. Charles intruded. "I'm waiting for the meat."

"Jesus didn't want sin to be restricted to a particular category, such as adultery. Jesus wanted to let them know that if you want to talk about sin and death, let's not single anybody out; let's talk about everybody's sin equaling death. 'Right,' he then says, 'which one of you is without sin? Let him cast the first stone.' The truth of the matter is that everyone—the accused and the accusers—are all participants of sin and should die, since sin equals death. If they desired accurate application of their doctrine, they would have just started throwing stones at each other because of the epistemological relationship between sin and death. It should have been a big stone fight until no one was standing. Because the truth of the matter is, ain't nobody without wrong—excuse my grammar. The Pharisees wanted to talk about the wrong of adultery, but Jesus wanted to broaden the category."

"What you say," several people called out.

"Yes, adultery is wrong, but so is hypocrisy. Jesus called the Pharisees hypocrites on many occasions, because of their saying one thing and doing another. Hypocrites are those who twist a wrong for their own benefit. It's funny—or sad—how you can kill two people in your nation and be called a murderer, and you can kill hundreds of thousands in another nation and be called a conqueror, freedom fighter, democracy pusher, and terrorist-preventer. That's not democracy; that's hypocrisy!"

"You're right," Rev. Ed agreed.

"Wrong is wrong, no matter how you slice it. Jesus wanted to broaden the category to include backbiting, fornicating, gossiping, coveting, lying, jealousy, debauchery, idolatry, envy, greed, as well as stingy, phony, selfish, stubborn, malicious, deceptive, and revengeful people."

Rev. Taylor reminded me of a truck—he was hauling everything in his path. He continued with the ease of a doctor but the attitude of a fighter. "While I'm along the lines of the double standard, let me associate it with gay issues. This may not slide with most of you, but who cares." Everyone look offended by his last remark but no one said anything, not even me, at least not yet. Even Rev. Ed took the smile off of his face and just stared at him. "When gays come into the church, why do we single them out like they're the only ones committing sin? Why do we attempt to stone them when we know we have some fornicators, lusters, liars, et cetera, in the church?"

"Talk about it!" Rev. Franklyn yelled out with a seemingly high pitched voice. His finger still in his mouth and his legs crossed as he swung it back and forth, by the looks of things he knew this subject well.

"If we were to be fair, if gays are subject to ridicule and discipline, then so are dirty deacons."

"Amen!" A couple of the women along with Rev. Franklyn almost fell out of their seats with the enthusiasm of their loud applause.

"And both should either be replaced or repent. But Jesus says the sick need a doctor, and that's what the church is supposed to be: a healing place and hospice for deliverance. The church is God's house, and if anything is wrong in the church, then God will take care of it. Jesus often spoke in parables because he knew only some would understand. Let me relate a parable to the situation of gays in the church and how we ought to respond. In the parable of the wheat and the weeds, some wanted to separate the wheat from the weeds but the owner says to let the wheat and the weeds grow together. Because while you are pulling the weeds up, you may also destroy the wheat. The good and the bad should grow together until harvest time. The owner says, 'At that time, I will tell the harvesters to first collect the weeds and tie them in bundles to be burned; then gather the wheat and bring it into my barn.'"

"Oh, what great wisdom you spout," Rev. Ed interjected, smiling again.

"The church is the storehouse where evil and good preside. The church can't separate the wheat from the weeds;

that's God's job. The church can only plant the seeds of righteousness, hoping that salvation and deliverance will branch out of sin and wickedness. The purpose of the weeds and wheat was to give the weeds a chance to grow, for you never know how the wheat will impact the weeds. We don't give people a chance to be delivered. We condemn them and lambaste them and dismiss them and burn them, as if we're God. Gays deserve a chance, and they constitutionally have a right in this nation to form civil unions—this is for material benefits and insurance purposes. The church does not have to marry them—according to biblical and spiritual understanding, gays can't marry in God, for the Bible says man and woman can form holy matrimony. But they still deserve a chance in the church to grow and convert."

Some gathered around the table nodded; others shrugged, as if they conceded that argument was valid but not necessarily agreeable. Rev. Taylor seemed to be waiting for us to voice our disagreement so he could cut us down like weeds. The strongest amen came from Rev. Franklyn's soft voice. When no one challenged him, he continued. "But we should also think about this as a people. We can't advance because we're too busy forcing the wrongs of God upon others, even though we've all fallen short of the glory of God. And I do believe in karma— what goes around, comes around. Jesus said, what you reap, you sow. That's why you have to be careful how you judge folks, for the same manner in which you judge others, it will be done to you. You have to watch at whom you throw stones, especially if you've got some junk in your trunk. Some bones in your closet. Some mess in your fence. Don't think that while you're accusing someone else, your mess won't surface."

"Amen," Rev. Charles called out.

"I remember when former president Bill Clinton got in trouble with Monica Lewinsky. All the Democrats stayed quiet except for one loudmouth, rambunctious congressman from California. He was outspoken and kept calling for Clinton's resignation because of Clinton's indiscreet involvement with an intern. He didn't succeed in his attempts to oust Clinton, obviously, but look how dirt comes around. A couple of years later, there was an intern that went missing. It was all over the news for weeks until they traced her to the congressman she had worked for."

"I remember that," Rev. Charles and Rev. Ed said in unison.

"Come to find out, she and the congressman had been in a relationship. He confessed to it but claimed to have had nothing to do with her disappearance. He tried to run for office again but was soundly defeated. You have to be careful when your own stuff ain't right, but you're ready to throw stones at others."

Lady Johnson spoke up. "So you believe there is never a time to condemn the wrongs of people? I mean, we condemn the wrong of the president all the time."

Rev. Taylor looked as though he'd been stuck. When he spoke again, his voice was harsh and reprimanding. "There is a difference between political and personal condemnation, Rev. Johnson. We have a right to object to unjust laws and unrighteous acts that hurt people—that's political condemnation. Political condemnation is not a personal assassination; it's a public denouncement of unfair treatment that hurts and oppresses people. Moses announced publicly and challenged outwardly the unjust acts of the pharaoh. Politics is a public game, so it is necessary to bring political disagreement to the surface. But personal embarrassment and public disgrace, which is what the adulteress was subjected to, was a disservice to her and to those who tried to humiliate her.

"They threw her laundry in the street, which resulted in everyone's personal business being challenged so they could see the shame in their game. Jesus brought up everyone's personal business to ask how you would feel if your stuff was put in the public for everyone to see. Jesus denounced personal public disgrace of sin and wicked acts. Remember when Mary, Jesus' mother, was found to be with child?" He shot a look at Lady Johnson, seeming to dare her to speak. "The Bible says that Joseph could have publicly disgraced her but instead, he kept quiet. Because he knew that family business is family business. And I must say there is a debasement of values in our society and our family if public disgrace is honored and glamorized. Look at the court shows that come on television. *Judge Joe Brown, Judge Hatchett* and the worst, *Divorce Court*. They glamorize public disgrace in the family, in the community, in our society. When you have to put your spouse in the news and on the television and in the tabloids, that's a disgrace before the eyes of God. Marriage is sacred, and divorce is secret. The person who publicly disparages another is equally disgraced. Because when you blast someone else, you're also blowing up yourself. Who would want a woman who publicly disgraced and revealed the issues of her last marriage? It makes you think: if she did it to him, she could do it to me. Then you women wonder why you can't find a good man, it's because you talk too much!" He blaringly and insultingly looked at Lady Johnson.

A strong and loud amen came from Rev. Charles, loud enough that heads turned in his direction.

Rev. Taylor would not be outdone, and his voice became louder. "That also says something about the person who is subjecting the person to shame: what was it about you that attracted that no-good man to you? How long does it take for a sheep to detect a wolf? Or could it be that the sheep is really a wolf, and the wolf attracted the wolf? Public disgrace reveals something about everybody—children and parents, all coming on television to bash each other in public; cruel and malicious insults being thrown from daughter to mother. It's a disgrace! *This*, Bishop Samuel, is where we should cry."

Bishop Samuel nodded vigorously, apparently in total agreement.

"Think about a daughter or son on the television, suing the parents. Those are your parents who raised you, who spent money on raising you and who diapered you, and you're taking them to court over a cell phone bill. What is this world coming to?"

"An end," Rev. Ed blurted out.

"Right," Bishop Samuel agreed. "Do you see the trouble we are in?"

Rev. Taylor turned to Lady Johnson and addressed her personally. "Your question is understandable. God doesn't need our help in punishing someone for his or her wrongs. God said, 'It is mine to avenge.' So this is not to suggest that the accused won't suffer the consequences of their actions. The adulteress was dragged out. She had her private business thrown into the street. She was made a public embarrassment before all the people. That is a consequence of her actions. Other women possibly attempted to kill her for sleeping with their husbands. That's a consequence of her actions. No matter that Kobe Bryant got off on the rape charges; he still faced public ridicule. Contracts for millions of dollars were withdrawn. His wife is mistrustful, regardless of how many diamond rings he buys her. Diamonds are forever, but trust must be renewed daily. If anything, his buying her gifts may cause further suspicion, because every time he comes home with a gift, she's going to ask, what did you do now?"

"Ain't that the truth!" Lady Johnson laughed out loud.

"Everyone will suffer the consequences of his or her wrongful actions. However, Jesus is saying, 'I don't need your help to bring anyone else to judgment.'"

"Amen!" Rev. Bryant came in strong.

"I don't need your assistance in bringing others down, especially if you got a plank in your eye. You hypocrite: first take the plank out of your own eye, and then you will see clearly so that you can take the speck out of your brother's eye."

"That's good," Rev. Ed said.

"That's biblical," Rev. Taylor demanded. "Matthew 7:5." He then continued. "One of the best things of the American justice system is that when you're on trial, your hand is placed on the Bible and you are asked, 'Do you swear to tell the truth, the whole truth, and nothing but the truth?' The Pharisees told the truth, but they didn't tell the whole truth. In a court of law, when you withhold information you can be brought up on charges of obstructing justice. The Pharisees were obstructing justice, trying to hold back on the whole truth. The whole truth was that they all were sinners. Even the man with whom the woman committed adultery should have been dragged out, according to the law of Moses. The Bible says we've all fallen short of the glory of God. So when the whole truth came out, the Pharisees started to drop their case against the woman; they began to back up and drop their stones. They dropped their sentence of death.

"Their use of the death penalty was relinquished, found to be unjustified and without sufficient evidence. This is a prime reason we should end the death penalty in America, because the truth of the matter is, we're all guilty. Christ determines the life or death of a person. And a person determines his or her own life-or-death sentence in Christ. God doesn't need government's assistance to kill people, because government is not the judge of man; God is. When government interferes, it is taking God's job, putting itself above God rather than under God. One nation *under* God. Christ died to take the penalty out of death, so who is man or nation to put it back in? Especially when no nation is without sin. The death penalty says you get no more chances.

"We're taking the power from God in a more significant way when we apply the death penalty." His hands now swinging violently. " If the death penalty is applied to one's life by the state, we never get to see the redemptive power of God upon that person. We're actually saying that God cannot help this person, so we kill him. God said that he would separate the weeds from the wheat. It is better to show the might of God upon the wicked's being transformed while they are living, than to die by penalty and not allow God to get the glory."

"That was nicely said" Rev. Ed commended.

"But not good enough," Rev. Taylor retorted, barely pausing to take a breath. He continued: "To put a person to death is to say that God can't correct the person, that he or she is irredeemable. We never see the correction of the person and the power of God. A nation cannot boast of Christ and redemption if it has killed a person because of illegal actions. We are no longer under the old Mosaic law in Christ. Christ died because the law was more condemning than redeeming. With the death penalty, there is no glory to God, only to death. Christ died to take the glory from death, but when we kill, we put it back in, giving glory to death. Christ never wanted a person's life to end in shame; he wanted a person's life to end in change, so that God would gain the glory. Man gets the glory and the shame with the death penalty."

"That was brilliant," Bishop Samuel interjected.

"Thank you, but I'm not done" Rev. Taylor answered poignantly. "Government through man is not righteous enough to kill, to take the life of a person. They got it wrong with Jesus. Jesus at Gethsemane was killing sin and taking the penalty from death through his death, so that there would be no more killing by man. Statistics have shown that many innocent people have died at the hands of governments' wrong decisions.

"Minorities are unfairly targeted; since the death penalty was reinstated in 1976, 76 percent of those sentenced have been minorities, and 99 percent have been the poor. Black men are three times more likely to receive the death penalty than are white men. Rich white men will never see the death penalty; they have a heavenly pass on earth.

"Since 1973, because of DNA testing, more than 120 inmates who were on death row have been released. They got a second chance. God allowed the evidence to grow. Just imagine if they hadn't had a second chance to prove their case." Rev. Taylor finally seemed to be slowing down. He smiled at all assembled and said, "And as I come to my conclusion, the story of Lena Baker comes to mind. I read it the other day in a book by Jimmy Carter. Back in the 1940s, Lena Baker, a black woman, was held in servitude against her will and abused by her master, a white man. In 1945 she was tried and convicted by an all-white jury and sentenced to death after confessing that she'd shot the man when he attacked her with a metal bar and threatened to kill her. In 2005, however, after a thorough re-examination of the case, she was granted a full pardon—sixty years after dying in the electric chair. America had plucked up the wheat, mistaking it for the weed."

"What a story," Dr. Smith whispered.

"It's true," Rev. Taylor confirmed. "It was the same with the Pharisees. Their theology was challenged and their reasoning was reversed. They decided not to stone the woman to death. I guess everyone deserves a second chance. Jesus was an equal opportunity chance-giver. The Pharisees got a second chance to walk away and think about their wrongs. Jesus looked at the woman and said, 'Where are thou accusers? Has no one condemned thee?' She said, 'No, Lord.' And Jesus said, 'Neither do I. Go away and sin no more.' She was released by man but pardoned by Christ."

Halleluiahs and amens blurted out the souls of all present at that last statement.

Rev. Taylor's roar got louder and his humming seemed to last forever, as if coming to the celebration of a good sermon. "She should have been dead, but because she had a good attorney, she was released from hell. Jesus saved her from hurt, harm, and danger, and gave her another chance. She got a second chance to live right, to do right, to live differently. Another chance to start a new job, another career. Another chance to pick her head up. Another chance to ask for forgiveness. Another chance to wake up married with her own man. Another chance to honor her body. Another chance to accept Jesus as her lord and savior." Rev. Taylor looked at Bishop Samuel. They gave each other the high five, and as Bishop Samuel began to sing, everyone joined in:

"Blessed assurance, Jesus is mine, oh what a foretaste of Glory divine, perfect submission …"

5

How Can We Sing?

Psalm 137: 1–4

How can we sing in a strange land
Don't want to sing in a strange land
No Liberation true democracy
One God one aim one destiny

—"True Democracy" by Steel Pulse

Rev. Ed's broad smile displayed an awesome endorsement of his two colleagues. His admiration of the men was clear by his jovial expression. With all the amens ringing out, it was hard to focus on anything else, but Rev. Ed finally raised his voice with an Amen which calmed the group.

"Bishop Samuel … Rev. Taylor …" he began, "you two just touched on every subject we will be dealing with in depth during this gathering. You both addressed the communal and the political. I thank you for diving right in with your biblical assessment of the conditions of our land and of our people, while at the same time showing hope for the future. It gives us something to think about, as well as sing about."

"But how can we sing?" asked Rev. Charles. The tone of his voice was hard-edged. He still looked as though he was not only on fire but burning with something to say that would set the whole place ablaze. With his shoulders upright and his hands palm flatly layed on the table his light eyes looked angrily at everyone.

Rev. Ed's eyebrows shot up in surprise. "Excuse me?"

"I don't know how we can sing, here in this land of greatness yet contradiction," Rev. Charles explained.

Rev. Ed extended his arm toward Rev. Charles, saying, "Please, take the floor. We'd all be interested in hearing what you have to say."

I had the sense that Rev. Charles would have taken the floor, with or without Rev. Ed's invitation. He cast his eyes accusingly on each one of us as he spoke. "We sing, and we are great singers; the world has not known better. But the question posed by the Israelites was, 'How can we sing in a strange land?'" Rev. Charles demanded; his frustration was evident. "Particularly on days like the Fourth of July. On this recent celebration, I saw black people jumping up and down, like they had something to rejoice about. How can we celebrate and rejoice and feel the miracle of liberty and the bells of glory? Over two centuries ago, America celebrated its independence from motherland Britain. That length of time—230 years—would be an incredible and unimaginable lifespan for a person, but for a nation, it is a drop in the bucket. Within this short period of time, America not only gained its independence, but it also built its reputation as one of the greatest superpowers on earth. A glorious accomplishment by any measure. It can be compared to Rome in its glory days or the Ottoman Empire at its height. This is a nation that is feared and admired. Its ideology has given it a place in history, and its military has given it supreme capability."

For a preacher, Rev. Charles had a radical style. Although his look was that of a military sergeant, his words were that of a black militant. He paused between sentences and placed heavy emphasis on his last words. He had a tenor voice that raised into an alto at times. He never cracked a smile as he spoke; on the contrary, his expression was one of anger. Still, as I looked at his face, I thought it was clear that he really felt for his people. He just was not going to take any mess. Not even from his own people. His light skin offset some of his militancy, but his tone of vocal denouncement brought the darkness back. "We must admire America for its rise to power," he added unexpectedly.

"Speak for yourself," Rev. Taylor interjected.

"We'll get there, but first let me finish this statement," Rev. Charles pointedly responded. "America's strength did not come easily. Its motherland felt ownership and desired control over the infant nation. Britain was not willing to loosen the grip it had over such a prized possession. As a result, America's freedom did not come through compromise but rather through excessive confrontation. Protests and rebellions. All these actions ultimately resulted in God's hand of deliverance on this land of the free and home of the brave. And look, America built its ideological constitution upon equality and freedom; that all men are created equal with inalienable rights, those of life, liberty, and the pursuit of happiness. Liberty and justice for all. But does anyone see a contradiction between the freedom fought for and the freedom given?" He looked at everyone with a hard face like he demanded an answer. When no one answered he continued.

"America has done wrong to members of its nation with the same cruelty and maliciousness that was bestowed upon itself. This land of the free and home of the brave should be known as the land of the thief and home of the slave."

"That's good," Rev. Bryant, applauding.

"While America was fighting for freedom, it was enslaving its residents," Rev. Charles continued. "When America received freedom, it continued to whip and hang and deny its own black inhabitants their rights. I won't use the word 'citizens' because we were not considered citizens—humans—at the time; we were three-fifths human, according to the Constitution. But we were residents and inhabitants of this land, humans in our own eyes yet denied freedom and equality as a people. With enslavement of its blacks, America scorned its own reputation and shunned its own ideals of democracy.

"Frederick Douglass, in one of his famous speeches, given on July 4, 1853, in Rochester, New York, asked the question, 'What have I or those you represent to do with your independence? Are the great principles of political freedom and of natural justice embodied in the Declaration of Independence extended to us? And am I to bring our humble offering to the national altar and to confess the benefits and express devout gratitude for the blessings resulting from your independence to us?"

"That, brother, was deep," Dr. Smith interjected with her own somewhat deep voice.

"Douglass went on to say, 'This is not my independence—this is yours. This is not my Fourth of July; this is yours. The rich inheritance of justice, liberty, prosperity, and independence bequeathed by your fathers is shared by you, not me.'

"Frederick Douglass warned them not to insult us or mock us by pretending we joined in the sunlight of jubilation while we lived in the darkness of despair. How could they ask us to sing and rejoice and celebrate on the Fourth of July? Douglass said, 'I rejoice with anyone who gets their blessings of independence. But I don't rejoice when the blessings of independence are not returned in common. I don't rejoice when those who understand the necessity of freedom deny it to others.'"

"I've read that, and I like it," Rev. Ed said.

Rev. Charles wasn't impressed. His stare was angry. "So then you know what I'm talking about! During the Israelites' captivity by the Babylonians, they were taken away from their land of Zion. Again, Jerusalem. The land that brought them happiness and prosperity was snatched away from them. And then they found themselves in a strange land. The description of their sorrow is well documented in Psalm 137:1–4. 'By the rivers of Babylon we sat and wept when we remembered Zion.'

"The Israelites found themselves by the banks of the Tigris and Euphrates rivers, filling them up with their tears of despair and abandonment. If you've ever felt despair and abandonment over loss, you would cry, too."

Amens rang out.

"That's sort of what the Israelites did when they sat by the water; they tried to hide their tears. Because when a tear goes into the river, it can't be found; it blends into the water and disappears. But the hurt of the heart cannot be drowned in water, and the sorrow of the soul will be challenged for its truth." Rev. Charles' words were poetic, even in his anger. "The Israelites said their captives required of them a song. In the midst of their sorrow and enslavement and displacement and wandering, their captives mandated that they should *sing*. It's the same here; America wants all of its citizens to sing. They require a song from us. 'My country 'tis of thee, sweet land of liberty, of thee I sing.' I sing. I *sing*?"

"Come on now!" Dr. Smith yelled out. "Talk that talk."

"They require a pledge from us. 'I pledge allegiance to the flag of the United States of America and to the republic for which it stands, one nation under God, indivisible with liberty and justice for all.' For all. For all. For *all*?"

"That's good," Lady Johnson and Dr. Smith both said at the same time. I had to agree. It was fascinating the way Rev. Charles wove his stern sergeant's tone around his words.

"It would be something if everyone who didn't believe in the actions of the nation just stopped singing its anthem. Unjust war? No song. Unequal education? No song. Tax cuts for the rich; nothing for the poor? No song. Trillion dollar bail out for corporations, couple of dollars for small businesses? No Song. Wouldn't that be radical?"

Rev. Charles was stepping into career-threatening territory, a place that most wanted to talk about but not be about.

He left it there, looking at each of us and then shifting his military foot to the next connection.

"But there is more." He pointed his finger at everyone at the table. "Not too long ago, the Pledge of Allegiance was challenged in the U.S. Supreme Court by an atheist who desired to take 'One nation under God' out of the pledge on the grounds that it violated his atheist beliefs and his daughter's rights. He stated that it coerced her into saying something she didn't believe. He could have just told her not to say it, but then again, he was fighting for all those who did not believe in God. The Supreme Court, instead of taking a clear stand on the matter to determine its constitutionality, threw the case out on a technicality. The father was not permitted to bring suit because he didn't have sole custody of his daughter. The Supreme Court dodged that bullet."

"They sure did; I remember that," Bishop Samuel said.

"Anyway, my point is this: I believe that 'One nation under God' should stay in the Pledge."

Most of the ministers nodded and voiced their agreement.

"But let me submit my reasoning, which may be different from any of yours. Some may say we should keep the words because of America's history as a religious nation. That's not it for me. For me, it's that the statement recognizes a superior power. That this nation, no matter how big and powerful it becomes, is still *under God*."

"Yes!" Dr. Smith said.

"No matter how mighty its military, nor how prosperous its economy, the United States is still under God," Rev. Charles explained. "No matter how many technical or scientific breakthroughs or medical miracles there are in this country, it is still under God. Science is not anathema to God; it is *because* of God. Can I get an amen?"

"Amen!" Came in like a congregational choir. It was as if he had said "Attention!" and everyone immediately stood up. That's the command he held over us as he proceeded. "Psalm 47 says that God is the king of all the earth, that God reigns over all the nations, that God sits upon the throne, that the kings of the earth belong to God. The phrase 'under God' keeps America submissive and humble. The proclamation speaks for itself: America is one nation under God. This means it is not the only nation; it is one nation, one among every other nation on earth that is under God. The Bible says, 'The earth is the Lord's and the fullness thereof.' America is not the only nation that is blessed by God or under God; it is simply one of the nations that exist on God's earth under God's authority. There are others. This land is not my land, and this land is not your land; this land is God's land!"

His words again forced amens to come forth from all present.

"When a nation is under God, it remembers the least of those on earth. Jesus says in Matthew 25, 'Whatever you did for one of the least of these brothers and sisters of mine, you did for me.' When a nation is above God, it no longer sings praises to God; it sings praises to itself, and it believes its own understanding to be true. The worst consequence of self-praise happens when a nation that's supposed to be under God instead goes over God, so it faces destruction from God.

"That's what happened to the Israelites; they disobeyed, went above God, and faced the wrath of God. And the reason many will suffer is because the righteous—those who proclaim to know and obey God—are either complying or are silent about the wrongs. The righteous are singing and dancing to the tunes of war and government, rather than to the melody of peace and righteousness"

"I like that," Dr. Smith offered.

"Yes. Such singing and dancing on the issues is expected of politicians. They worship the party rather than the Creator. This is even to be expected of corporations, because they're looking to profit rather than to prophets to determine their decisions. It's all about the bottom line for corporations. They're greed has caused a breakdown in the nation's economy. Even the media can easily be silenced and forced into touting certain perspectives for fear of representing and encouraging unpatriotic positions. And to be viewed as unpatriotic is the worst sin in America. Remember what happened to Dan Rather when he revealed the story on Bush's not serving in the military, and they found it to be untrue?"

"Yes, I remember." Rev. Minor whispered in a small voice as if she didn't want to attract to much attention away from Rev. Charles for fear of reprisal.

"Rather resigned from his anchor position not too long after the inquiry, but we all know what happened. The media is scared of political power. Even academicians and educational institutions can be expected to go along to get along, fearing retaliation from the government in the form of funding for their institutions. Many college boards, including liberal ones, are run by very conservatively connected corporations and legislatures.

"But principles of freedom are grounded in biblical truth; they may be compromised and even disregarded by others, but never by the truly righteous. John Adams said, 'Statesmen may plan and speculate for liberty, but it is religion and morality alone which can establish the principles upon which freedom can securely stand.' But when those who purport to have God as their head begin to submit and sing to the tunes of unrighteousness, the nation is at great risk of grave destruction. What will destroy the nation are the silence and submission and singing of the righteous to unrighteous acts of a nation. The singing of the nation's song over God's psalm."

"Amen. I like that." Rev. Bryant led the applause.

"If the righteous do not speak, who can God rely upon to defend his truth? How can his truth be marching on if everyone is going wrong and singing the nation's song? If God can't find truth, God will be forced to lift his leg" Rev. Charles lifted his one good leg above the table. "and crush the nation that is under him." Then slammed it to the ground until a big thump was heard.

"Are you relating it to Sodom and Gomorrah, when God could not find the righteous number of people that he was looking for?" The voice of Bishop Samuel interrupted from the left.

"Exactly my point, thank you, Bishop. And when God could not find the righteous, the nation fell." Rev. Charles paused for a moment, smiling to himself. "I remember a joke," he told the group. "God sent Peter and Paul down to look at the condition of the world. And Peter came back with a bad report, saying there was too much sin; hatred and envy and disease and lies were torturing all of the people's souls. Paul came back with another report. He said it was not as bad as Peter said; the people still had love and faith and many were doing good by one another. Peter and Paul argued their point before God. Each built his own case. While Peter demanded destruction, Paul demanded salvation. Finally, God said, "This is what I'll do: I'll send a letter to all the righteous and tell them of my coming and that I want the people to tell me of their joy or sorrow." So God sent the letter to the righteous and the letter said ..." Rev. Charles paused again, pointedly looking around the table at the assembled clergy. "Oh, I don't have to tell anyone sitting at this conference what the letter said. All of you got the letter, right?"

Rev. Bryant looked confused. "No, what did it say?"

Everyone laughed—except Rev. Charles, who remained serious. "My point exactly," he said. "The righteous who are purporting to be righteous did not get the letter from God. The Bible says 'Not everyone that says to me "Lord, Lord" is going to heaven.' It's a joke, but it makes a good point. The situation is worse than we think. Too many of the righteous are not truly righteous, and this is what is causing the fall of the nation. We need the righteous to speak. How can we sing jubilantly, knowing that America has put itself above God? How can we sing joyfully, knowing that God has been replaced as head of the state? How can I sing of a sweet land of liberty when I have not tasted its brown sugar? How can I sing of justice for all when I have not felt it? Nor have many of my brothers and sisters. How can I sing that all men and women are created equal when the facts do not support the statement? Discrimination persists as we speak.

"When they ask me to sing of their freedom I am like the Israelites; how can I sing in a strange land? Strange, because they say one thing and do another. As you stated, Rev. Taylor, this nation is full of hypocrisy. Strange, because the ideology and philosophy of the Constitution are not consistent with the actions and policies of that nation."

"Oh, you are preaching now, doctor." Rev. Taylor supporting his every word.

Rev. Charles' voice became heavier and urgent. "It's strange, because those who are under God know that when God speaks, words and actions connect. When God said, 'Let there be light,' there was light!"

"Preach! Preach!" Several of the ministers called out.

"When God said, 'Let there be a firmament in the midst of the water,' it was so. When God said, 'Let us make man in our own image,' dirt jumped to attention and landed on God, and God stepped away from the dirt and left his image." His radicalness did not limit his creativeness. He stood up with a wobble because of his artificial leg and began to slowly move around the table.

"That's what you call the *Imago Dei*," Rev. Ed called out, watching him as he made his way around the room.

"Yes!" Rev. Charles confirmed. He paused and allowed his hands to sculpture the image his mouth described. "Inside the image, a scaffold of bones was structured to support the flesh that reflected God's pattern. Sinews and nerves began to form, and the bloodstream flowed and circulated in a slippery, rhythmic motion. God then inhaled" He took a deep breath "and exhaled" He let his breath blow. "And blew the breath of life into his formation, which then became a living organism." He began moving around the room again.

"Oh, when God speaks, things happen. Words and actions don't collide; they connect for the creation of a healthy manifestation. There is no contradiction. That's Jesus at

Gethsemane, willing to show the correlation and the connection of God's salvation through his humanity no matter how much his agony. Jesus did not say one thing and do another. He said he would die, and he died. He said he would rise, and he rose. If I were to sing for the nation it would be a false act of cooperation rather than a true sense of celebration, because of these contradictions."

Rev. Taylor and Dr. Smith stood up with him, and walked behind him. As he bellowed on they gave their amens and pats on his back.

"It's hard to shake hands with folks who do you wrong. It's hard to smile at folks who talk nasty about you. It's hard to eat with people you know are out to get you. And it's certainly hard to sing with folks you ain't in tune with."

"That's good talk." Rev. Taylor yelled as he walked around with him.

"Bring it home!" Rev. Ed yelled out.

"I'm already home; I just haven't gotten to my seat yet!" Rev. Charles shouted back. The entire group had risen to their feet by this time, following Rev. Charles' lead. He continued without pause. "The reason why I sing is the reason why Moses and Martha sang when God delivered them out of slavery. Moses began to sing, and Martha got all her girlfriends with their tambourines, and they began to sing and dance. When all my people are free and the enemy drowns in the sea, then I'll sing— because I'll be happy and we'll all be free. His eyes are on the sparrow, and I know he watches me."

Rev. Charles began to walk around the room faster, hopping and jumping on his peg leg and shouting, "We must all be free before we sing about being happy! That's Gethsemane— to risk one's life for others. Even in his agony, Jesus made the decision to risk his life so that we might be free." He made it back to his seat, sat down, and put his peg leg on the table, while everyone applauded him and praised God.

6

What It Means to Be Free

Romans 6:6–7

Do the David Dance
He jumped on his feet
Pulled off his grief
Put up his hands
And started to dance
Others looked at him
Said you are the king
You're acting quite crazy
You're out of your league
He looked right back at them
While he was still dancing
And said, when God sets you free
You dance just like me

The conference was off to a good start. The three most revered participants had spoken, and they had set the stage and proved that this was for the heavenly minded and heavy minded. No boys or girls; just men and women.

Rev. Ed looked at Rev. Charles. "Thank you for your verbal militancy and physical energy."

I had not said anything during this first part of the conference, although I had laughed when necessary and celebrated and applauded from time to time. I kept my eye on each participant. Most seemed encouraging yet intimidating—and arrogant enough to not mind if I stayed quiet the whole conference. I noticed everyone's confidence and style. They looked as if they'd come well prepared. From the look of things, this was not a gathering for the immature or uninformed. This was for the mature in faith and focus, for those whose reading and experience had brought exceptional enlightenment to otherwise unknown territory. The theological framework and creative understanding would make the conference inspiring, but at the same time the competitiveness of the participants and degree of their insightfulness would make it challenging.

Rev. Ed kept looking toward the door; I think he was anticipating the entrance of the two who had not yet arrived. He then signaled to Rev. Franklyn.

Rev. Franklyn seemed caught off guard by the call, and he responded hesitantly. "Yes, I would like to get a piece of that freedom discussion."

"No problem," Rev. Ed responded, "but I think the food is ready." He raised his voice so we all could hear him. "Ladies and gentlemen, do we want to pause and eat, or do we want to continue our discussion while we're eating?"

"What's the purpose of stopping?" Bishop Samuel asked. "We're going to talk while we're eating anyway, so I'd suggest we just continue."

When we all voiced our agreement, Rev. Ed said, "Okay, then, let's go. The waiters will serve the lunch, and we'll continue when they're gone."

Immediately, the waiters rushed in with the lunches. Orders already had been taken, so the waiters only had to look at each place card and match it with the appropriate order. They also left extra food and drinks. As quickly as they'd come in, they filed out of the room and were gone.

"Rev. Franklyn, you were saying." Rev. Ed asked as he stuffed food in his mouth.

"I just wanted to piggyback off of that independence piece."

"Oh, but turkey back would go better with independence," Rev. Taylor said slyly. Everyone laughed, except Rev. Franklyn, who perhaps didn't get it or didn't care. He continued, opening with a comment that confused me and, judging by their expressions, others also.

"I wanted to add more of an orthodox, theological approach to the discussion." He had a very high-pitched yet soft smooth, almost feminine-sounding voice. He sat in his seat with his legs crossed and one finger in and out of his mouth as he spoke. "I believe back when our country was founded that Americans realized that the control Britain had over them was not only a moral wrong but a religious sin. Any time a person or a people are bound and restricted in such a way that their freedom of expression and opportunity for resurrection are restricted, then they are not only prisoners of society but slaves to sin." He spoke cautiously, and appeared to be taking time to think about each word or phrase. "Hate, malice, envy, oppression—all are part of the wicked terrain that puts one under sin. And the wickedness not only affects the nation but the soul of the nation. So in essence, what America was fighting for was freedom from sin."

"Talk about it," said Rev. Ed, his words slowly working their way through the food in his mouth. "You're really going somewhere that I haven't connected to before."

"Sin is something of the soul. That's where the saying 'sin-sick soul' comes from. Our souls are diseased and infected with the spoils of greed, selfishness, and malice. So in order to get free of sin and gain independence, the soul of self has to be transformed. Sin not only affects the person, it affects the soul of the person. It's the same for the nation. The nation is sick whenever it indulges and accepts the oppression and suppression of a people. It is not only a national tragedy but an internal national infection. And you would think that a nation so taken by freedom and so inspired by liberty would follow its own course of history and extend the invitation of liberty and justice to all in doctrine and in action. As Rev. Charles stated before, America should share the grace it has been freely given. Remember, God shed his grace on thee."

"Yes. Make the connection," Bishop Samuel blurted out. Food coming out of his mouth along with his words. "You would think the nation would shed its grace on me."

"I like that," Rev. Ed said.

"But the societal control and enslavement that Britain placed on America are the same restrictions and oppression America placed on the souls of black folks. America the Great found itself not only in its own moral crisis but also committing sinful actions. So the same tyrannical, controlling force of sin that bound America was the same act of sin that enslaved blacks. The same sin that America escaped is the same sin that America perpetuates. It is perpetrating the fraud."

"Very good, preacher," Rev. Ed commended him, as if he knew Rev. Franklyn needed encouragement.

"Thank you," Rev. Franklyn responded while looking down at his plate as he picked up bits of food with his fingers. His loud squeak at times became irritating to the ears, and I found it hard not to focus on his voice. But what he said somewhat masked the pitch of his voice, and his revelation and theological perspective was clearly conveyed. It seemed to me that he had a little self-esteem problem, but he didn't allow it to stop him. I suspected that's why he looked down as he spoke—so as not to be disturbed by the facial expressions of his listeners.

"Sin keeps one's soul in slavery," Rev. Franklyn continued, "so that true praise, honor, and worship cannot be given to God or the nation. If a soul is strangled by sin, it cannot give God the glory. It is hard to give praise when the sin of society keeps the soul in captivity. That's why you can't sing to the nation, Rev. Charles." Rev. Charles abruptly looked up when his name was called as if he was now paying attention to the high note coming from Rev. Franklyn. "Because of the sin of the nation. The sin of the nation is the lack of freedom and overwhelming suppression that takes away from soulful expression. So it's impossible to praise this country. How can we sing? How can we dance? The truth is, as long as the gag of oppression and racism is over the soul, we can't! It's just not logistically, linguistically, lyrically, or even 'gospel-ly' possible."

Bishop Samuel applauded that last statement which seemed to give Rev. Franklyn more confidence. Now, he began to look up as he spoke. "I like the way Dr. James Cone says it in his book, *A Black Theology of Liberation*. Cone says 'If the content of the gospel is liberation, human existence must be explained as being in freedom, which means rebellion against every form of slavery, the suppression of everything creative.' I think that was on page 87." He became a little bit presumptuous at that point. Removing his fingers from his mouth and now looking at each one of us. Rev. Ed and a couple of others lifted their head from their plates and directed it towards his face to see if he had more to say. And he did. Dr. Smith and Lady Johnson were impressed and told him to go on.

"Sin is evil that keeps us oppressed and captive and immobile and, to a large extent, paralyzed in a position of soul poverty. Sin restricts our progress and preys upon our weakness and results in ultimate death. The Bible says, 'Therefore, just as sin entered the world through one man, and death through sin, and in this way death came to all men, because all sinned.' The power of sin is its ability to attract and captivate us. The penalty of sin is its ability to kill and condemn us."

"Good analysis," Lady Johnson confirmed while stuffing her mouth with her last piece of chicken.

"Once we are under sin's control, then we are out of God's control. Because sin is contrary to God." His high pitch voice was getting preachy. While speaking he uncrossed his legs and kept his fingers away from his mouth and used them instead to make his point. "The sin of racism and discrimination keeps

America away from God. What Jesus did at Gethsemane was take us from the enslavement of sin to the emancipation of the spirit. And those who understand our emancipation from slavery will understand that we are no longer under the old selves, where sin controlled us, but we are under the new creation, where Christ controls sin. The Bible says he who had no sin became a sin offering so that we might be saved from the power and the penalty of death. When we identify and connect with Christ, we are no longer under the old self. The fullness of our independence and freedom came by accepting and declaring that Christ died to sin, and we, too, being baptized, share in the emancipation of our salvation from sin."

Rev. Franklyn was on a doctrinal roll. Everyone kept eating, but a few blurted out an amen to let him know they were still with him. I myself was hoping he would move quicker from doctrine to real life situation soon. "So now, after accepting Christ, our souls are no longer sin-sick but set free." His voice seemed to become much deeper and less annoying as he transformed into the preacher he was. Everyone caught his vibe, and amens began to ring. "My application is this: once the soul is set free, then the body not only desires emancipation but demands it. It yearns for it. In fact, it cannot live without it. It has no choice but to seek it because of a transformed internal."

"That's a really impressive thought," Rev. Ed said while pausing from his food to show his amazement at that last profound statement. Others gave similar approval and Rev. Franklyn gave them a nod of gratitude. Rev. Taylor muttered something under his breath, but I couldn't tell what he'd said. He, however, didn't look impressed.

Rev. Franklyn ignored the grumbling and gravitated to the gratitude that he received from the others as he continued with his orthodox position. "During slavery, many slave masters were opposed to baptizing the enslaved because they felt it not only freed slaves doctrinally from sin but legally from slavery. So they withdrew from baptizing for fear of being compelled to set the captives free. But their doctrinal understanding was correct: once you've been set free from sin, there is a yearning and a burning for liberty in society."

"That's good," Bishop Samuel commended.

"So whether or not the slave masters set the enslaved free, if conversion were to occur, they would seek freedom instinctively!"

Rev. Charles and Bishop Samuel along with Lady Johnson and myself stood up at that last remark. He had hit a cord not only with us but with the volume and the strangled bass by which he said it. His words were profound and his voice was strong as if he had transformed from David Banner to the Incredible Hulk.

"Many slaves escaped right after Sunday service. Because if they heard the word and accepted its power, they not only desired freedom but actually were forced toward freedom."

"I like this orthodox stuff," Rev. Minor whispered.

Rev. Franklyn continued. "The story is told of a young woman who kept escaping from the slave master. He would catch her and whip her until the skin peeled off of her back. But a couple of months later, she would be on the run again. He would catch her each time and whip her something horrible. But it wasn't the body she was concerned about; it was the soul she was ushered by."

"Good God! Yes!" Dr. Smith hollered. She was looking upward and praising.

Rev. Franklyn paused briefly just to witness her reaction and then resumed his spiritual connection. "The Bible says fear not those who can destroy the body but not the soul; rather, fear the one who can destroy both soul and body in hell."

There was a collective "Amen" from the group.

"She was free; she was just trying to get to the place where the spirit and body could meet in liberty. That's Gethsemane—the place where the spirit and the body meet in liberty, in unity rather than being in controversy. Once the spirit leads toward liberty and the body follows, then both body and soul have been set free. Because who Christ has set free is free indeed. Being *set free* is the internal release from sinful captivity; *free indeed*, is the external emancipation in society, which means all aspects of freedom must manifest from the soul to the surface, from the spirit to the nation."

"I'm loving it," Rev. Charles said while wobbling to sit back down.

I'd been somewhat bored by Rev. Franklyn's initial analysis but now I was amazed by it. He'd taken his time but eventually made the connection. Only Rev. Taylor still seemed unimpressed—he kept stuffing his mouth with food, seemingly uninterested with the lesson coming from Rev. Franklyn. "The soul is free, so the body demands freedom, even if it has to die for it. Americans who rail against immigration really do not understand the spiritual connection. The bodies of the immigrants are moving to where their souls can be free, just as Americans did when they freed themselves from the tyranny of Europe. We're all aliens and should be treated fairly. God says to the Israelites in the book of Exodus 'Do not mistreat an alien or oppress him, for you were aliens in Egypt.'"

Everyone had resumed eating. As our forks hit the plates, Rev. Franklyn's transitional voice sounded as if it was singing to the beat of the tapping utensils. "As Cone stated, 'Inherent in freedom is the recognition that there is something wrong with society, and those who are free will not be content until all members of society are treated as persons.'"

"You must be a James Cone fan," Rev. Charles suggested. "Did you memorize all of that?"

"Yeah, and more," Rev. Franklyn responded.

"I guess when you don't go to school, you can memorize everybody else's stuff," mumbled Rev. Taylor. Throwing the spirit of the discussion off and embarrassing Rev. Franklyn. Just then, Lady Johnson jumped to his defense. "He went to school," she stood up "Can't you tell? Since when has formal education become the only education for God's kingdom. Maybe it's you who need to take some classes in edict and respect. What good is it for a man to gain the whole world and lose his soul. I'd rather be a wise servant than an educated fool!" She then sat down while others applauded her for her defense of Rev. Franklyn. Rev. Taylor who looked as though he was going to harshly respond was interrupted by Rev. Ed who forcefully held his hand up by saying "wait, let's allow Rev. Franklyn to complete his analysis, we can get to the subject of education later Rev. Taylor. Rev. Taylor bowed his head and mumbled something else under his breath. Rev. Ed, being the expert moderator that he was, redirected our focus. "You were saying, Rev. Franklyn?"

Rev. Franklyn didn't say anything for a moment. I wondered if he was too embarrassed to speak, but suddenly he picked up the thread of his logic but had gone back to his squeaky rather than mighty voice. "What seeks freedom for all and risks itself is the internal baptismal transformation that we have gained. Esther had this! Moses had this! Jesus had this baptism! We became a new creation with the demand of emancipation. Freedom is essential to the human and divine experience. This is Jesus at Gethsemane: the human and divine experience, both on the verge of release. Freedom is not an option; it is an obligation that must be taken if not given. Once the spirit speaks, we seek freedom at all costs. Nat Turner, in his spiritual revolution, sought freedom with a rebellious, violent vengeance. Frederick Douglass sought it with an educational and political mix of radical and diplomatic persistence. Harriet Tubman sought it through a clever escape route. Marcus Garvey sought it through the motherland. Malcolm X sought it by any means necessary. And Martin Luther King, Jr., sought it through legislation. How are we seeking it?"

"Good question," Rev. Bryant said.

"If the body does not prevail because of fear, the soul and the body will be at war. This is where we return to the struggle between humanity and divinity at Gethsemane. The persistent demand of sin is what prevents our bodies from following our souls' desires. Sin reaps fear, and fear causes war with the faith. Just because we are no longer controlled by sin doesn't mean that sin doesn't want to control. Just because we are no longer enslaved by sin doesn't mean that sin doesn't want to enslave. Just because we've been set free by the blood and buried in the baptism doesn't mean that sin has died. We have died to sin, but sin is still very much alive."

"Very well stated. That's brilliant give us some more" Rev. Ed encouraged hoping to bring out the lion in him over the lamb.

"And it seeks to rob, kill, and destroy, even in our freedom. Watch this," Rev. Franklyn pronounced, his confidence being restored. His voice was building up the muster and the might as he spoke. "You ever had something or somebody in your life that you got rid of because it was no good, yet it still tried to get back in?"

"Yes," Lady Johnson quickly responded.

"That's how sin is. Even though the baptism declares our freedom and the blood has cleansed and given us independence, sin still tries to enslave. It's just like when the Israelites tried to get away from Pharaoh. God had set them free, but Pharaoh kept coming. It's just like black people, when we try to get away from the oppression and racism of this nation, hate and indignity and poverty and ill reputation still runs after us.

"But look how the soul of conversion works. There is something about the soul, once it's been set free, that keeps it fighting and agonizing for its continued emancipation. A set-free soul does not bow down easily. It fights its best not to be entangled in sin or in society again. That's why immigrants keep fighting for freedom. That's why African Americans keep fighting for civil rights. That's why women keep fighting for equality, and that's why the poor keep fighting for economic prosperity.

"Because the set-free soul demands to remain free. When the soul is free and the body is free, then the mouth can sing and the body can dance, like David danced." He got up, tipping over his plate and began to dance. Everyone looked at him and most of the women smiled. "The soul wants to be able to soar and fly like an eagle. The soul wants to be able to push the body forward into schools and jobs and neighborhoods and positions without difficulty or interference." His voice had gone from high squeak to mighty roar as he spoke.

"The soul does not want to be caged. It is like an eagle that wants to spread its wings and fly. Fly to the White House without being stopped because of color. Fly to the corporate boards without hitting a glass ceiling. Fly down the highway without being stopped by racist cops." All of a sudden, Rev. Franklyn became a singing angel. He lifted his head and spread his arms and began to flap his wings as he made his point. All the women in the room caught his spirit, jumped on board, and began to flap their arms and fly along with him. He started singing an old spiritual:

Some glad morning when this life is over,
I'll fly away;
I'll fly away, O Glory, I'll fly away in the mornin'
When I die, hallelujah, by and by,
I'll fly away.

7

Look What the Blood Has Done

Matthew 26:28

I get down for my grandfather who took my momma
Made her sit in that seat where white folks ain't want us to eat
At the tender age of six she was arrested for the sit in
With that in my blood I was born to be different

—"Never Let Me Down" by Kanye West

When the applause for Rev. Franklyn died down, Rev. Ed turned to Dr. Smith, who had been applauding and encouraging others' truth and doctrine but had not had an opportunity to present her case. "Dr. Smith, I think now we'd all like to hear your topical reasoning," Rev. Ed encouraged her.

She smiled in acknowledgment but waited to speak until the waiters had cleared the plates off the table. Once the sound of gathered dishes and cutlery had subsided, she began: "Well, thank you, and it couldn't be at a better time, now that I've filled my stomach with that good food. I thought Rev. Franklyn was going somewhere else in his reasoning, but I'm glad he gave me an introduction."

Her easy style made you smile. She was relaxed, and the pitch of her voice was deeper than one might have expected— like a cigarette smoker's voice, coarse and rough. Still, at the same time it had a nice, melodic harmony. I noticed that she pronounced every word slowly, as if she were teaching a class of third-graders. "I, too, believe in the orthodox approach to religious doctrine, so let me teach. I want to take it from the spirit of freedom to the blood of liberty. And I do believe the two work hand in hand, but let me just talk about the blood in relationship to freedom."

"Sounds good. We're listening." Rev. Franklyn said.

"I do believe that we often associate blood with fear and death, which is justified, because when most people think of blood, that's exactly what it represents. But God has somehow, throughout the ages, used blood in a magnificent, lifesaving, transformative way. God has fixed it so that blood is not disturbing but necessary for reconciliation and changing the landscape of human existence. God has turned things upside-down once again, so that instead of being life lost, blood dripping is life gained. God has showed us the wonder of the working power of the blood by taking us from an old system of death to a new covenant of life. Let me give a little history."

She was grandmotherly yet tough. She raised her thick voice a notch and dove into her discussion.

"Under the old system, when one sinned against the law of God, sacrifices had to be made through goats and calves. When one violated the rights of God or humans, the wrong had to be corrected. If you robbed somebody, you were guilty of a violation of the law, and a guilt offering had to be made. The guilt offering required that you get a lamb without defects and pour its blood over the surface of the altar. If we had been living in that time, a lot of us would have had to kill a whole lot of lambs in order to correct our wrongs and atone for our sins. It would have been a lamb over here and a lamb over there, here a lamb, there a lamb, everywhere a lamb, lamb."

She was also funny. Rev. Taylor laughed so hard he almost fell out of his seat. So did Rev. Minor, who for the first time went from smile to loud laugh. Dr. Smith laughed along with us, unable to contain her laughter, as if her own humor had surprised her. Along with her laughter came coughing which she tried to stop by sipping on a glass of water. She finally got herself together with the help of Rev. Ed patting on her back. She continued where she had left off.

"Somebody say, 'Thank you for Jesus.'" We all complied as she continued in what seemed an even deeper voice. "The sin offering or guilt offering made atonement to God, and when it made atonement, it temporarily covered up the wrongs and made peace with God."

"Ok, I see where you're going." Rev. Bryant called out. "No, you don't," She responded abrasively. "because I haven't made my turn yet, wait and see where I'm going, son." Like a grandmother to a grandson he was put in his place as she continued with a smile.

"Understand that atonement did not erase the wrong or pay for the wrong; it simply covered up the wrong. It's as if you want to buy something, and so you write a check. The check satisfactorily covers the amount of bill, but it does not take away the debt—that doesn't happen until the check clears. That's why some of us used to pay by check because we had at least two or three days to get the money in the bank to cover the check. But now, the stores check to see if money is in the bank before the check can be used. In the old testament, atonement was a check that covered the offense but it didn't have enough power to take away the debt or sin. It was merely reparation.

"That's why it really doesn't matter if they decide to give us black people reparation for the past sin and enslavement of our ancestors." Just then she made a right turn, throwing everyone off course. "The reparation would be a monetary gift to atone for slavery. If they gave us a billion dollars each, it would possibly cover the expenses of living and clear us from poverty. Some of us could get a good education and homes to live in. We could buy land and live comfortably. But it could not clear the damage that was done historically or mentally. It does not take away the rape of our women, the breakup of our families. Women and families are more valuable than silver and gold. It doesn't erase the inward hurt, the psychological damage as a result of the ghetto and poverty that was inflicted upon us for so long. The culture of hedonism and materialism is overwhelming in our communities—Cornell West calls it the culture of consumption. It is the debt of the problem. If we got the money, I fear—because many of our people are so damaged psychologically and warped internally and weak spiritually—we would give the money right back to the capitalist nation and oppressors. A lot of us wouldn't invest in houses and land and stocks and bonds or build businesses and acquire corporations. Instead, we'd buy a bunch of clothes, a billion dollars' worth."

Rev. Charles and Rev. Bryant stood up on that point. Her voice got deeper as if she was scolding rather than analyzing. Even though her words were spoken with humor she was serious. Rev. Ed listened intently along with the rest of us because she was so knowledgeable and passionate about the situation.

"Closets full of Nike and Reebok and DKNY and Gucci and Nine West shoes. Cars with the latest wheels and Bose sound systems. Every time you walked down the street you'd hear music blasting from another car. Us leaning back in the latest model." She put her hand out as if she was driving a car, leaned back, and started making music with her mouth.

"That's funny," Rev. Taylor again almost falling out of his seat chuckled.

"No, that's for real," Rev. Bryant insisted. The rest of us had tears in our eyes from her comedic enacting of the streets.

"As soon as we got it, we'd spend it," Dr. Smith continued even more serious. "We haven't learned what it means to save and invest. Most of us know nothing about stocks and bonds. We'd use all the money to make white folks richer, and there still would be a class difference. The atonement would make repairs and cover the wrongs, but it wouldn't make up for the damage that was done psychologically, because it isn't strong enough."

"Say what you want, they give me a billion dollars, I'm taking it. Quick, fast, and in a hurry," laughed Rev. Taylor.

"Well, I never said don't take it; I just said it's not strong enough," Dr. Smith responded. "Reparation has no teeth to eliminate the weak and frail minds of our people; it's just a front without power. It's like the United Nations."

"The United Nations?" Rev. Ed asked, clearly surprised. This time she took a left turn and threw some of us off her path.

"Yes, the United Nations," Dr. Smith assured him. "The United Nations is just a good front with no teeth. I believe the United Nations is a false act of international cooperation. It is a body that is weak. Talk about Gethsemane and the body being weak—well, the United Nations' body is weak! If they had any might they would have gone into Iraq before America did and detailed their search and conclusion of whether or not there were weapons of mass destruction. They would have had the power to hold America off until they concluded their search. If they would have concluded their search, they would have been able to prevent—through force, if necessary—the United States from entering militarily into Iraq, prematurely and falsely. But because the United Nations doesn't have an enforcing bark or a military bite, nations are able to dismiss it and take matters into their own hands. There is no verbal or tactical force to prevent defiance from the United States. The United Nations did nothing to America, so what can they do to other rebellious nations?"

"That was a good connection," Rev. Ed commended her. "You shed light on a matter that is often shrouded in darkness. Thanks."

Dr. Smith nodded, even as she continued with her thought. "It's like the Emancipation Proclamation," This time she took a U turn back to black people's history. "which inscribed the termination and abolishment of slavery. When the Emancipation

Proclamation was issued on January 1, 1863, the atonement was worded in clear verbiage, but the Emancipation Proclamation did not have the power to take away the unjust, unfair, inhumane, unnecessary, and uncivilized treatment of enslaved African American people. That's because the proclamation was backed by nothing concrete; it was a promise without substance."

"Yes!" Rev. Ed confirmed with excitement.

"Under the old Mosaic law, atonement didn't take away sin; therefore, death still reigned. One was still confined by the boundaries of death. There were no opportunities for life—or life more abundantly. There was no talk of the here and after, no hope for the future, no talk of many mansions. No sacrifices for life, and no mediator for justice. Death still had victory, and the grave still had its sting." Dr. Smith reminded me of a seasoned poet. I could hear the poetry in her logic and rhythm. "After the Emancipation Proclamation, there were no opportunities for good-paying jobs; African Americans were restricted to domestic work. Dilapidated housing. Separate bathrooms and ill-prepared health and legal representation."

"I feel you," Rev. Minor postured.

"All the stuff that we've been through with the Proclamation, but no power and restitution. I tell you, if anyone should believe that there is a God, it is black people." She paused, then coughed before she continued. "Although the atonement was weak, the blood was strong." She looked around at all of us. "I should have gotten an Amen right there" She told us.

And just then at her request she got it loud and clear.

"Jesus told his disciples that his blood was poured out for the forgiveness of sins. Jesus had to shed his blood for us to be free from the power and the penalty of sin. This is where I thought you were going, Rev. Franklyn. Jesus became the ransom for the check so that it wouldn't bounce. He became the deposit to give the check substance, so that it would cover the debt of sin. Jesus was no ordinary currency. First Peter 1:18–19 says, 'For you know that it was not with perishable things such as silver or gold that you were redeemed from the empty way of life handed down to you from your forefathers, but with the precious blood of Christ, a lamb without blemish or defect.'

"The monetary currency with which we're all familiar is used for purchases and transactions of goods and services. It would be hard to live without this currency, because that is what the world operates by. Money talks and bull crap walks, if you know what I mean."

Heads nodded in agreement, and "yeah, we know" was heard from more than one person.

"Money is able to get you the needed and desired possessions. The more of the currency you have, the more purchases and transactions you can make. You can redeem almost anything in this world at a price, and that goes for people as well as products."

"Talk about it," Rev. Ed unabashedly encouraged her.

"Once the purchase is made, money switches ownership from person to business. Some people even worship money—that is why it's called the 'almighty dollar.' The O'Jays used to sing about that." With her rough yet catchy voice, she began to sing the song: "'Some people got to have it, they really need it, do thangs, do thangs, bad thangs with it.'"

"Oh, that was one of my favorites by them," Bishop Samuel said, tapping his foot.

Dr. Smith coughed again and then continued. "I believe it was in 1803 that with a stroke of a pen by Thomas Jefferson, America made its biggest acquisition of land with the Louisiana Purchase. This agreement allowed America to go beyond its constitutional powers and purchase from France over six hundred million acres of land for fifteen million dollars. The new territory doubled the size of America, and the country became stronger and more powerful. Today, that purchased land makes up over thirteen states between the Mississippi River and the Rocky Mountains. But some things cannot be purchased with monetary currency. You cannot purchase freedom from sin and death. The devil is not accepting money for your liberty; he's giving money for your captivity."

"Amen" resounded through the room. She had broken it down and come to her destination with flow and fluency. And from the looks of things she wasn't near her conclusion.

"The enemy doesn't need money; he needs souls. And he gives money to get souls."

"That's right," Rev. Franklyn agreed, loving Rev. Smith's orthodox connection.

"There's only a certain type of currency that can free us from sin and death. It's not money—it's bloody." Rev. Smith looked around the table and settled her gaze on each one of us in turn before continuing. "This is what Peter points out in verse eighteen: 'that ye know it was not with perishable things such as silver and gold that you were redeemed.' However, it was through the precious blood of Christ, without blemish or defect, that we were purchased. In other words, there are some things that money can't buy and only blood can supply."

"You preach, Doc." Rev. Charles exclaimed while waving his hands up in the air.

"Even with our own freedom from slavery in America, it was money that was used to buy us and sell us, but it was blood that was used to free us. Marcus Garvey once said, 'Any sane man, race, or nation that desires freedom must first of all think in terms of blood. Why, even the Heavenly Father tells us that "without the shedding of blood there can be no remission of sins." Then how in the name of God, with history before us, do we expect to redeem Africa without preparing ourselves—some of us—to die!'

"Civil wars had to be fought and blood had to be shed and people had to die. Money was used to keep us in slavery for economic reasons, but blood was used to set us free for moral reasons. Gethsemane is Jesus' spirit pushing his body to die for freedom." She paused again and looked at us like a chastising grandmother before she resumed.

"No death, no blood. No blood, no freedom! In order to gain freedom, spirit must be willing, but body must be strong to endure the punishment that comes with shedding blood. The blood of Jesus became the currency that freed us from sin and death. The power of purchase came through the blood of Christ."

Amens were heard around the room, and I was impressed by her weaving of the biblical with the historical.

"Jesus redeemed us with his own precious blood—precious, because it was worth a lot; it had strong backing. It wasn't empty, like the United States treasury. And he redeemed us with our sins. The Bible says, 'While we were still sinners, Christ died for us.' He didn't purchase us while we were good or perfectly put together. Jesus purchased us when we were broken and beat up, and defective, misplaced, and no good, and of no value, and some of us of no use." Dr. Smith had everyone's attention, and she knew it. She went on, obviously feeling the energy of her own words.

"Listen! I went to the supermarket the other day and bought a can of corn. When I got to the cashier, I discovered a dent in the can. I said to the cashier, 'Let me exchange this for a better can because I don't want any dents in anything I buy.' But I'm so glad Jesus is not like me." She picked up her hand and pointed to her chest, shut her eyes, poked out her lips, then opened her eyes and continued with her deep melodic voice. "He saw us with dents of sin and said give me that one. Broken like glass; give me that one. Alcoholic, drug addict; give me that one. Abused and misused; give me that one."

"Yes!" Lady Johnson gravitated to Dr. Smith more than anyone.

Dr. Smith's deep voice became demanding. And the louder she got, the louder we all got, with "amens" backing up her every word. She persisted, because the amens gave her permission.

"Liars and thieves—give me them, too! Heavily burdened and disconsolate—give me them, too! Unhealthy and lowly—I'll take them, too. I'll take all of them—murderers and mentally damaged, all of them. Jesus said, 'Come to me, all you who are weary and burdened, and I will give you rest.'"

Cries of "Amen!" and "Thank you, Jesus" rang out.

Dr. Smith kept going. "Some of us, he picked off the shelf; others came off the streets or out of the hospital bed. Jesus purchased us while we were no good and sinners and sinking and sick. Then he took his used purchases and left with the receipt, for proof of purchase."

"Thank you Jesus! Halleluiah! Thank you Jesus!" Lady Johnson cried out unabashedly and undeterred.

"When you buy something used, like furniture, you have to fix it up and smooth it over. When Jesus purchased us, he had to sand us down from our sins. He separated us from our wrongs. Jesus started stripping and forgiving. He stripped us of our lies. Stripped us of misusing and abusing. Stripped us of our selfishness and greed and said you're forgiven. After stripping, he washed us with the blood. We all needed washing from all that dirt we used to get into when we were in the world. We opened ourselves up to some stuff that made us feel filthy and trashy. Filth and dirt left spots and stains in our lives."

"Talk!" The quick shout again came from Lady Johnson, who couldn't take her eyes off Dr. Smith.

Dr. Smith met Lady Johnson's eyes. She must have realized then that she was touching somebody. "Sin doesn't feel good after you come to Jesus; it feels dirty and stinky and nasty. It feels disgusting. It's like the woman-at-the-well story in John: 'Jesus said to her, "You are right when you say you have no husband. The fact is, you have had five husbands, and the man you now have is not your husband."' After he told her all about herself, he offered her some living water. And she said desperately, give me some of that water, because she needed cleansing. She needed washing from her past. She needed scrubbing from all the men who had gone up in her womb."

"Good God!" Lady Johnson exclaimed.

Dr. Smith smiled slowly and then continued."Ntozake Shange has this brilliant, poetically choreographed line in his book, *For Colored Girls Who Have Considered Suicide When the Rainbow Is Enuf*."

"I read that years ago," Rev. Charles interrupted.

Dr. Smith closed her eyes and out of the crevices of her cranium began to recite the poem with drama and emotion.

"'At 4:30 AM, she rose, movin the arms and legs that trapped her, she sighed affirm the sculptured man, and made herself a bath, of dark musk oil Egyptian crystals, and Florida water to remove his smell, to wash away the glitter, to watch the butterflies melt into suds and the rhinestones fall beneath her buttocks like smooth pebbles in a Missouri creek. Layin in water she became herself, ordinary.'

"And then Shange goes on to say, toward the end:"

'And now she stood a regular girl, fulla the same malice, livid indifference as a sistah, worn from supporting a would be horn player or waiting by the window, and they knew, and left in a hurry, she would gather her tinsel and jewels from the tub, and laugh gaily and vengeful, she stored her silk roses by her bed, and when she finished writing, the account of her exploit in a diary, embroidered with lilies and moonstones, she place the rose behind her ear, and cried herself to sleep.'"

Everyone was silent, except for Lady Johnson, who wailed quietly, and Rev. Ed, who gasped. Dr. Smith had tears in her eyes from rendering the poem, as if she were telling her own story. But in a passionate yet sympathetic tone, unmarked by her tears, she continued and made the connection to the Bible. "The woman at the well was tired of being used and abused by men. She was tired of being touched by dirty hands and sprinting feet. She was tired of being an open receptacle of male dominance and fluids. She was tired of being an incinerator of male waste."

"Hallelujah, oh God." Lady Johnson was now down on her knees, with tears in her eyes and holding her stomach. She felt every word of Dr. Smith's sermonic selection.

"She needed something that would cleanse her and free her and get the spot out. I remember the part in Shakespeare's *Macbeth*, in which Lady Macbeth had the illusion of blood on her hands. The blood haunted her. She cried, 'Out, damned spot! Out, I say! ... What, will these hands ne'er be clean?' The woman at the well wanted to get the spot out—the filth out from between her legs and off her breast and out of her mouth. But no faucet water, no vinegar, no mouthwash, no douche, no bleach, no doctor, no Ivory soap, no Tide detergent would work; she needed the living water ..."

"Yes! Yes!" Lady Johnson yelled out again.

"... which had heavy-duty bleach and cleansing power. The ingredients of the living water made it pure and strong. It was scented, yet relieving. It was expensive, yet easily gotten. It did the job. It was a certain type of currency."

"Yes!" Lady Johnson was now yelling even louder. Tears streamed down her face. Her hands tried time and time again to clean them to no avail. After awhile she just let it pour. Her beauty was now overshadowed by her sorrow. Her story was told by her tears rather than her own words. Dr. Smith, however, continued through all the commotion.

"After you've been dipped in the blood, you come out looking new and good. New flesh, free of the odor of the past. New body, free of the dirty hands of the past. New breasts, new legs, new mind, free of the fear of the past. The blood will make you new. Talk about extreme makeovers! Well, this is one from the inside out."

"But don't think that the devil is finished with you or is going to leave you alone. He wants you back. You mentioned this earlier, Rev. Franklyn—when evil just won't let you go. That's Gethsemane, trying to keep an eye on the enemy. The only way to keep an eye on the enemy and beat the enemy is to live by the spirit and allow the spirit to guide the body. Because the enemy is looking to rob, steal, and destroy. If you're not careful and prayerful, the devil will rob you in your face and steal when you're not looking. He'll foreclose on your house right in your face, and then steal your furniture right behind your back."

"Ain't that the truth," Rev. Bryant spoke up.

"Let me tell you how slick the enemy is. Brothers, you got some men that as soon as you turn your back, they're checking out your wife."

"Don't we know it." That came from Rev. Charles. "Might as well tell the truth."

"And sisters, you got some women that will try and take your husband right in front of your face. They sweet talk, with breast showing, legs unstockinged, skirt two sizes too small, and a Bible in their hand."

"Hello, everybody,"

The voice from the doorway was unexpected and a little jarring. Dr. Smith's words seemed almost prophetic, as our tenth participant—young, and by any standards an attractive sister—walked in the door. She looked like a cross between a hip-hop vixen and a Wall Street businesswoman. She strutted slowly into the room, smiling broadly and walking as though she was accustomed to being the life of the party—and getting attention. It reminded me of parishioners who come to church late and walk down front, just so everyone can look at them. That's the type of vibe she sent. She finally made it to her seat, where she crossed her legs, with the skirt inching up her thighs, right next to Rev. Taylor, who smirked and said, "Oh, we were just talking about you."

When everyone broke out in laughter, she looked puzzled, but Rev. Ed immediately jumped in and said smoothly, "We were just wondering when you would get here."

She apologized sweetly, saying that her plane had been delayed and that she had called his office phone, but no one had answered.

Rev. Ed then took the liberty to briefly introduce her. "This is Rev. Michelle Mellowin, whom I told you had to perform a wedding."

Rev. Mellowin greeted everyone with a wave of three-inch nails and a soft yet sweet hello. Everyone responded with a cordial welcome.

Rev. Ed then called to Dr. Smith, who now a little confused and flustered, but she quickly refocused and continued from her last thought. "As I was saying," she said, "the devil can leave you with nothing and naked. Stripped and bare. Broken and bruised. But as long as you have Jesus, you can say, like Job said, 'Naked I came from my mother's womb, and naked I will depart.' Job says in a later verse, 'I know that my redeemer lives.' Jesus is the redeemer, the one who died, the one who purchased my salvation with his blood. I know he lives."

"Hallelujah!" Rev. Mellowin awkwardly yelled out.

Dr. Smith smiled in her direction, then continued. "The good thing about the blood is that it provides protection against theft and damage. Ephesians 1:7 says, 'In him we have redemption through his blood.' When you have been redeemed by the blood of Christ, you can get on the main line and call him up and tell him what you want."

"Amen." Bishop Samuel blurted out.

Dr. Smith began to act out her talk with Jesus. She pretended to hold a phone to her ear as she said, "Say, Jesus, the devil is messing with me. He robbed me and stole from me, and I need your help. I'm standing here, naked and with nothing." She looked up from her "phone" and explained to the group, "And Jesus will look on his receipt, because he has proof of purchase. When he sees your name, he'll say 'Yeah, the devil is not only robbing from you, but because you belong to me, he's robbing from me, because I purchased you with my blood.' Jesus is a strong brother. He will get gangster and all in the devil's face. Because there is a time for sophistication and education but there is a time for the hood and Vaseline on the face." Her description of a fighter in the hood caused all of us to break into laughter; even Rev. Bryant, who knew the hood, cracked a smile.

"The Bible says there is a season for everything," Dr. Smith continued. "A time to build up and a time to tear down.

Some folks you have to tear down to build up." She put her fists up and began boxing and hitting into the air while she was speaking to the image in her mind. "Jesus got hood and says, 'I heard you been messing with my servant. I bought her with my blood! I bought him with my blood! I died for their surrender.'" She pointed her finger as if she were actually talking to someone and ready to rumble. "How are you going to rob and steal from me? You took her joy—give it back! Took her peace—give it back! Took the children—give them back! Took her home —give it back! Took her husband—give him back ... if she still wants him back." The laughter grew in intensity, and Dr. Smith kept going, with heavy breathing and bronchial coughs at times, but little pause.

"The blood has set us free from the devil's hand and it has set us free from a racist and stubborn society. But herein lies my relationship: just as we were free from sin by blood, we also are freed from society by blood. In order for us to be free from sin and death, Jesus had to bleed. In order for America to be freed from British tyranny, it had to bleed. In order for us to be free from slavery and inhumanity, Nat Turner had to bleed. In order for us to be free, Martin Luther King, Jr., had to bleed."

"Oh, God, I'm feeling you, Doctor," Rev. Taylor interjected. Dr. Smith worked her way out of her seat, her heavy set and her bronchial cough made her move even slower. But she got up.

"In order for us to be free, four little girls in Birmingham had to bleed."

"Talk, doctor!"

"In order for us to be free, Medgar Evers had to bleed. The marchers over the Edmund Pettus Bridge in Selma, Alabama, had to bleed. Fannie Lou Hamer had to bleed. Emmett Till had to bleed. Michael Schwerner, Andrew Goodman, and James Chaney had to bleed."

"Yeah!"

"Farmers and domestic workers and garbage collectors all had to bleed." Her breath was labored, but her power persisted.

"There's blood in the trees! There's blood in the fields! There is blood in the restaurants! Blood in the oceans! Blood in the churches! Blood in the houses! Blood in the streets! But look what the blood has done!" When she yelled, she expelled a loud cough and what seemed her last breath.

"Tell us!" we egged her on even in the midst of her coughs.

"Because of the blood, we can sit anywhere on the bus. We can attend any school we want. We can vote. We can live in any neighborhood. We can get any job. We can go to restaurants and hotels and resorts. We have gone from slave ships to cruise ships."

"Yeah!"

"Look what the blood has done!" She bent over and yelled at the top of her voice. We can become doctors and lawyers and mayors and governors and senators and run for president—big up to Barack Obama. Look what the blood has done! We can win Grammys and Oscars and own television shows."

"You preach, sister."

"Look what the blood has done, we can teach white children and supervise white folks. Look what the blood has done—we can drive big cars and live in big homes. And go to big universities. Look what the blood has done; it has erased our sin. And I will never forget those who shed their blood, because I know they shed their blood for meeeeeee." Wheezing and with labored breath, she began to sing the old hymn:

I know it was the blood,
I know it was the blood,
I know it was the blood for me.
One day when I was lost,
Jesus died on the cross,
and I know it was the blood for me.

8

Shall I Go?

1 Samuel 30:8

All I need is one blunt, one page, and one pen
One prayer—tell God forgive for one sin
Matter fact maybe more than one, look back
*At all the hatred against me, **** alla them*

—"One Mic" by Nas

T hat was brilliant, informative, creative, and deeply
inspirational," said Rev. Ed to Dr. Smith. The applause
continued, and she looked encouraged yet exhausted, she
coughed a couple more times until she drank the water Rev. Ed
handed to her. He praised her for her literary and historical
knowledge and for adding so much richness and drama to the
discussion.

Rev. Ed turned to face Lady Johnson, who looked as
though she was ready for some action. Rev. Ed gestured toward
her as he said, "The Reverend Stacy Lee Johnson, a.k.a. Lady

Johnson, it's good to see you. I know you have a lot to say, but before you begin, I need to make a call. I was just beeped."

"Go ahead," said Rev. Taylor. "I'm sure we can wait for your return."

"Thanks for your permission," Rev. Ed joked. He excused himself, tapped on the door, and was buzzed out.

Lady Johnson spoke up loudly, yet smoothly and melodically so her voice could be heard across the large table. "So, Bishop Samuel, I read your recent book. It was an unkind criticism of the position of the nation on war," she said abruptly. "Do you really believe this nation is harsh and uncaring, obsessed with lies, arrogance, and self-righteousness?" Lady Johnson seemed to be launching an attack, but perhaps it was because she was riding the energy from Dr. Smith. Her voice was direct, yet because of its seductive tone, it was hard to over look her beauty and take her seriously.

But Bishop Samuel, being the wise old man he was, responded politely to her probing. He chuckled and answered her with a simple "No, Mrs. Johnson."

"*Reverend* Johnson!" she corrected him.

"Excuse me, Rev. Johnson," Bishop Samuel calmly responded. "To answer your question, I feel this nation is hurting because it is absent of truth, humbleness, and righteousness. And its victims of oppression suffer the sting of its misdirection." Bishop Samuel's reply was quick yet humble. I wondered if he was testing the wind to see if she was going to pursue her attack.

"But it sounds as though you're trashing the nation." She came back at him with force, as though she had been waiting to confront him about his position. The beauty in her voice was irresistible, however, the accusation in her voice was unmistakable. It seemed like a showdown was brewing? I scanned everyone's faces to see if anyone else looked worried.

Bishop Samuel offered her a smile. "No, I'm not trashing the nation," he responded courteously. "I'm observing the current administration in regard to the ideology of the nation, and it's coming up stink." Now taking the smile off of his face and his voice deepening. "That's why you think I'm trashing the nation. But in all seriousness, my reaction is based upon the constitutional and biblical demands of peace and justice for all. Jesus said, 'Blessed are the peacemakers, for they will be called sons of God.'"

"But you must remember, Bishop," she sniffed, "they attacked us first."

"When you say 'they,' to whom are you referring?" asked Bishop Samuel.

"I'm referring to terrorists!," she shot back.

"To which terrorists are you referring?"

"The terrorists who attacked us."

"Well, I have a problem with what you're saying. When you say terrorists, I need more specifics."

"Well, Bishop Samuel, when innocent people die so horrifically, how many specifics do you need? Do you need each name, specifically? We must strike back; that's elementary!"

"But is it supported, biblically?"

"I believe so."

"So you believe in an eye for an eye?" he asked

"No, I believe it is natural to retaliate when you've been attacked."

"Lady Johnson, you're a biblical scholar. Justify your reasoning theologically and politically, not emotionally. You sound like you're reporting rather than assessing."

"Talk about attack," Rev. Taylor muttered with a smirk. He seemed to be enjoying the back and forth.

The bishop's remark hit Lady Johnson like the Japanese hit Pearl Harbor. Without warning. "Excuse me!" She glared coldly at Bishop Samuel.

Bishop Samuel spoke up before she could say anything more. "If you say that we must strike back, Rev. Johnson, then how do you substantiate your argument using your scriptural knowledge, mixed with theological reasoning, to come to a justifiable conclusion?"

"I will give you my answer, but I hope we can keep this above insult," she said, rather imperiously.

"I understand," Bishop Samuel replied.

"I recall the story of David in his fight against the Amalekites," she began.

"Good start," Bishop Samuel said.

"The Amalekites raided the lands of Negev and Ziklag. They attacked and burned Ziklag and took the women and children hostage. They didn't kill them, but they took them. In our case, the terrorists killed them. When David and his men came to Ziklag, the home of many of his soldiers, they saw their land burned, possessions stolen, and their wives and children taken captive. Bishop Samuel, the Bible tells us that David and all his men began to cry aloud until they had no strength left!"

"I know what it says," Bishop Samuel said confidently.

She continued, her voice filled with emotion. "Can you imagine? Mighty men breaking down and weeping! These were soldiers, but they cried. Why? Because their land was burned, and their families were destroyed. Here is the correlation, Bishop Samuel. Terrorists came to our land and destroyed our towers and took the lives of innocent people. Those lives were taken regardless of ethnic background or political persuasion. When Americans saw the planes crash into the towers and people jumping out of windows and running out of the buildings on fire, they began to break down and cry. Cry like babies. Husbands began to cry because they had lost their wives, wives because they had lost their husbands. Parents cried at the loss of their sons and daughters. The land was filled with fire and tears. And the tears couldn't put out the fire. When the smoke finally cleared, there were ashes of buildings and bodies. The whole nation cried because the type of death the victims suffered was inhumane and savage. You would have to be cold as ice not to feel the agony. Like the Israelites, I beat my chest when I heard of the suffering. They took more than lives. They took dignity, safety, and a sense of invulnerability from the nation." As she spoke I could feel her every word, its emotional outpouring made the story relevant and real. She spoke looking directly at Bishop Samuel not giving him a chance to interfere with her words.

"America, once a triumphant and dominant nation, became a country of vulnerable and fearful people after the attacks. And the distressing factor about the disaster was that nobody could stop it or save the victims. It's just like at Ziklag. Nobody was there to protect the women and children from the enemy. People on the planes and in the towers were trying to call their loved ones. One wife said her husband was able to tell her good-bye. Then there was silence. Imagine how agonizing that is—to know that you heard a last call from your son or daughter, mother or father and then—boom! That's the agony of Gethsemane, for Jesus to know that he was about to die. To know that it would soon be over in a brutal and devastating way. Jesus cried for God to take this cup away from him because what was to come was no joke. It was going to hurt—real bad. The anticipation of devastation is what caused the agony. And the people who died, as well as the families who cried, felt that pain." She wept as she spoke; ironically, the kind of weeping that Bishop Samuel had described earlier. Her emotions drew attention to her sorrow. Dr. Smith leaned over and put her hand lightly on Lady Johnson's shoulder so as to comfort her but not interfere with her lesson.

"Those who tried to rescue the living were themselves victims of horror and death. Firefighters and police officers ought to be honored. The men of Ziklag who lost their families wanted more than tears. They wanted revenge. Somebody had to pay for the loss of their land and family. At first they looked to David, the leader and administrator, blaming him for the loss. The Bible says the men wanted to stone him out of bitterness and anger. David was highly distressed and hurt over their thoughts. And we, as a nation, must question the present administration, in our bitterness and anger, and ask: Did the administration do enough to guard our families and land from the attack? To this day, reports suggest that much more could have been done to protect the people. So it is justified, emotionally and constitutionally, when people blame the administration. The nation's declaration that it provides sufficient protection and takes all necessary precautions to prevent such atrocities is questionable and far from substantial. But the Bible then said that David found strength in the Lord his God. There's nothing like when you find strength in the Lord."

We all came in with "Amen. Amen again," as if to suggest she was winning this battle and converting anti-administrators into believers.

"David, the executive arm of the administration, found strength in the Lord because of the demand of the nation. Catch this, Bishop Samuel."

"I'm listening," Bishop Samuel said.

"The Ziklagians wanted retaliation against the administration because of their frustration over the destruction and kidnapping. This caused David, in his distress, to seek strength from the Lord to come up with an alternative target for retaliation. If David had not been the target of their frustration then he would not have sought out God for strength and an alternative method of retribution. Our president was pushed into seeking God for strength to deal with the anger and bitterness of the American people. If the nation had not pressured the administration with talks of political stoning, then the administration would not have been forced to go to God for strength and direction. But because of the nation's talk of retribution upon the administration, the administration was coerced into finding an alternative target of retaliation."

"That is deep. She got you there," Rev. Charles commented. "I'm a liberal and I'm thinking twice."

Lady Johnson ignored our show of support and continued on with perfect biblical correlation and presentation for the slam dunk. "God heard the nation's cry for retaliation because of the destruction—not because of the administration. The nation was hurting and saddened by the obliteration. The nation was full of fury and ashes. It was not the administration's call to retaliate against the perpetrators, because any talk of retaliation from the administration would have been seen as an attempt to save and protect the president from political persecution. The administration was forced to find strength and look to God for an answer that would refocus the people's anger and energies toward the terrorists. David went to God and asked, 'Shall I pursue this raiding party? Will I overtake them?' 'Pursue them,' God answered. 'You will certainly overtake them and succeed in the rescue.' So David and his men pursued the enemy. David fought them from dusk until dawn and the only men who got away were four hundred young men who rode off on camels. David recovered everything the Amalekites had taken, including his two wives. Nothing was missing; every possession was returned and every family reunited." "She's good, Doc." Said Rev. Taylor rubbing his head and leaning back. Bishop still just listening, looking like he himself agreed and respected what she had to say.

"America got the go from God and pursued the enemy. We also claimed the victory. Although we could not get families back in the flesh, their souls and our souls are at peace, knowing the perpetrators were caught and seized. When America came home, it brought its safety back. Its credibility and dignity was restored. God said, 'It is mine to avenge.' I got my assurance back. I got my faith back. Not because of the nation, but because of a nation under God! Now, I hope I have supported my position with scriptural and theological reasoning." She abruptly ended the conversation, leaned back in her chair, and fanned her hand quickly in front of her face, as if she was overheated from her oration.

"She got you there, doc," Rev. Taylor sniped, which immediately cut through the tension.

"You must be an administration supporter," Rev. Franklyn suggested.

Lady Johnson stiffened. "No, I'm a victim, a sufferer. I lost my mother."

"Your mother!"

"Yes," she said, "my mother."

"Oh, I'm sorry," Rev. Franklyn apologized.

Lady Johnson wiped a tear from her eye. Everyone became quiet. I wished she hadn't been pushed to that degree. Bishop Samuel looked perplexed and penitent.

"It's okay," Lady Johnson said. "I demanded that the administration take action or I would take action upon the administration."

"I'm sorry; I can understand your emotions." Bishop Samuel said hesitantly

"I hope you will also understand my biblical and theological cementing," she retorted.

Rev. Charles tried to lighten the mood. "If I may say, that was a brilliant connection and understanding."

"Well," Lady Johnson said, smiling slowly, "we weren't chosen to be here for our good looks."

9

Heal Our Land

2 Chronicles 7:14

The People's in Terror, the Leaders made the error
and now they can't even look in the mirror
Cause we got to suffer, while things get rougher
and that's the reason why we got to get tougher

—"Beat Street" by Grandmaster Melle Mel

The mood was tense. Bishop Samuel decided to clarify his perspective about the nation. He began with smooth precision. "Rev. Johnson, I feel for you personally and as you know, I am agonizing just like you, but I feel that we as a nation, because of the administration, are heading in the wrong direction." He seemed to be treading carefully, being cautious with his words. "Our land is hurting and needs healing. And although I respect your analytical and insightful theological presentation, and I feel your personal pain, I must, in all sincerity and truth, disagree with you."

"I never asked you to agree!" Lady Johnson snapped at him, still fanning herself.

"I understand, my sister, but please hear me out." Bishop Samuel said quietly. "Let me tell you why."

Lady Johnson glared at him for a moment, then dropped her hands into her lap. "I'm listening," she said.

"So are we," said Rev. Taylor.

"And this better be good," said Rev. Charles, "because she got you beat by a mile."

"Who are you betting on? I've got five on her," Rev. Taylor said to Rev. Charles. Their bantering seemed to lighten the mood. Even Lady Johnson and Bishop Samuel smiled.

"As I stated, I believe this nation is hurting," Bishop Samuel began again. "It is hurting because of its arrogance, wickedness, and self-righteousness. When someone hurts you, it is natural to want to strike back. I must agree with that secular and psychological reasoning and truth, although it is by no means absolute. But when your payback is misguided and misdirected, it not only leads to self-destruction but also to national disaster. National disaster then leads to the destruction of innocent lives because of the mistakes of a nation. After the administration identified its target, it should have dealt severely with its objective and concluded and restricted its attacks upon its assailants, such as David did. But the administration seemed to take advantage of a bad situation. They began to tie another nation into the conflict, justifying it with information that later turned out to be false and intentionally misleading. This is where it becomes wicked and dangerous. Biblically, any time a nation became disobedient and unfaithful, it lost a battle. Remember Achan's sin?"

"I remember. Joshua 7," Rev. Taylor offered.

"Thank you, Rev. Taylor. God told Joshua not to touch the devoted things of Jericho during the attack. But Achan decided that he was going to be disobedient and take more than what God permitted. Achan figured that since it was war, he could take anything he wanted, that he could reach beyond God's permission and instructions and conduct his own invasion. By taking the devoted things, he separated himself from the initial target of war and God's purpose for his own personal gain. But his sin of taking more than he should, in fact, did not hurt him, not at first. It hurt the soldiers; it resulted in the defeat and death of three thousand innocent soldiers at the hand of their enemies. Speaking of crying! The Bible says the people's hearts melted and became like water when they heard of the deaths. Joshua tore his clothes and fell face down from morning until evening."

"I'm back with you, my brother," Rev. Taylor agreed, but Bishop Samuel paid him no attention.

"This is what you call a national disaster. Mothers are crying and weeping. Over four thousand soldiers have died in Iraq. They are hurting, not knowing that someone's personal greed resulted in their children's deaths. Not knowing that someone was conducting his own search for his own gain, rather than the true protection and principles of the nation. The plan was made way before the attack. The attack played into to the plan of invasion and other operations, such as spying on Americans, which, again, was declared to be unconstitutional. Achan was later caught and dealt with severely. It's just too bad he wasn't caught before the men went to war or before he took the devoted things. America has taken more than it should. It went from targeted retribution to personal invasion. Retribution could be justified biblically and supported nationally. But invasion without the master's permission is itself terrorism and self-destruction."

The Bishop's observation and analysis were as usual flawless. I along with others found ourselves glued to his reasoning and his rhythm.

"We have seen the enemy, and it is us. We took more than we should. We took for granted the devoted things, such as obedience to God and trust and faithfulness and love for humankind. We took more than we should have taken—and misled the people. We took more than we should have taken—and gave false information, took the oil, and gave friends the contracts. Most of all, we took advantage of a bad situation to justify our position, which resulted in selfish invasion, rather than divine intervention. As a result, innocent soldiers are dying, and mothers are crying. Like the Israelites, their hearts are melting like water."

Rev. Charles straightened himself in his chair. It seemed that war talk put him at attention.

"It reminds me of Luigi Pirandello's short story, 'War,'" Bishop Samuel continued. "Although the setting is Europe, this story of parents who have children on the front lines resonates with people of all lands. The story highlights the disturbing feelings of parents who must send their children off to war. The setting is a group of parents on a train; some are going to see their child off to war, others are on their way to identify the remains of their child killed in the war. Such a gathering provokes twisted and uncomfortable conversations. They speak of their sorrows and of the heroism of their children. They share their fearful and horrifying stories of their children being sent to an unsupported war. And not only to war but to certain death because of their positions on the front lines. One woman in the story states that she is suffering for one of her sons who is leaving for the battlefront. Another woman sternly retorts that her son has been on the frontline since day one and was wounded twice, only to be returned to the frontline. Another woman rejects all other claims and sympathies to tell of her two sons and three nephews at the frontline. Her pain is larger than theirs in her mind.

"But suddenly there is an abrasive reasoning mixed with satisfaction, patriotism, and delusion. A heavyset gentleman raises an argument in defense of country and independence of children. He dismisses all sorrow and pain, and highlights love for country and patriotism. He has lost his son but has found it in himself to display gallantry over resentment, and valor over bitterness—not only for himself but for his son who died with much bravery. But with all the talk of patriotism for country and independence for children, there is a sudden realization when a question is asked of him by a hurting woman, who listens more than speaks and cries more than sleeps. She asks him, 'Is your son really dead?' Darkness seems to cover the train, and silence is awakened while eyes turn in his direction. Then silence is broken upon true confession from the heart. The man breaks down and cries, freeing himself of denial and delusion. The love of child is stronger than the love of country, and the mouth may talk but the heart won't lie."

"Very impressive, Bishop," Dr. Smith told him, "and powerful." Rev. Johnson looked down her nose at Dr. Smith. I imagined she was offended by Dr. Smith's praising the bishop but maintained her own defensive posture.

Bishop Samuel continued smoothly. "Many of the parents of soldiers in Iraq tout patriotism and protection against terrorism, but when the truth is revealed, and neither weapons nor reason is found to justify the war, oh how the heart will bleed over the lost loved ones. A justified war is a cause for celebration of patriotism, but a questionable war is cause for extreme defection and lost faith in a nation. Cindy Sheehan, whose son died in the Iraq war, recognized the contradiction between patriotism and the dishonesty of a nation. She not only stood in front of the president's residence, she stood in front of justice and judgment upon a nation."

"That is brilliant." Rev. Minor who hardly said a word ushered in."

And there was no doubt Bishop Samuel was brilliant. As far as I was concerned, his mind and his metaphors were unmatched. He went on, still in his humble yet decisive tone. "And I, like Joshua, fall down and cry until evening for the innocent and misunderstood lives that are lost—one of whom is my nephew."

With that, voices of sorrow were again raised, saying, "We're sorry to hear that," and "We didn't know."

"I figured since the good Lady J. got personal, so would I." Bishop Samuel's personal partition put everyone firmly on the fence, rather than standing on either side. "But let me not stray from my point. What's hurting this land and can destroy this nation is not outside terrorists; it's its own wickedness. Greed, lies, cheating, hate, injustice, inequality, and unfaithfulness on the part of leadership and citizenship."

"Excuse me," Lady Johnson said, "but don't you think terrorism can destroy this nation?"

"No!" Bishop Samuel's retort was surprisingly coarse. "We must remember that no matter how many people try to attack God's nation, they will not succeed, because as the Bible says 'What God has put together, let no one put asunder.' The winds may blow, the rain may fall, but if it's built upon a rock, it will withstand the enemies' snares. If this nation believes that it's under God, then it must also believe, as the word says, 'No weapon forged against you will prevail.'"

"You preaching now, boy. I like that answer," Rev. Taylor interjected.

"This does not mean that the nation won't get hit or sick from other nations' actions; it means it won't fall because of other nations' tactics. The only people who can destroy God's people and nation are God's people and nation. This is witnessed again and again with regard to Israel in the biblical text. We mentioned it earlier in talking about Nehemiah. Unfaithfulness led to their exile and the destruction of their land. But to be sure, if God does not permit anything to happen, it won't happen.

"But speaking of that, let me just interject this little revelation that I'm getting." Bishop Samuel interrupting his own words. "Sometimes a hit means that there is not only a military and security breakdown where terrorists can get through, sometimes it also means that there is a spiritual breakdown where enemies can get in. God could be allowing the hit as a warning that America's spiritual defense system is down or weak. When a germ gets into the body, if the immune system is not strong enough to fight it, it can spread and cause sickness and ultimate destruction. Terrorist germs got into the nation's body and hit the towers, and the fear spread throughout the nation because of a weak immunity of the spirit. Because if it were strong, no one could get in no matter how hard they tried. So this could be a wake-up call, not for America's military but for America's spirituality.

"I agree." Said Rev. Taylor. "Me too." Said Dr. Smith. "Me three." Said Rev. Bryant. "Me four" Said Rev. Charles. "Me five." Said Rev. Minor. Before the rest of us could say anything Bishop Samuel continued.

"When God is on your side, he is so good that he will break down other territories to let his people in. Read Joshua. God is a provider and protector to those who love and obey him. Jesus at Gethsemane knew that God was with him. He went forward with spirit and body because God was on his side. The only time the hands of God are withdrawn from the nation is when that nation dismisses God with its arrogance, disobedience, wickedness, and self-righteousness. Therefore, the nation is not dying from external attacks but from internal infections. The only people who can hurt and make sick the foundation of the nation are its own people. It kills itself from the inside.

"When justice is not for all, the nation is sick! When peace is compromised, the nation is sick! When mistruths are accepted and not challenged, the nation is sick! When innocent people die as a result of misinformation, the nation is hurting! When mothers are weeping over the loss of their sons and daughters in war and can't explain why, the nation is sick and hurting!

"America is hurting, not at the hands of outside antagonists but at the feet of its own disobedience. The longer it takes to diagnose the problem, the worse the condition gets. We have seen the symptoms, for they are visible on America's face. They show up like swollen pimples filled with pus, waiting to burst. Psychological hemorrhaging of the poor. Depression and further regression of working families. Greed of the rich, increased oil prices. The breakup of families. The breakdown in community. A culture of consumption, hedonism, materialism, and violence. Increased hunger and homelessness. Wars and rumors of wars. Parents dishonored by children. Ghettos growing. Wealth gap increasing, generational mobility decreasing, morality falling, and increased hate and mistrust of the political system, judicial decisions, and legislative actions."

"Talk, boy!" Rev. Taylor feeling the Bishop's vibe.

Bishop Samuel was now on his feet. Amens were heard but no comments, just praises. The bishop continued in a voice that was set for preaching. "The Constitution has warned the nation of the consequences of spreading disease. In one section it states that if a government seriously threatens the interests of society, the people can overthrow it and substitute another government in its place. Those of us who speak of America's wickedness are only trying to get her to the doctor before the infection worsens and kills everyone. Once arrogance spreads, it cripples America's economic, political, and judicial systems. Once wickedness increases, America's moral and spiritual immune system breaks down. And once self-righteousness and disobedience multiply, the spirit of justice, mercy and grace is no longer abiding within the nation. It's just a matter of time before it perishes like other great nations before it."

"Good God." The words of amazement came from Rev. Ed.

"Let me conclude like this: The only way to heal the nation is to subscribe to the prescription of redemption that God gave to the Israelites in 2 Chronicles 7:14. This is where God said, 'If my people, who are called by my name, will humble themselves and pray and seek my face and turn from their wicked ways, then will I hear from heaven and will forgive their sin and will heal their land.'"

It was clear from the shaking and quaking in Bishop Samuel's voice that it was preaching time. He thundered and held his notes like he was singing a tune. He bent over as he stood to allow the spirit to flow from his hands to his feet. His sweat showed that his soul was crying. He went on.

"There is a remedy. There is a way out. There is a prescription for the sickness. And most of all, there is still time. That's because somebody's been praying, but their prayers are hanging on by a very thin thread. All the nation has to do is take four tablets—one: humbleness; two: prayer; three: seek his face; four: turn from wicked ways."

"Oh, preach, that's good talk."

"I'm preaching now. The *humbleness* tablet will fight off arrogance. The *prayer* tablet will restore God's grace. The *seek his face* pill will build up righteousness while fighting off disobedience and self-righteousness. What the last tablet, *turn from wicked ways*, will do is obvious: it will kill off the infections—decimate lies, greed, deceit, and selfishness among others. America must drink the prescription with holy water."

"You go, preacher!" Dr. Smith yelled out, while most of us stood up to praise along with him.

"It's better to take it on an empty stomach, because it's always good to fast and pray if you want real change. Since the pain has been worsening, the nation has to put itself on a schedule when taking the tablets. Just like all medicines, you have to take a certain amount for a certain amount of time before the infection will go away and the healing begins."

"Okay, now!" Rev. Mellowin was now on her feet.

"America will need to take four tablets, every seven hours, for seven times seven days. Seven is the number of completion. Don't rush the cure; if you do, it may do more harm than good. Because part of getting well after you've been sick so long is patience. But if America does it right and follows these instructions, she will feel and see the difference. The healing will be obvious. Sores on black folks will be cleared. Hemorrhaging from the hurting will cease. Justice starts rolling down like a mighty stream, righteousness like thunder."

"Preach!"

"People will begin to feel at peace with themselves and trust in the system. Statistics on the direction of America will rise favorably. There will be restored dignity of the oppressed. People will walk with a smile of confidence in the nation, a laugh of happiness to be an American, and a song and dance of praise for the administration."

"I like what you're saying!" said Rev. Taylor.

"Outside agitators and terrorists will be rebuffed; their weapons will turn on them."

"Oooh, good God. This is good, Bishop!" Dr. Smith couldn't help but gasp.

"It will be like John, when he was locked in prison and darkness, and he sent the question to Jesus: 'Are you the one who was to come, or should we expect someone else?' Jesus told them go and tell John what you've seen and heard. The blind receive sight, the lame walk, those who have AIDS are cured, racism is ineffective, discrimination impotent, the deaf hear, the dead are raised, the good news is preached to the poor, the oppressed are prospering! All these will be signs of a healthy nation."

"Yes! Yes! Yes!" Said Rev. Franklyn, jumping and shouting as if he were under the holy spirit.

"All we have to do is take and wait! Take the prescription, and wait on the Lord. Take the medication, and wait on God. Take the redemption, and wait on Jesus. For they that wait upon the Lord to renew their strength. They shall rise up with wings as eagles. They shall run and not faint. They shall walk and not be weary! Teach me, Lord! Teach me, Lord, to wait! God bless you." Bishop Samuel dropped into his seat, wiped the sweat from his brow, and slipped a piece of gum into his mouth, all at the sound of loud praise.

10

Why Do We Hurt Each Other?

Exodus 2:11–13

We got ourselves together
So that you could unite and fight for what's right
Not negative 'cause the way we live is positive
We don't kill our relatives

—"Self Destruction" by KRS-One

L ady Johnson glared at Bishop Samuel, "I still stick to what I said regarding the retaliation, aside from the administration."

"I understand, but I still feel that it is the natural response to want to retaliate. When you're dealing with the spiritual it directs the natural. That's Gethsemane" Bishop Samuel, who could not be outdone, responded."

"Yes, but—"

Just as she was about to argue her point again, Rev. Ed came back into the room. "Is everything okay?" Rev. Ed looked around the room at everyone. When no one responded, he sat down, saying, "I'm sorry. It took longer than I thought. You all look like you've gotten to know each other … a little too well." Rev. Ed looked at Lady Johnson, who looked annoyed.

Rev. Taylor quickly confirmed Rev. Ed's suspicions. "All I can say, Doc, is that a referee ought never to leave a boxing match." Rev. Taylor laughed, amusing himself.

"It got that bad?" Rev. Ed inquired.

"No, I would say that it got that good," Rev. Taylor responded.

Lady Johnson's face, although quite beautiful, clearly showed her irritation and embarrassment.

"Okay, we can proceed." Rev. Ed first pointed to Lady Johnson because that's where he had left off. But when he saw the anger on her face, he skipped to Rev. Bryant. "Rev. Malik-Haj Bryant, would you like to speak?" asked Rev. Ed.

"Yeah. Why not? You wasn't here, but it got a little heated up in here. Up in here. Up in here," he said, displaying the street slang and rhythm of the hood. Rev. Bryant's tone was concerned but rough. "And I don't mind the heat or the controversy, 'cause where I'm from, I'm used to it. I just don't understand why we can't agree to disagree without hurting one another. Or putting each other down." Those were unlikely words coming from a person who looked like he had physically hurt a lot of people in his life.

"Well, don't take it out of context," Rev. Charles scolded, as if disciplining a child. "No one put anyone down!"

"There were insults," Rev. Bryant insisted, squinting his eyes and looking menacing.

"Yes, there were. I'm a preacher, and I can't lie," Rev. Taylor confirmed.

"Okay, okay," said Rev. Ed. "Please continue, Rev. Bryant."

"My question is this," Rev. Bryant began, "why can't we just get along?"

"Okay, Rodney King," Rev. Ed teased him. "Why don't you tackle that issue?"

"Well, in my contemplating, I ask this question often: why? And I know there is the inquisitive why that we use when we're asking a question and looking for an answer or satisfactory response. Why is the sky blue? Why is there night and day? But then there is that rhetorical why. Here, you're not looking for a specific answer per se but a reason as to why things happen. The purpose for asking the question is because there seems like there would be no good reason or justifiable answer as to why things happen the way they do. Why the tsunami that killed over 250,000 people? Why Hurricane Katrina that killed thousands of our people? Who can answer those questions with compassion, intelligence, and biblical might and still have the sensitivity and pity the victims deserve? What could be the reason or the justifiable good answer for such tragedies? Why one minute you're up, and the next minute you're down? Why does the sequence of life flow in such complicated and unexpected channels, leaving us desperate and dying for a reason? Why?"

"Good questions," Rev. Ed agreed.

Rev. Bryant continued, "A drastic change in status is what happened to the Israelites. Why did it change? It's hard to say, but we can see that it did. And it was a change that went from prosperity and freedom to poverty and enslavement. And whenever I read the book of Exodus, I can't help but connect it to the struggle of African people in America. How we too had the withdrawal of prosperity and the deposit of slavery and poverty put on us. The Bible tells us that Joseph, an Israelite, rose to power in Egypt. As a result, many of the Israelites, including all of Joseph's family, migrated to Egypt and chilled there. That's like us—you know how we do, when one goes and gets a good job or a position of power, we're all going. During the years of the 1920s through the '50s, a great migration occurred for black folks from the South to the North. When one of us went up North and found a good job, eyerbody came—moms, pops, uncles, aunts, brothers, sistahs, best friends, and dogs."

"Amen. That's the truth." We couldn't help but agree.

"If they heard Uncle Jesse got a good job, eyerbody was going to move up to where Uncle Jesse was."

"That's the truth. I did it, and so did my sisters," Bishop Samuel said before Rev. Bryant continued.

"I always say, just imagine now that a black man is president."

"And black woman! Don't forget his wife." All the women said the words in unison.

"Iaight, and black woman with her husband is president," Rev. Bryant conceded. "There are going to be major changes to the way things operate. We'll have the whole black hood in the White House. White folks will trip out. They will hire extra security and extra cleaning people. We'll tear the presidential pictures down and put the family portraits up. The only pictures that will stay will be John Kennedy's and possibly Bill Clinton's, and we would make Martin Luther King an honorary president. And Barack Obama would be the first not the forty fourth president. You know the first shall be last and the last first."

"Amen," Dr. Smith said, laughing along with the rest of us.

"We'll have family all over the White House lawn and barbecues eyry weekend."

"You know that's right." Rev. Taylor chuckled as he spoke.

"We would pull up in Hummers, blasting rap music," Rev. Bryant continued, his face breaking into a smile. "Uncle, aunt, niece—eyerbody would just pop up all times of the night. Three o'clock in the morning, crack-a dawning, here comes Shaquana, who left her boyfriend for the fifth time, and her three kids. They snuck past security to get in. We'd have chicken, watermelon, church services on the lawn." Rev. Bryant laughed at his own words. I hadn't thought he could loosen up his rough look, but his laughter achieved that. "And don't let the outcast of the family visit. That is the drunk, the prostitute, the drug addict, the flamboyant lesbian or gay, the thug with pants hanging down. All hell would break loose."

"Yeah, you're right, doc. Talk about national security," said Rev. Charles.

Rev. Bryant laughed and continued. "Talk about a war on poverty and curbing deviant behavior—they would experiment with the president's family. Maybe now they'll focus on us, now that we're in the White House, and they see some of our people's condition. They would say them negroes really do need help; even the president is a thug."

Everyone burst out laughing, including Rev. Bryant, who was amused by his own humor. He then quickly sobered and said, "The Israelites made a home for themselves and began to grow and prosper in the land of the Egyptians. The Israelites and Egyptians lived comfortably and harmoniously for about two hundred years. However, after some two hundred years, a new king rose to power who wasn't cool with the prosperity of the Israelites. Just like today, people ain't cool with our prosperity. The king figured that if war broke out, the Israelites would join with the enemy and defeat the Egyptians and take over their land. So the king decided it was time to deal with the Israelites like an old car: harshly. The king decided that the Israelites would no longer be free but be forced servants with no rights—in other words, slaves. The king oppressed and put heavy labor on them. The Egyptians physically and mentally abused the Israelites and made them work in the fields, sometimes from sunup until sunset.

"Check it. America worked our Africans ancestors in the field, picking cotton for no pay, oppressed them and abused them, and forced them to do work even when they were sick. Slaves didn't have sick time or comp time or vacation time or holidays. They didn't get days off. It was either do or die. But the glorious thing is that even in the midst of all the hardships and dangers, the Bible says the Israelites, like our ancestors, continued to grow in number. The impositions didn't make slaves impotent. Children were still being born and lived."

"All right now!" Dr. Smith yelled out. I leaned a little closer so I wouldn't miss a word, his slang could be misunderstood at times.

"It is ironic and nothing short of the power of God how under pressure, you can still rise. If any people is a testimony to rising under pressure, it is the African American community. Throughout history, we've been under pressure from the government and still managed to rise to corporate heights. We've been under pressure by racism and still risen educationally. We shouldn't be afraid of pressure, because many times it is under pressure when we are most focused, most prayerful, most desiring, and truthful. Jesus rose under pressure. At Gethsemane Jesus was under pressure. Who wouldn't be? Jesus had the world on his shoulders. At Gethsemane, Jesus showed us that under pressure, you can still beat the body and follow the spirit. The spirit will help you rise under pressure. When Jesus' enemies were coming, he rose up after being under so much pressure and went toward them. He didn't back away or run; he went toward them. That's because the spirit works best under pressure."

"Amen. You're talking a little something, young doc," Dr. Smith called out. She seemed to be becoming his biggest supporter.

"Well, let me get a little poetical for you, Dr. Smith. Maya Angelou wrote, 'You may shoot me with your words/You may cut me with your eyes/You may kill me with your hatefulness/But still, like air, I'll rise.'" Off the top of his head, he quoted more portions of Maya Angelou's "Still I Rise," a recitation that made Dr. Smith smile.

"I like your connection," Dr. Smith said with a grin that seemed flirtatious.

Rev. Bryant smiled but his face then became expressionless as he went back to his text. "The Israelites grew under oppression so much that it disturbed the king even more. So he decided that he would authorize the killing of the Israelite babies. He summoned the midwives and ordered them to kill the male Israelite babies but to let the baby girls live. It is disheartening how they targeted the children, especially the boys. Damn. I mean, really. Even today, it seems they want to annihilate the boys. Our boys to men are in trouble. Particularly the black brothers. They treat us the rawest. If you can get rid of the boys, then you cut off the future generation of that nation. Have any of you seen the movie *Hotel Rwanda*?"

"I did," said someone.

"Me too," said another.

"I haven't been able to catch it," Rev. Ed admitted.

"Well, I checked it out the other day. It was about the fighting of the Hutu and Tutsi in Rwanda, Africa. The whole situation was shattering and emotionally disturbing 'cause the Hutu were massacring the Tutsi. But the most troubling was when they killed the children. They used machetes to kill the people. A sad sight to see. It brought tears to my eyes. Neither America nor any other nation intervened to prevent the killing of over eight hundred thousand people in Rwanda in 1994, half of them children. And Bill Clinton, friend of black people, was in office at the time. They killed the children, and many of the young boys were their targets.

"But in Egypt, the midwives were afraid of God and would not take the Israelite babies and kill them. As a result, the Egyptians decided that they would order all of their people to throw baby boys into the Nile River. And although they succeeded, I'm sure, in drowning many babies, God had other plans for one of the babies."

"Yes!" said Dr. Smith. Looking deep in his face and continued with her yeses and yeahs as he spoke.

"An Israelite child was born and his mother, after hiding him for three months, decided to wrap him in a basket and send him down the Nile River. She used the river as an escape route rather than a grave site. Sort of like Harriet Tubman with the Underground Railroad."

"Yeah."

"The baby flowed down the river and ended up in the arms of the pharaoh's daughter. She took the child and named him Moses and raised him in the king's house. She gave him the finest foods and Egyptian Southern cuisine and a Harvard education."

I enjoyed the way that Rev. Bryant related the story in current terms while making excellent exegetical connections.

"But as Moses grew," he continued, "he still felt a kinship with his people. He knew who his family really was. He felt a sensitivity, love, and connection to his brothers and sisters. He despised their condition and the nation's treatment of his peeps. Moses was not a sellout, Uncle Tom, or Clarence Thomas."

"Watch it, now," Rev. Ed cautioned him.

"I'm just keepin' it real," Rev. Bryant responded, as several of those gathered applauded. "As Bishop Samuel stated earlier, you have some who get into the big house and forget about their people. They don't even pass by the hood anymore. But not Moses; he felt a genuine connection to and concern about the Israelites' condition. And he hadn't even grown up in the hood. It was just a natural or spiritual connection. So much so that one day, he was passing by along the desert coast, crying at the condition of his peeps, and he saw an Egyptian beatin' down one of the Israelites. Moses scoped out his surroundings to make sure no one else was around and then proceeded to intervene and look out for his Israelite brother. Moses ended up killing the man who was assaulting the Hebrew. And that's what we all should be doing when we see our people in trouble. We should try and help them."

"Yes."

"When we see our brothers unjustly beaten by police officers, we should help them. When we see our people suffering in poverty, we should help them. When we see our children doing the wrong thing, we should help them. But instead of helping each other, we're hurting each other!"

"Amen, I see where you're going," Rev. Ed said.

"Instead of looking out for each other, we're looking down on each other. Instead of helping each other, we're pissing on each other!" He was harsh but real. Everyone just stared at him because of his coarseness. "Check it. Look what happens," Rev. Bryant continued.

"Tell the story, Doc!" Rev. Franklyn screamed out.

"The next day, Moses was walking and, the Bible says, he saw two Hebrews fighting each other. He was shocked. He intervened and said to them, 'Yow, why are you hitting your fellow Hebrew? Why are you fighting each other?' To Moses, it did not make sense for two people from the same family, history, and oppression to be tearing each other apart. And putting each other down. And virtually killing each other."

"I like your connection," Bishop Samuel spoke again.

"When I look at us as an African American people and see how we fight and tear each other apart, I ask, like Moses, why are we fighting each other?"

Amens rang out like bells.

"The biggest pressure we're under right now is not the Man but our own mother, father, brothers, and sisters in the hood."

We all jumped to our feet, applauding wildly for that perfect connection he'd related with such raw eloquence.

Rev. Bryant held out his hands to quiet us, and he continued as we all took our seats again. "Why do we hurt each other? Why do we hate each other and exploit each other? Why do we rape our sisters? And why do our sisters hurt our brothers? Why do we keep each other from rising and put each other down?"

"Oh, this is good; this is the heart of what we came here for," Rev. Ed interjected.

"Why do we cuss each other out? Why do we tell each other off? Why do we kill each other and treat each other like nothing? It doesn't make sense. I can't think of a justifiable reason. We're all black people, tanned by the sun and molded by the dirt. Even during slavery, you had slaves fighting each other rather than fighting the enemy. Field negroes fighting the house negroes, and the next-door slaves fighting each other. They were all under the same system of dehumanization and oppression, and they were attacking each other. It doesn't make sense! I must admit, I am just as guilty. Growing up, I hurt a lot of my brothers and sisters. If I knew then what I know now, I would have been helping rather than hurting my peeps. All those days on the streets, robbing and stealing and harming my own people. I was a fool, but I'm so glad I know better now. The spirit has taught me a lot about the body."

"Amen, young brother, we've all had our days," Rev. Minor stated.

"Anyway, as I was saying, we're fighting against each other when we should be fighting against the oppressor. The system of oppression. The system of 'mis-education.' The system of no occupation. The system of incarceration."

"Wooo, I like that," Rev. Mellowin came in.

"Why do we put stress on each other and put no fight against the system that's oppressing and hurting us? Even in the church, we fight each other, and it makes no sense. We're all part of the body of Christ. We're all a people of God. A royal priesthood. Citizens in the kingdom. Aliens in this world. Believers in Jesus Christ. We're supposed to love each other in Jesus' name, not tear each other down in the name of God."

"Amen."

"We're supposed to see each other as sisters and brothers. We're supposed to feel each other's pain. Paul says to the Corinthians in 12:25–26, 'there should be no division in the body, but that its parts should have equal concern for each other. If one part suffers, every part suffers with it; if one part is honored, every part rejoices with it.' We're all the same body, we're supposed to feel each other's pains and rejoice with each other's successes."

"You're right; I feel you. Brothers need to hear this," Rev. Mellowin interrupted. I wondered if I was the only one who caught the connection.

Rev. Bryant just flowed on. "The nation is hurting us all. Let's fight the system of suffering and oppression. Moses fought the oppressor. He killed the oppressor. The oppressor was part of the system. While Moses was killing the oppressor, all the anger and hate of Hebrews who were killed at the hands of the Egyptians was running through his mind. All the babies who were drowned in the Nile. All the sons who were snatched out of their mothers' arms at birth."

"Good God," Lady Johnson moaned.

"I remember the indie film *Sankofa*."

"Yeah, I remember that one," said Dr. Smith.

"You watch a lot of movies, Doc," Rev. Ed noted.

"Yes. In the film there was this sister who was constantly being raped by her slave master. Harshly violated and rammed into like a shovel into snow. But toward the end of the film, all the brothers and sisters decided they were going to get those slave masters back, and that sister caught that slave master and beat the hell out of him."

"Woo, are you advocating killing the nation and administration?" Rev. Ed quickly challenged him.

"Nah! That would be political and physical suicide. We could never win a physical battle against the nation. I'm encouraging killing the oppressive, racist, sexist system!" Rev. Bryant shot back with his face squinting and his finger pointing at Rev. Ed as if he was the enemy. "You know what the word of God says in Ephesians 6: 'we fight against spiritual wickedness in high places.' We must fight the wickedness with the whole armor of God. Public Enemy, the rap group, used to sing that song 'Fight the power. We've got to fight the power that be.'"

"That is good!" Rev. Mellowin cried out.

"No. God is good. God always sends someone to get us straight. The Bible says Moses broke up the fight between the two Hebrews and brushed them off. God interceded with his servant. God will always bring someone to bring us back together and refocus our energies. He brought us Frederick Douglass, who taught us to demand—together. God sent Marcus Garvey, who taught us to love the motherland—together. James Weldon Johnson, who taught us to sing—together. Martin Luther King, Jr., who taught us to march—together. Fannie Lou Hamer, who taught us to vote—together. Malcolm X, who taught us to stand—together. A. Philip Randolph, who taught us to organize—together.

"I think we need a prophet who will teach us to live together and love ourselves and love each other. We've had the political, but we need the family and the moral leadership. So we can learn to treasure each other rather than kill each other."

"Boy, you are good!" Lady Johnson yelled out.

"No. God is good. That's Gethsemane for me," Rev. Bryant continued. "Jesus struggling with humanity to show us his love through divinity, so that we can love ourselves and others. It was God's love that gave his son. 'For God so loved the world that he gave his only begotten son.' It was Jesus' love that gave himself. 'Not my will, but yours be done.' That is love. To know the Father's will is that you die for the love of others. We shouldn't be fighting and hurting and killing one another. We should learn to love and die for one another. Our ancestors loved us enough, as Dr. Smith said, to shed their blood to show their love."

"I like that," Rev. Charles cut in and shouted out to everyone. "Shed your blood to show your love!"

"Now turn to your neighbor," Rev. Bryant instructed, "and say these words over and over: Shed your blood to show your love."

"Shed your blood to show your love!"
"Shed your blood to show your love!"
"Shed your blood to show your love!"

11

God Can Stop The Bleeding

Mathew 9:18–22

A thousand words or more
Seep through the floor
And then take root in the soil
Growing trees of doubt
Helpless people shout
Until their blood starts to boil

—"If We All Get to Heaven" by Terrence Trent Darby

R ev. Minor, I know I've introduced you," Rev. Ed began, "but you really have done a lot to help the personal lives of women, as well as the political life of the nation. No one has made that correlation better than you. Please render your articulate existential knowledge to this discussion."

"With that type of introduction, who could refuse?" Rev. Minor smiled at Rev. Ed; it seemed to be a natural part of her expression. I guessed that she must be in her late forties, early fifties. When I'd spoken at a conference in California, she'd been part of another panel discussion. She was great—I don't remember the essence of her speech, but I do remember that she had a big smile and real sense of the issues.

"You all are so great, and I believe that we all are here with our own special understanding and interpretations, but at the same time, we share the hurt and pain of our nation and of our people. I thank God I am here. I sense so much hurt and turmoil and unease in our nation." She began with a soft tone that was almost a whisper, and she was very calm in her manner. "I thank our young brother for that marvelous, analytical assessment and significant conclusion. We all need to shed our blood to show our love. But the blood that's dripping is more from pain and remorse. Gethsemane is Jesus' knowing that he would soon shed his blood, and the thought provoked the agony. But many of us are shedding blood not as a thought but as a symptom of a greater problem. This hemorrhaging is from the heart, and the weight upon the wound causes ripping and an increase in the flow of blood. But I believe that God can stop the bleeding."

The amens that came from the group matched Rev. Minor's tone—it was confirmation, yet calm.

She continued with a mellow modulation. "Imagine if you had a health condition, but everything you tried to cure it did not work. The best doctors and professionals couldn't come up with a treatment for your sickness or a cure for your condition. It is not only lack of a cure but absence of a treatment that's the issue, because even if the disease can't be cured, treatment would help relieve some of the pain. No treatment and no cure would not only bring physical pain but psychological strain. I am reminded of the woman with the issue of blood."

"Oh, I know where you're going, sister." Rev. Charles couldn't help himself. His interjection disturbed her peaceful flow, but she effectively hushed him with a look that took the smile off her face but not the calmness from her voice. She was Presbyterian; she believed in speaking over shouting and rationality over emotionality.

"Listen for a minute, if you will. I know all you scholars and preachers know the story, but you still want to see this little Presbyterian girl put the exegesis and the extra-Jesus on it."

"I like that," Dr. Smith supported her. Then she put her hands over her mouth to comply with Rev. Minor's request to listen.

"Jesus was busy talking to a number of his disciples. All of a sudden, he was interrupted by a ruler. The ruler was powerful and undoubtedly had access to any medical doctor that he desired. But in this moment, he was not only asking Jesus; he was humbling himself and begging Jesus to come and touch his daughter, who was dead. Not sick, not dying, not sleeping—she was dead. Apparently, all the influence and power and people he had, had not been able to help him. At this point, the only person he could rely upon to help his daughter in her death was Jesus.

"America, as a ruling nation, has achieved scientific miracles. It has advanced technologically. It has outpaced others militarily and become a superpower, economically and politically. As was stated earlier, on earth and in space, America is on top. But there are some things that are beyond this great nation's ability. There are some things rulers can't do. They can't resurrect the dead."

"A—" Lady Johnson caught herself before she got an amen out, as did most of us. Everyone seemed to be finding it hard to listen without verbally confirming. But with a smile and look from Rev. Minor, Lady Johnson was quieted.

"Whether it be the death of a person or the death of nation, resurrection is out of the rulers' hands and in the hands of the Creator. The ruler in the Bible was intelligent enough to know and humble enough to realize that only God can raise the dead. So that's why he went to Jesus.

"To some extent, we can't help but say that this nation is spiritually dead. One pastor in New York calls it 'spiritual malaise.' Even with all the mega-churches springing up around the nation, including mine, we still have a considerable amount of malaise in the nation. Everyone knows that the life of any nation, just like the life of any person, is in its spirit. That's Gethsemane, bringing life to the body through the spirit. Without the spirit the body is dead. Jesus was assuring us that the body would live with the spirit, not without it. The body wants to live without the spirit, but little does the body know that without the spirit, it is dead.

"When a nation is living only off of its economy, military, and policy, that nation is like a beautiful corpse. It looks good, but in truth it's going nowhere. It is hollow; it is empty. Just like the little girl who was dead—she was still there in body but her spirit was gone, which caused the breakdown of her functioning. America is still here, but its spirit is waning and it is causing the breakdown of its body policy. America looks good but without the spirit, it's not going anywhere good."

"Okay, you're going somewhere," Rev. Taylor slipped one in to the surprised looks of others.

Rev. Minor continued. "Jesus, being the considerate and hard-working man that he was, got up and followed the ruler to his home, with his disciples in tow. Jesus knew that the ruler, like all rulers, needed help. But look what happened. While Jesus was on his way to the ruler's house, another interruption occurred. The Bible talks about a woman's condition to give her description so we can focus on her desperation, rather than her interruption."

I wanted to say amen, but I strained to refrain from an outburst.

"This woman had been subjected to bleeding for twelve years, had an issue of blood. The Bible relates that she was in a very different socioeconomic class from the ruler. She, unlike the ruler, undoubtedly didn't have the best access to doctors and medical scientists and politicians. In fact, such known cases of infections and medical conditions as bleeding were shunned and the afflicted disgraced at the time. She was considered an outcast. Many people—and even doctors—didn't accept her syndrome. She was like those who had leprosy, one of the most shunned diseases of the time. Not only were those with leprosy considered hideous to look at, but they were so scorned that no one would speak to them. The woman with the issue of blood possibly didn't get the same scorn or shunning because she could hide her bleeding. Only when a drip slipped was she discovered and insulted and rebuked.

"But she and he—the peasant and the ruler—met at the same place and went to the same person, not because of their class but because of their crisis."

"That was good." Even Rev. Ed slipped and then repositioned himself with a smile.

"The woman's outcry for a healing was different from the ruler's; he was begging for his dead daughter. She was begging for herself. Both just as painful. But this woman's outcry was more desperate and more aggressive. Not because of her condition over his daughter's but because of her desperation, which led to an aggressive interruption that made Jesus attend to her first. It was like a last cry for justice. A last cry for healing. A last cry for wholeness. She was helpless and defenseless and bleeding. Woke up every morning—blood on the bed. Laid down every night—blood on the sheets. Walked down the street— blood on the clothes. Clothes had to be thrown out daily because it's hard to get blood out of clothes. She had to wrap herself up real tight so that when she walked down the street, no one would see the blood dripping."

Rev. Minor made the story come alive. While she spoke I felt the pain of the woman but also the pain she felt for the woman. Her description filled with emotions almost made you want to cry for her.

"Although we know of the physical drain, we can't miss the psychological strain. Years of living with any type of sickness not only affects the body, but it also affects the mind. Think of the detrimental psychological impact she felt, knowing she had suffered from this ailment for twelve years. No relief. No breaks. She could've been emotionally disturbed, depressed, distant and friendless, hopeless and ashamed."

Her voice rose with her degree of excitement, but she seemed to be restraining herself. "We all have our issues, our sorrows and pains. Even we who gain public praise, no matter how much we smile or how bold or bad we may seem, we still have private pain. Bleeding. I'm a witness."

We all shook our heads in affirmation.

"Bleeding occurs from some incident or occurrence in your life, and it's still hurting. Or dripping. When you hold on to past hurts and pains and hates and mistrusts, you are bleeding inside. Hurt causes hemorrhaging. Hate causes hemorrhaging. Fear causes bleeding. The bleeding is on the inside, and people can't necessarily recognize the blood because we know how to cover our pain. We buy the best clothes, and fix our hair, and exercise our figure, and buy the best makeup in order to conceal the dripping blood. And many times, bleeding people don't get close to other people because what's inside might drip out. Bleeding keeps you alone and secretive. I knew a beautiful sister who suffered with HIV. She had the disease but no symptoms. And she covered her malady with the greatest happiness. Brothers would seek her companionship, and sisters would wonder about her relationships. She was the most cheerful person in the world. She confided in me one day, admitting that although she desired friendship, her secret kept her from connecting with people. She was bleeding inside."

"I hope they caught the guy who gave it to her," Rev. Mellowin spoke out of order with a harsh attitude. "I'm sorry, but it's a shame sisters have to suffer like that because of some man."

Rev. Ed quickly quieted her down. "We'll get to that. Allow Rev. Minor to continue."

"Thank you, Rev. Ed," Rev. Minor said calmly. "It's like this brother on the train I was talking to one time. He said, 'I will never fall in love again. She hurt me, took all I had. Left me lonely and alone.' He was crying and needed someone to talk to. I just sat there and listened and when I was about to get off, I said, 'Just give it some time and healing will come.' He asked, 'How much time? It's been five years.'"

"Oooh!" Rev. Ed came in shockingly.

"I just told him to have faith, and it would come."

"I hope they caught the sister who gave it to him," Rev. Charles shouted out while looking at Rev. Mellowin.

"But a lot of us are bleeding like he was," Rev. Minor continued "especially sisters, which is why I founded my ministry—to heal and help wounded sisters. Sisters can carry around misery and mistrust for years."

"Amen. My wife is still mad at me for not telling her about that girl in our church who kissed me when I was thirteen," Rev. Taylor interjected, hoping to lighten the mood. And he did; everyone burst out laughing. Even Rev. Minor smiled before reverting back to her serious tone.

"I meet with sisters every day, and they help me confront my own history of hurt. I remember this sister who told me that every time she saw a black man with a bald head, she hated him. And she meant it; you could see it in her burning red eyes."

We all looked at Bishop Samuel's head, including Rev. Minor. He apparently understood the stare and rubbed his bald head.

"Then I realized it was an incident of brutality that had caused her hate. Late one night, while she was walking back to her dorm room, someone snatched her and violated her for three hours. The news reported it, and the police said that it was the worst case of brutality they had ever seen."

"Oh, God," Lady Johnson blurted out.

"Her body was warped with bites, and her head was bashed from a blow that knocked her unconscious. Between her legs were rips and scars; the abuse was violent and animalistic. The perpetrator got away and was never apprehended—at least not by the police. I believe that God took care of him." She had everyone with the story, which she told with calmness yet passion. I could see the blood in her eyes as she spoke. "Her connection of hating any black man with a bald head was because the one who violated her was a black man with a bald head."

"I see why she hates him," Rev. Mellowin came in strong again. But she was hushed by Rev. Minor, who continued with an even more stern expression.

"Although the actual bleeding from the harsh abuse she endured was contained and eventually healed, the bleeding from her heart and mind because of the violation endured. She was bleeding profusely on the inside, fifteen years after the rape. Holding on to her pain, which caused hate and mistrust. She had an issue of blood that was dripping and killing her inside. I know … because that girl was me."

"What!" Yelled Dr. Smith. The rest of us stood there stunned. Lady Johnson with tears in her eyes, then got up and fell on the ground by her feet and started weeping loudly. Rev. Mellowin looked angry, perhaps too angry to say anything because she was silent. Everyone else just stared.

Rev. Minor lowered her head, probably to avoid the stares. She herself began to weep. "No, don't be sorry, for sorry is as sorry does," Rev. Minor said quietly, while helping Lady Johnson up. "Thank God I didn't allow it to take up the rest of my life. But I'm sad to say that it took up a great part of it. All those years of hate for my brothers who had nothing to do with one person's degenerate actions. If I could have been healed psychologically earlier in life, it probably would have prevented me from mentally killing other good men who came into my life. My bleeding resulted in my hurting many of my brothers through disrespect, dishonesty, and disengagement—including many of my own family members. I've cried, but I've repented, and I'm glad to say, God has stop the bleeding. I am healed."

Her face showed a relieved smile along with her tears. She continued with more boldness, as if to show she had overcome her bleeding, and she didn't want anyone sitting in her blood. "Rev. Bryant, you asked, 'Why do we hurt each other?' Well, the truth of the matter is that when we're hurting, we hurt the people closest to us. When we are broken, we break the people nearest to us. When we are disgraced, we disgrace and abandon and beat those closest to us. Our mothers and fathers, sisters and brothers. Wives hurt husbands, and husbands hurt wives. Mothers hurt their children. Children hurt their mothers. Black-on-black crime is real, but so is white-on-white crime. Because we have been put into a system that is broken and a family that is ruined. And hurt does as hurt is. We need God to stop the bleeding."

Her voice, though small, was controlled. It made me cry, even though I tried to restrain myself. I couldn't help but think how I had hurt someone close to me or been hurt by someone close to me. She was real. When she continued in that same calm yet collected voice, she had my attention, as well as that of my fellow participants.

"Our churches are filled with bleeding folks. Folks who have come with heavy loads of blood on their backs, between their legs, in their hearts, and on their minds. People who are hemorrhaging from the inside out. People who have held on to their hurts and hates, fears and mistrust, and it's killing them and hurting others. They drop blood everywhere they go. On the surface they may look good, but deep down inside they're crying, 'Somebody, please, please help me.'

"It's the same in America as a whole. Look at America. Because of racism and sexism, black people, Hispanic people, and women are bleeding. Because of wars, everybody is suffering—including white people. Many prescriptions have been tried, and many promises have been made. Many politicians have sworn, and much legislation has been passed. But we're still bleeding. One out of every four people in America is said to have been diagnosed with some form of depression. And those are just the ones who have been diagnosed. You'd be surprised how many black people are taking anti-depressants."

"Amen," Bishop Samuel, Lady Johnson and Rev. Franklyn all said at the same time.

"That's because if not controlled, severe hurt can turn a pleasant woman into an irate enemy. It can turn a decent man into walking dynamite. It can turn a loving heart into a revengeful spirit. I remember the movie *The Joy Luck Club*, Rev. Bryant.

The story of four Asian women telling their story of relationship and family."

"Yes, I saw that," Lady Johnson said while still wiping the tears from her eyes.

"Do you remember the scene that represents the highest act of bleeding and revenge? Well, one of the women was being mistreated by her husband, and instead of loving him, she grew to hate him. Her hate, however, did not allow her to conquer her fear to confront him directly. She grew cold and withdrawn and heavily depressed. It caused her to become psychotic. The baby that she bore with her despised husband became the source of her retribution. She took that baby and while bathing that baby, slowly drowned that baby."

"Yes, I remember." Lady Johnson said.

"That was her psychotic response to her hate for him. That was her wound shedding blood. Damage to children is the worst scenario and a real cause of pain in itself. In our communities, cases of hurt and abandonment exist, where the mother takes her anger out on the child because of the father. That's hurt at its worst. Fifteen years of my life I spent hating black men because I could not have children after the incident. My womb, my creation spot, was ruined. I hated them all for what he did." Tears welled up in her eyes, even as the rest of us filled the room with our own tears.

"But I'm healed," she repeated. "I adopted two wonderful children from my sister, who died while giving birth to twins—a girl and a boy, who since have given me grandchildren. The devil tried to take my family, but he didn't succeed."

"Amen! God is good!" Came from Lady Johnson and Dr. Smith.

I found this too deep. She seemed to speak as a psychiatrist who had us all in session. At this point, I felt that each of us needed healing more than she did.

"The Bible doesn't state what happened in the woman's past that caused the bleeding. It doesn't say what drugs she was on to contain the bleeding. But it does say she met Jesus."

Amens resounded again, we all seem to come out of our sorrowful state and entered one of hope and joy because of Rev. Minor's words. "Jesus was walking down the road with the ruler, and the woman interrupted to get her healing to stop her bleeding. And sometimes the poor must take their blessings before the leaders get their blessings, for fear of no blessings being left. Or fear that the rulers won't share their blessings with the poor. God bless America, but America didn't bless God. How America blesses God is by sharing wealth with the least of these."

"Yes, great connection." Rev. Ed said.

"Jesus said in Matthew 25, 'Whatever you did for one of the least of these brothers of mine, you did for me.' So the woman, out of desperation and fear, took her healing. Jumped the line and grabbed her blessing. She didn't want to wait on legislatures to distribute health care; she felt she was entitled, just like everyone else. So she took it from Jesus. She reversed the norm. Instead of waiting in line, she jumped the line, broke through the crowd, and took her blessing."

"I like this talk!" Rev. Taylor yelled out.

"She had tried the waiting game for twelve years but, the Bible says, her condition went from bad to worse. And I believe that if the situation gets bad enough, it will move us from waiting to taking."

"Yes!" said Rev. Ed again and others now feeling free to verbally express their support for her words.

"Martin Luther King, Jr., captured this brilliantly in his book *Why We Can't Wait*. He stated that 1963 became the pivotal year for demanding change because of all the promises that had been made and hardly delivered. The year 1963 was nine years after the Brown vs. Board of Ed decision, which saw little progress for integration in education. According to King, only 9 percent or less of the schools had been integrated. And 1963 was three years after the Democratic Party announced major civil rights legislation on its platform, only to find the administration backing away from major campaign promises in housing discrimination. Additionally, on the international front, by 1963 the number of independent, decolonized African nations had gone from three to thirty-four in thirty years. But the biggest, and I believe the most profound, exegesis of Dr. King's analysis is when he pointed out that it had been one hundred years since the signing of the Emancipation Proclamation, yet although the Negro was without chains, the Negro was still in bondage. King made this point to suggest that the winds of change would demand when it was time to stop waiting and start taking. For King, that year—1963—became the time because the climate triggered the labor pains, and the labor pains gave birth to liberation. We can't wait."

"That's good history," Rev. Bryant commended.

Rev. Minor just bowed her head, briefly acknowledging his compliment, then rolled on like a Baptist preacher rather than a little Presbyterian girl. "Many woman are hurting from some of the same scars I encountered in my life. And they're looking for the first man they can trust and with whom they can feel comfortable to touch. And usually, they're disillusioned by the pastor as their man, rather than as their minister."

"That's right!" Lady Johnson interrupted. The women seemed to connect on a female level.

"Many women are hurting so badly that they cannot love again, trust again, or feel again. They don't want to be involved again, engaged again. Their wounds are too wide; scars are too deep. Bleeding is too profuse. And when the wounds become wide and scars deep, blood begins to gush out like a fountain. And when blood is leaking, life is losing. When you drip blood, you lose life. You lose joy. You lose peace. You lose strength. A wounded soldier won't be good for too long. A healing must take place before you move on. The woman with the issue of blood knew she could not go on in life unless she had a healing from heaven. And she got it, or should I say, she took it. She couldn't wait any longer for her healing."

"Amen," Rev. Mellowin called out.

"But I didn't forget about the ruler." Rev. Minor paused, making the connection to the biblical text with woman and the ruler. "God is so good, he can heal the person and the nation. The peasant and the ruler. The ruler was bringing Jesus to his daughter. That's the kind of rulers we need—those who see a dead situation and decide that instead of just bringing talk, to bring Jesus. Leaders need to know how to bring Jesus to a dead economy. To a hopeless people. To a morally decaying nation.

"When Jesus got to the ruler's home, he healed the daughter. He put the spirit back in her. This nation needs the spirit back in it. That's Gethsemane—the spirit being poured into the flesh to heal the rulers and the bleeders. Look at this: if leaders know how to come to Jesus, and bleeders know how to reach for Jesus, then the nation will rise, and the people will be healed. The combination of the dead and the wounded coming to Jesus can only result in resurrection and restoration. God can stop the bleeding. God can raise the nation. God can stop the hemorrhaging. Let's get leaders and bleeders to Jesus."

"Good God, I'm not going to ask you where that came from. I'll just say, God bless you," Rev. Ed said.

"All I'm trying to say," Rev. Minor explained, "is that we must, like the old hymn says, lift him up." She began to sing, adding her own words to the verse. "How to reach the masses/men and women of every birth/peasant and ruler on earth. Jesus gave the key: he said 'If I, if I be lifted up from the earth, I will draw all people unto me.'"

12

Have Mercy on Me, Lord

Matthew 5:7

What about Us
We are God's children too
What about Us
We have feelings just like you
We can breath and we can bleed
We have wants and we have needs
We need protection for our family
We want out of poverty
We need to be treated with dignity
We want the blessed opportunity
To seek life and liberty
So we can live and be happy
In the land of the brave and free
That is blessed with God's mercy
What about Us

Rev. Minor, you raised something pertinent in your assessment and made the perfect biblical connection," Rev.

Ed complimented her after the singing. "The leaders don't give to the bleeders. This has been the cause of the fall of many nations. There is no mercy. For mercy shares, mercy cares and mercy distributes equally. The Bible says we should love mercy." With that and without preamble, Rev. Ed turned to me and said, "Rev. Parks, we're ready for your prophetic condemnation, for which you are so popular."

He'd caught me off guard, but I recovered quickly. "Well, it's about time," I joked. "I was beginning to think I was part of the chair."

Everyone laughed politely, and I began: "According to the law of disobedience, we all should be condemned!" I looked around the table and gazed at everyone as I spoke. "The leaders and the bleeders. As was raised earlier, according to the file, we all have fallen short of the glory of God, and as such, we should all be destroyed! All of us have violated the law and ignored the Commandments, even the most basic and simplest summary of the Commandments: Love the Lord your God with all your heart and with all your soul and with all your strength and with all your mind; and love your neighbor as yourself.

"We all have criminal records for doing the unrighteous. Some of us have longer rap sheets than others, but it's not the length of the offense; it's the intent of the offense."

"Break it down," Rev. Bryant encouraged me.

I knew I was speaking forcefully, punctuating every word and pausing after each sentence. "The Bible says out of the heart comes evil thoughts, a point Rev. Franklyn raised earlier. Murder, deceit, pride! The intent is what condemns! We all have done wrong intentionally at some time or another! And because of our intent, we don't deserve God's salvation or deliverance! We don't deserve God's compassion or forgiveness! There ought to be no forbearance or clearance of our record. David was right in Psalms 8:4, when he asked the question, 'What is man that you are mindful of him, the son of man that you care for him?'"

"That's a good point." Rev. Ed leaned over to me and said. I looked at him and bowed my head in gratitude then went back to my assessment.

"According to the law and according to the establishment, justice demands that we die!"

"Ooh, that's harsh and true," someone yelled out.

"But what has saved us from the law and rescued us from the fall is God's mercy."

Amens rang out.

"Nehemiah called it 'the great mercy of God' because with all the wrongs the Israelites had done, God should have put an end to the Israelites, but because of his mercifulness, God saved them. If it had not been for God's mercy, we would be in the dark pits of our lives! This is where David in the twenty-eighth psalm says, 'Hear my cry for mercy,' so that I will not go down into the pit like others. David cries out and lifts up his hands and surrenders to God and says, 'Lord, I need your mercy!' David, in all honesty, as at Gethsemane, committed the acts of frailty through his humanity and should be condemned."

"Tell the story, Doc." Without looking I knew it was Rev. Taylor's voice.

"David often followed evil over God, and the result of his arrogance caused the death of his people and the destruction of his nation. It's like what you raised earlier, Lady Johnson. If you look at First Chronicles 21, you will see that David, the ruler, listened to Satan rather than to God in taking the census. As a result, the Lord's wrath came upon Israel. The angel of the Lord pulled his sword out of its sheath and a plague fell upon the land, killing seventy thousand people. More ruin was going to take place, including the destruction of Jerusalem. But God had mercy upon them and called off the angel of death. And David looked up and saw the angel of death suspended between heaven and earth with a sword in his hand extended over Jerusalem.

"Many people were destroyed but many were saved by the mercy of God. And I often think we look at the devastation that occurred with Hurricane Katrina in New Orleans and

Mississippi and Alabama, but we don't look at the mercy that was extended to save the rest of the land from destruction." Hearing nothing but praise, I got into the spirit of the message. "If the destruction were to equal our nation's sin, then more land should have been taken, if not all of it."

"You're talking real," Bishop Samuel said as he patted me on my back.

"If it had not been for the mercy of God, the waters would have kept rolling along from land to land and from sea to shining sea. God did it in Noah's days and promised not to do it again. God in his mercy called off the death angel. And now that angel is suspended between heaven and earth, with a sword in his hand extended over Washington DC, waiting for instruction from God on how to proceed."

"Ooh, good connection and relevance," Rev. Ed stated. "I've never heard it that way before." Rev. Ed looked amazed at my every word. I simply, in order to stay focused and humbled, continued with my point so as not to disappoint my admirers.

"Because this nation, just like us, doesn't deserve God's forgiveness. God is so good that he honored David's request for mercy and saved him from his fateful pit. In the psalm, David cried in joy at the mercy of God. 'Praise be to the Lord, for he has heard my cry for mercy.' And I believe that all of us can testify to God's mercy—how God forgave us when we should not have been forgiven; how God saved us when we should not have been saved."

"That's right. I got a testimony." Said Dr. Smith.

"Mercy is when you realize that the consequences of your actions should have led to your destruction. Unprotected sex can lead to AIDS. People have to wait in agony a whole week to find out their test results and cry to God for mercy during the misery. And God has been so merciful that he can blot out our transgressions and hide our sins so that no one knows about them. And I'm sure many of us have been there before, where we beg God not to let our sins get out the closet."

"Oh, you're talking truth, Doc," Rev. Bryant called out.

"We beg God and plead with God and tell God we will never do it again! Because if certain people knew of our past transgressions and present indiscretions, some of us would not be married today!"

No one said a word, perhaps for fear of exposing themselves, except Rev. Charles, who unashamedly confessed, "That's why I'm not married today." I ignored him and kept going with my lesson.

"Some of us would not have a job today," I continued. "Some of us would not have as much respect as we do today. Because although folks say they don't care what happened in your past, the truth is, if they ever found out any stuff on you, they would criticize and judge you through the lens of your history, rather than by your transformed reality."

Everyone gave their hearty amens. Then Rev. Charles stomped in with his military foot. "Especially church folks!" he interjected angrily. "Church folks will condemn you and stone you worse than the world will! The ones who have received mercy are mercilesssss." He pronounced "merciless" with a long hissing sound at the end of the word; his point was clear. As I was about to continue with my statement, he rushed in without regard to my turn. "I am not going to lie: many of you probably already know I was a pastor and was married but got into trouble with women in the church. It was wrong, and it cost me my family, my church, and my reputation. I was ridiculed by the community, which I expected, but the church, which I had grown and taken to higher heights, was merciless. They voted me out two days after hearing of my indiscretions."

"What do you want? Pity?" Rev. Mellowin asked scornfully. "That's your punishment! You should have kept your stuff in your pants. You don't deserve mercy." Rev. Mellowin then condemned him and the whole male population with complete judgment. "You men, including pastors, think that you could stick your stuff anywhere, and people are supposed to just forgive you. No!" She pointed her finger towards his face. "You deserved everything you got! And more! As far as I'm concerned, you did get mercy because if I'd been your wife, not only would you be peg-leg, but you'd be peg-penis!"

"Hold it, hold it!" Rev. Ed shouted. Everyone was going wild. All the women gave Rev. Mellowin a high five. All the men, except Rev. Charles, couldn't help but laugh out loud.

Rev Charles looked agitated. Talk about no mercy. Rev. Ed tried to calm the disturbance, but Rev. Charles was too incensed. He stood up and wobbled while pointing and hollering at Rev. Mellowin. "I wasn't looking to get away with any damn thing young lady! I deserved what I got, and I got what I deserved! I was just saying that even after all I had done, I didn't expect the church to be so merciless!"

"You're still trying to get what you expect, but you got what you deserved, you damn fool!" Rev. Mellowin could not be hushed. She stood up and pushed her face close to his. "The church didn't give you what you expected because God gave you what you deserved. Don't blame the church; blame yourself for that thing in your pants or that messed-up mind in your head or that lust in your heart. Stop blaming others! You stupid, ignorant, impulsive ass! You got what you deserved, and mercy saved you from the worst!"

Before Rev. Charles could say another word, Rev. Ed jumped between them with hands outstretched, like Jesus on the cross. The two guards at the door busted into the room—they must have seen the commotion through the window. They asked was everything alright. Rev. Ed told them everything was okay. They looked around before departing.

"Rev. Parks," Rev. Ed motioned to me, his breathing heavy. "You started this, so why don't you finish it. I don't think we mind the confession, but I don't think we need the commotion."

"Well, confession begets commotion," Rev. Mellowin threw in.

"Can't we all just get along?" added Rev. Bryant, making everyone, except Rev. Charles, giggle.

"May I just say one more thing?" Rev. Charles asked, looking at me, with less anger in his voice.

"If I were you, I wouldn't say a word," Rev. Taylor suggested. "I would protect my other leg … if you know what I mean."

Since it was my floor, I waved Rev. Charles on. Rev. Ed looked at me with annoyance for permitting Rev. Charles to continue, but I wanted to hear what he had to say.

"We all have our issues, and mine was women. I carried the church and my family to greatness and then to embarrassment. I struggled throughout my ministry with my lusting—a battle for me. I could not beat it at times. That's Gethsemane for me—the spirit willing but the body weak. I allowed the body to prevail and the spirit to fail. And it has cost me more than you know."

"You still alive, ain't you?" Rev. Mellowin sniped at him. Rev. Ed placed his hand gently on her shoulder as Rev. Charles continued.

"But I've recuperated with a new love of salvation. I stayed away from the ministry for three years—celibate, fasting, and praying, and asking the Lord to 'take this cup away from me.' And I'm glad to say that God has honored my request. But thank God, he saw fit to move me to another location to complete my ministry, restart my family, and regain my reputation. And the reason I am not upset at Rev. Mellowin is because I understand that this is part of the continuous punishment, so that I will never forget and never fall from the mercy God has granted me."

Rev. Mellowin didn't say another word. It was suddenly up to me to get back to where I had left off. I was so anxious, I forgot what I had last said. I didn't realize personal confession would come from my political disposition. Slowly, I organized my thoughts and found my place; then, calmly, I went back to my original thesis of mercy.

"God has been so merciful that he has given a forbearance to our files of defilement and clearance to our sin and shame." I glanced at Rev. Charles. "But the mercy that God extends to us is the same mercy God expects us to extend to others." I looked in the direction of Rev. Mellowin and hoped she had caught that. "Mercy is one of the cardinal virtues of mankind. When we are compassionate and show loving kindness and forgiveness to our brothers and sisters, it is an act of mercy that God is pleased with. That's why God said, 'Blessed are the merciful, for they will be shown mercy.' Mercy begets mercy."

"I like that," Rev. Ed said.

"The more we give, the more we receive. God encourages mercy upon others. God encourages the strong to help the weak. The well-fed to feed the hungry. The seeing to assist the blind. The well-off to support the poor. When we extend our hands to others, God extends his hand farther to us. That's why God said to Hosea, 'I desire mercy, not sacrifice,' because many can sacrifice for themselves but can't help someone else. God wanted them to have mercy upon the people. Mercy not only showed the loyalty to God, it showed the love of mankind."

"Excellent exegesis," Bishop Samuel complimented me.

"When we don't extend mercy to others, we can't expect God to have mercy on us," I continued, realizing I sounded accusatory. I felt that neither Rev. Charles nor Rev. Mellowin cared about what I was saying. I expected one of them, at any minute, to cut in on my analysis. But I fixed my eyes on first one and then the other as I spoke. "If anything, the lack of mercy causes judgment upon us."

"Teach," Dr. Smith broke in.

"The book of James shows in chapter 2 how the believers discriminated against the poor by showing favoritism to the rich when they came to meetings. To those who had more, they gave the best seats. But to the poor, they gave a floor at the feet of the rich—similar to today's tax cuts for the rich and spending cuts for the poor. James asked, 'Has not God chosen those who are poor in the eyes of the world to be rich in faith and to inherit the kingdom he promised those who love him?' James then said sternly, 'Judgment without mercy will be shown to anyone who has not been merciful. Mercy triumphs over judgment.'"

"Yes! Good connection," said both Rev. Ed and Bishop Samuel, who appeared to be loving the logic I was offering. This was their type of talk.

"That was really creative," Rev. Ed said appreciatively. "Rev. Charles, do you realize all the mercy you were given?" Rev. Mellowin stated, pointing and glaring angrily at Rev. Charles, and he exploded. "I realize it, but I don't need you to keep reminding me of it!" He pointed his finger in Rev. Mellowin's face as he continued. "Ain't nobody perfect. So get out of my face!"

I found the strength to continue from where I left off, while they whispered back and forth. "Instead of attending to the dire needs of the people during the hurricane, the government left them on roofs, in sewers, in a stadium like they were wild animals. Left them to drown and die. Called them 'refugees' rather than victims of the storm. Portrayed them as looters instead of survivors. Babies and the elderly died after the flood, waiting on the government. The government has murder on its hands!" My roar was heavy, chastising, and rough. I continued with a fury that came from my soul. "And its judge won't be Congress or the Supreme Court, for the bias of Congress prevents it from judging itself impartially. The judge will be an independent Creator, a divine moderator who will weigh the soul of the nation against the hurt of the people. Alexander Crummell once said, 'When the sins of a people reach a state of hateful maturity, then God sends upon them sudden destruction.' The sins of the nation are growing, and their height is reaching heaven's door. And when they mature, the sins will knock down the door and out will pour the awesome wrath of God. And such fury will cover the land with fire next time!"

"That's rough. Go on," Rev. Ed urged possibly seeing I was being disturbed by the two whispering and silently arguing.

"Where is the mercy of America that has received so much mercy from God? God had mercy—he could have destroyed all of our cities. New Orleans was just one of the filthy fifty that got hit. There were many others. Las Vegas should have been gone a long time ago. There is no doubt that New Orleans is known for its lewdness and lasciviousness. The city celebrates its streets of darkness. It glorifies its acts of defilement, and it relishes its reviled reputation. If I were speaking bluntly, I would say there is a biblical connection to the lewdness of the land and the flooding of the city. Sodom and Gomorrah. The city was dirty. God washed the city, and in the midst of washing the city, lives were disrupted and destroyed. God is not interested in hurting the innocent, but in the midst of cleaning the corruption and lewdness, the innocent got hurt."

"That's condemning indeed." Lady Johnson said.

"When I clean the house, some good stuff may get thrown out with the bad. Some medicines can help one thing in the body and destroy something else. And you mentioned earlier, Bishop Samuel, that the nation can be hit by other nations because of its low spiritual immune system. Its defense is down. The way America bullies other nations, God can also beat up this nation with natural disaster, whether with water or fire. We have to remember from our schools days, no matter how big you are, there is always somebody bigger." I pointed my finger around the room, not out of maliciousness but as a message and a warning for the arrogant. Rev. Charles and Rev. Mellowin still were making rude gestures at each other. I continued, in spite of them.

"Other nations may be scared of America, but God is not. God did not intend to destroy this nation with the flood but rather to discipline it. God did not intend to annihilate it, but rather to chastise it. As Crummell said, vengeance crushes and annihilates, but chastisement, however severe, saves and at the same time corrects and restores. God's mercy is still perpetuating and functioning in favor of this nation but warning against its wicked ways."

"Nicely stated," Rev. Bryant said. "Crummell is a new one to me." "Yes. Read about him sometime, young man," I suggested. "It is wicked to dismiss the concerns of the poor.

When you clean, certain things are found. The very area the administration hides and ignores most was brought to the surface. It was as if God were saying, 'You do for the rich but forget about the poor.' You pay attention to the corporations but what about the lowly in the nation? The city touted its tourism and hid its poverty. But just like God can blot out transgressions with his mercy, he also can reveal the dirt of the merciless. The Bible says secrets will be yelled upon the rooftops. The city kept the poor under a rock and its problems in the closet. But water will bring rocks to the surface and bones out of the closet. When the water filled the city, blacks and the poor came to the surface—literally upon rooftops."

"Wooo. You are cleaning house," said Lady Johnson.

Rev. Mellowin again cut in, asking Rev. Charles, "How did you feel when your mess was shouted upon the rooftops?"

Before he could answer I jumped in and spoke louder. "The city of sin was touting its attractions while hiding its poor residents. If America had concentrated more on jobs and construction during the election than just gays and abortion, maybe funding would have gone toward strengthening the city's levees."

"You talking now."

"But only mercy would have shown how to prepare for the poor. Look at what happened when America's filth came out: other nations witnessed our dirty laundry. The world now knows of the racism that America often has tried to hide. Thirty-seven million poor people in the world's superpower were introduced to the world. Thirteen million poor children were revealed. The nation that's pushing freedom from terrorists all over the world couldn't save and free its own people from a flood."

"How sad is that," Rev. Ed said simply.

"America is the big dog, top notch, and to not have been prepared and responsive makes America look sad and embarrassing. We should be ashamed of ourselves!"

"We really should," Dr. Smith agreed, and others nodded in response.

"Jesus at Gethsemane went forward because of the sad state of mankind. We needed mercy, and at Gethsemane, Jesus found the strength to give us what we needed. I pray that God has mercy on me!" Everyone looked up at me, and I suspected they thought that I was ready to confess. But my statement was more theological than personal. "Mercy is what keeps the nation standing. God said to Moses, 'I will have mercy upon whom I will have mercy.' God chooses whom to give his mercy. The reason I pray that God has mercy on me is because the merciful will uphold the nation. If God can't find mercy in the government, he has to find it in the people. If God can't find it in the leaders, he has to find it in the bleeders. As long as God distributes his mercy, we can assure a future on earth."

I felt compelled to end it there. I had a feeling that although my words were of great revelation, some participants were still focusing on the confession and continuous confrontation between Rev. Charles and Rev. Mellowin. But then a song came to mind, and I began to sing loud to blot out the other noise. Dr. Smith backed me up, which gave more resonance to the song.

"Your grace and mercy brought me through/I'm living each moment because of you/And I want to thank you and praise you too/Your grace and mercy brought me through."

13

Believing While Broken

Jeremiah 20:8–12

Lord, I've really been real stressed
Down and out, losin' ground
Although I am black and proud
Problems got me pessimistic
Brothers and Sisters keep messin up
Why does it have to be so damn tuff
I don't know where I can go
To let these ghosts out of my soul

—"Tennessee" by Arrested Development

We thank you, Rev. Parks, for giving us food before the food. We should all be spiritually full," said Rev. Ed.

"I'm still physically hungry," said Rev. Taylor, ever the comedian. "What do you have to eat?"

"I understand, Rev. Taylor," Rev. Ed responded. He explained that the research center had prepared a table of hors d'oeuvres, chicken wings, and drinks in the lounge next door.

Rev. Ed whispered to me that the different atmosphere of the lounge would spark a whole new form of relaxed discussion, which would encourage people to interact freely. Rev. Ed was not only a master divinity, he also was a master psychologist.

"Feel free to sit or stand where you please," Rev. Ed continued. "For this one, we can be more casual and get to know each other individually, personally and professionally. We can eat in the lounge where there are couches and chairs."

"You go ahead," Rev. Charles called out. "The men's room is calling me." He picked up his cane and hopped out.

Rev. Taylor said, "I'll race you," and hurried out just behind Rev. Taylor.

I led the way to the lounge. If the discussion was to continue, I wanted to make sure I had a good spot right by Bishop Samuel, so I could absorb his extensive knowledge. But Rev. Bryant ran toward Bishop Samuel before I could get to him. I stood next to both, hoping to capture the conversation and work my way in.

"Where are the drinks?"

"What do you need, Bishop Samuel? I'll get it."

"Pass me that water."

"No problem." Rev. Bryant was acting like he was looking to get in Bishop Samuel's favor. He knew the extent of the bishop's connections and status. Who wouldn't want to be in with him? I myself was hoping for the opportunity. But Rev. Bryant was more aggressive, and I didn't want to go up against a truck. After handing Bishop Samuel a drink, we three sat on the couch. Rev. Ed stood nearby, and I felt he was listening in.

"I really enjoy listening to your sermons on Sundays over the radio," Rev. Bryant told Bishop Samuel.

"Well, thank you, and I enjoyed your picturesque performance and exceptional regard for our people that you conveyed, son. How long have you been pastoring?"

"Five years; in October it will be six."

"How are you finding the experience?" Bishop Samuel asked him.

"It's been iaght. I mean, all right." It seemed to me that Rev. Bryant was trying to impress upon the bishop that he could speak proper English. His tone was clearer and less rough than when he had addressed the group. "You know, I can't complain. I've been blessed with a good congregation of loving people at the church."

"What are your challenges?" Bishop Samuel pursued.

"I guess getting people to really believe, to be faithful and courageous," Rev. Bryant responded without hesitation.

Bishop Samuel looked confused. "What do you mean, Rev. Bryant?" He seemed to have expected a different response.

"I don't think that people truly believe in the mission of our people, of our Jesus, of our salvation."

Just then Rev. Taylor came into the room with Rev. Charles in tow. They both sat on the couch facing us.

"Oh? And how are you able to detect this?" Bishop Samuel asked, showing his concern.

"I can feel the absence of faith. Not that I'm God and should judge, but I check it out in people and agonize over it. I've seen some people who will go with you just so far; they half-step. They support the idea but do not believe in the mission. The mission goes beyond idea and into vision, and vision take risks to get to."

Bishop Samuel's only response was "Ummm."

"You know, I don't think the people believe enough to take risks for our people or for our Jesus. For example, recently in my town there was a development taking place, and part of the land they wanted to acquire involved some of the church's property. I had seen the vision of our own development on that property, but the developers had seen the prospect of a new market. Most of the other landowners sold their property to the developer. However, I held out as long as I could—not for more money, but for the vision. But then they threatened eminent domain and taking me to court. My people supported me until they heard 'eminent domain and court.' I had to fight my own congregation for months because they didn't want to battle the court system. I was used to such battles when I was in the world. I thought of little David taking on and beating Goliath. Finally, because of the political pressure and other clergy from the community giving in, I decided to go along. But to this day it hurts my heart that we did not go to the end. More than that, it left me broken spiritually. That's why I don't think we will ever overcome our situation with this nation. We have followers and supporters but no true worshippers and believers. Worshippers and believers are willing to take the cross all the way to the grave."

Bishop Samuel nodded and said sagely, "I understand; you must've felt as Jesus felt when he was at Gethsemane. His supporters were sleepers, unwilling to pray with him. Jesus had a lot of walkers and talkers and most of all, a lot of eaters—folks who followed him for bread rather than for belief. That's why Jesus challenged their faith so often. He wanted them not only to follow him for what he fed them nutritionally but also for what he could give them spiritually and eternally. I remember Jesus' suggesting in John 6, after feeding the five thousand, that they were following him because of the bread of land, rather than the bread of life." I thought Bishop Samuel was great with words. He could turn a little rock into an awesome structure. "So your question, son, is not necessarily for them but for you. For people will do what people will do. But how do you deal with *you* in connection with what people will do?"

"Yes!" Rev. Bryant blurted out. "Because people can leave you feeling broken. It can be like Jesus at Gethsemane; they can leave your faith waning. I've had more support from brothers in the hood than I've had in the church at times."

As Rev. Bryant finished, Lady Johnson and Rev. Mellowin came rushing over. Rev. Mellowin asked me to move over so she could sit down. Lady Johnson sat across from us, next to Rev. Charles and Rev. Taylor.

Rev. Franklyn, who had apparently been listening from a distance, joined us, too. He interrupted the discussion with his high voice. "I feel the young man's pain. I've experienced such measures in my own ministry and at times it has been really daunting, to the point of depression. I felt like nothing could be done about our situation or our people. The more time went by, the more the challenges occurred, rather than progress and promise being realized. For me, there is still this yearning, this absence, this brokenness and emptiness and uneasiness while believing. Do you think it's possible to believe while broken? And what effects does it have on our salvation when conveying the message to our people?"

It was a good question, but one of the brilliant, more mature minds would have to answer it. Rev. Taylor, chicken wing in hand, jumped into the conversation after hearing the topic. Bishop Samuel encouraged Rev. Taylor's dissection of the question. They were the ultimate tag team.

Without hesitation, Rev. Taylor began. "A recognizable story comes to mind. If we've been around for a little while, we understand that there is no easy road in life, especially as pastors; we take a peculiar road as a peculiar people." Because of the chicken in his mouth, his words were garbled, but he made his point. "We have a difficult and challenging road, which requires of us a certain strength, endurance, behavior, manner, fortitude, and expectation. This road challenges our faith, it confronts our fears, and it solidifies our relationship with God. Many look at us differently—justifiably so because many looked at Jesus differently because of his manner, his lifestyle, his presence, and his words and actions. So this road is hardly ever crowded or filled because of its requirements; that of trust, hope, and holding on to the unseen. Robert Frost, the great poet, wrote, 'Two roads diverged in a wood, and I ... I took the one less traveled by; and that has made all the difference.'

"Jesus expressed a similar sentiment by stating, 'For wide is the gate and broad is the road that leads to destruction, and many enter through it. But small is the gate and narrow the road that leads to life, and only a few find it.'" Rev. Taylor seemed to love teaching others. "I don't think being broken has any negative effect on our salvation or calling; it shows our humanity.

In fact, it shows reality. The reality that Jesus showed us at Gethsemane was the struggle toward promise and prosperity. Jesus was broken at Gethsemane; it showed his humanity without taking anything away from his divinity or destiny. Sometimes brokenness is part of the plan for our progress. As Romans 8:28 states, 'And we know that in all things God works for the good of those who love him, who have been called according to his purpose.'

"Jesus showed us this reality of brokenness, so in our times of tribulation, brokenness is expected but prescriptive. Brokenness becomes a dose used to advance our cause and test our faith. We can still believe while broken." As before, the chicken bits in Rev. Taylor's mouth kept him from being as articulate as he might have been. He quickly swallowed, dropped the bone onto his plate, and then went on. "Now, Jeremiah was one of the major prophets of God, and compared to all the prophets of the Old Testament, Jeremiah's life was described in greater depth and detail. Jeremiah came with a message of judgment from God upon the Israelites, but he and the message were sternly rejected, with much fierceness and abuse. Such is the case for many of us prophets who try to bring the word of judgment to the nation or to the congregation. It is rejected and suggested as unpatriotic, unsympathetic, and ungrateful. And our judgment is never a personal attack, like judging. Judging is personal disintegration of a nation or person. But judgment is divine proclamation upon a nation or person for its betterment, protection and advancement. It is what the world would call constructive criticism. But the nation confuses judgment with judging, and therefore denounces all aspects of constructive criticism of its system and decisions. As a result, the nation deals harshly and uncaringly by assassinating character and breaking spirits, which prevents true challenge and eager supporters of a democracy."

"There goes freedom of speech," Rev. Franklyn joined in. "Too much judgment and condemnation on the congregation will cause people to leave the church."

"In this passage," Rev. Taylor continued, "Jeremiah goes to God, shattered like glass and scattered like grass, because he is battered and broken. He's been thrown in jail. He's been beaten and falsely accused, and he goes to God with concern for his own life. Looking through Jeremiah's eyes, we, as pastors and people, can see that this life can be hard, disappointing, and abusive. This life can bring you to pieces. It can break you down and make you cry. It would be good if this life was one of peace and beauty, love and serenity, but the reality is that this life can be harsh and life-threatening. Saul D. Alinsky, in his book *Rules for Radicals*, quotes Henry James as saying, 'Life is in fact a battle. Evil is insolent and strong; beauty enchanting but rare, goodness very apt to be weak; folly very apt to be defiant, wickedness to carry the day, imbeciles to be in great places, people of sense in small and mankind generally unhappy.'"

"That's deep. Who did you say quoted that?" Dr. Smith was intrigued; the poetry had caught her attention.

"Saul D. Alinsky," Rev. Taylor repeated, "a former organizer of the prisoners, the poor, and the middle class. If you've ever heard of the Industrial Areas Foundation, which helps communities organize for rights, that's one of Alinsky's babies. A true warrior of our time."

Dr. Smith took out a piece of paper and pen and wrote down the name of the author.

"But that quote is relevant to what Job said in Chapter 7, verses 1–5. He said, 'Does not man have hard service on earth? Are not his days like those of a hired man? Like a slave longing for the evening shadows, or a hired man waiting eagerly for his wages, so I have been allotted months of futility, and nights of misery have been assigned to me. When I lie down I think, "How long before I get up?" The night drags on, and I toss till dawn. My body is clothed with worms and scabs, my skin is broken and festering.'"

"That is poetically incredible but agonizing," Rev. Bryant jumped in. "It sounds like what the rapper Jay Z once said when he adapted a verse from *Annie* some years ago for his song, 'It's a

Hard Knock Life.' Rev. Bryant began to sing: 'It's a hard knock life for us. Instead of kisses we get kicked. Instead of treated we get tricked. It's a hard knock life for us.'"

Everyone joined in to finish the tune. Guessing the ages of the singers, I decided that most of us knew the *Annie* version rather than Jay Z's. Rev. Taylor, however, seemed to dismiss the reference as he rerouted the conversation back to his own discourse.

"One word in that fifth verse by Job stands out and speaks volumes to the description of life. And that word is 'broken'! Get out of bed, and bones don't move like they used to—you feel broken."

"Amen!" Dr. Smith yelled out.

"Disappointments and discouragements throughout the day make the spirit feel broken. Lay down at night—brokenness is your only cover. Get up in the morning—brokenness is your breakfast."

A soft amen came from Bishop Samuel.

"Jeremiah, in the midst of being beaten, went forward with the will of God and with boldness and uninterrupted passion. Even though he was hurting deep down inside, his distress was not on public display. Even though he was crying for help, you never heard the screams to his friends or saw his tears in public. Jeremiah kept it in and complained and frowned only to God. God knew his pain, while people saw his strength. But others, like Job, let it out. Everybody knew he had lost his fortune and his children. His wife saw his hurt and pain, and she told him to let go and cuss God. His three friends saw the scars on his body and the tears in his eyes. Job let it out."

"I like that comparison," Bishop Samuel complimented Rev. Taylor, who bowed and went on.

"And, I guess, just like Jeremiah and Job, as we go about this life we all have our own expression of the situation, and it can either be mute or thunderous. Acknowledged or veiled. Some may decide to keep it in, like Jeremiah. Others may decide to let it out, like Job. Some may decide to keep silent. Others may decide to shout. Some may decide to meditate. Others may decide to stomp. Some may fold their hands and pray. Others may clap their hands and praise. Some may decide to cry in silence. Others may decide to wail out loud."

"You go, Rev." Dr. Smith admiring his rhythm and wording. He looked back at her and with a smile said "I'm going."

He did, and his voice became almost thunderous. "Some may go into the closet. Others may go before the congregation. Some may look to the hills. Others may make a joyful noise. Some may hide their bruises. Others may show their scars. Some may stand, like Paul. Others may dance, like David."

"Preach the word." Again Dr. Smith loving it encouraged him.

"But whatever you decide to do, that's between you and God. What connects us is not our expression but our brokenness."

"That was good," Rev. Ed complimented.

"But what distinguished Jeremiah is that in the midst of his pain, he kept praying," Rev. Taylor continued. "That's Gethsemane. That's Jesus in the midst of it all; he's still seeking the face of God. Gethsemane is where brokenness of humanity interacts with willingness of divinity and finds energy. In the midst of Jeremiah's brokenness, he kept on believing and kept on moving. If anyone read the recent book on Mother Teresa, you know how she struggled with her faith in the midst of her ministry. But you would not have known it from observing her, because she kept it in and suffered while helping those who suffered."

"I've suffered in silence for many years," Bishop Samuel abruptly interrupted. Everyone's attention immediately turned away from Rev. Taylor and to Bishop Samuel. "My ministry has been a dichotomy of pain and praise—pain on the inside while being praised on the outside. As I stated earlier, I've cried for my people, for many families and for many issues, but my loudest cry has been for me—a cry to God for me to stop crying. I've been diagnosed with depression. Maybe it has to do with my mother dying at an early age, or my having to grow up mostly alone. I don't know, and I've never really analyzed it. But I, like many others, choose to keep it hidden, and at times it burns me up inside. Suppression of emotions is a dangerous commotion that leaves one convicted. I want to talk to someone but at times, I don't feel like I can talk to anyone, which allows the sadness to build up inside.

"Like Jesus at Gethsemane, I've prayed to God to either 'take this cup from me' or 'not my will, but yours be done.' And God's been good to me. Even at its deepest, my misery never stopped my ministry. In fact, some of my best sermons came out of my withdrawal."

He received a hearty amen from those who sat closest to him. Dr. Smith with her grandmotherly self began to hug him.

"Some of my best books came out of my low moments. Some of my best visions for the church, for the community, and for my life came out of gloom and darkness. It is incredible how in darkness, the imagination can create so much greatness."

"Amen!" The word resounded through the room. I felt like they were not only praising his confession but also confirming his statement. I wondered if that was God's plan for us—to break us, darken us, and then enlighten us. Like the earth—it was once void and without form, then God created it. Gethsemane is Jesus' going from broken body to resurrected savior. "That's because I kept on believing while broken," Bishop Samuel continued. Standing and loosening Dr. Smith's arms from around him. "I kept on trusting while busted. I kept on struggling while suffering. That's Gethsemane: the spirit willing to go on while the body is weak and going wrong. Depression will try to keep the body weak and immobile. It will try to keep the mind worried and wandering. It will try to keep the emotions expressionless."

"Yes, yes, yes," Lady Johnson confirmed.

Bishop Samuel was confronting his own malady, and he did it with force and fierceness. "But ... but ... but like at Gethsemane, the spirit has enough energy to pick the body up and lead it to victory." He stood up even straighter and spoke louder. "The spirit picks the mind up and leads it to creativity. The spirit picks the emotions up and leads them to joy, unspeakable joy."

"Amen!"

"This joy that I have—the world didn't give it to me, and the world can't take it away! I said, this joy that I have—the world didn't give it and the world can't take it away!" He dropped back into his seat, and slipped a piece of gum into his mouth. Then he looked at Rev. Taylor and said, "Take this cup away from me."

Rev. Taylor grabbed the cup and ran with it. "Jeremiah said, 'The Lord is with me like a mighty warrior, so my persecutors will stumble and not prevail. They will fail and be thoroughly disgraced, their dishonor will never be forgiven.' Jeremiah kept believing while broken. When you can believe while broken, while torn, while dysfunctional and disappointed, that's when God gets to see what you are made of—see whether you're a real Christian or an imitation brand."

"Okay, now."

"Whether you're quality silk or synthetic."

"You talk!" Dr. Smith shouted out.

Rev. Taylor continued, slowing down to make his next point. "I remember seeing a program on television that reflected a true and realistic case of believing while broken. The program was regarding Sierra Leone in Africa. The government and the rebels were in civil war, mostly fighting over the diamonds of the land. And the innocent civilians were caught in the middle of the fighting. And what the program showed was highly disturbing, just as in Rwanda. The rebels in Sierra Leone, in order to keep the civilians from supporting the government, would take their machetes and chop off the limbs of civilians—their arms and legs. They would attack the parents and the children and everyone who might support the government. The children were chopped and left screaming. Many had scars down their faces, and you could see the bone."

Rev. Taylor described the scene so dramatically that I could feel the pain in his voice and the pain of the people. We all had wet eyes.

Bishop Samuel repeated his famous phrase, "Do you see the trouble we are in?"

Even Rev. Taylor, out of character, began tearing up as he told the story. "But one scene, through all the tears of madness, conjured tears of joy to my eyes. During the church scene, they were having a spirited service and you could see those with cut-off hands, clapping their elbows and praising. You saw those with no legs, banging their knee bones and worshipping. Some rolled around in the dirt—babies whose limbs were no more—and praised God anyhow. Some hit their bodies up against the wall and made a beating sound as if to say, 'I'm going to praise him anyhow.' Then others with broken arms used their splints to clap on each other. They were broken, but they kept on praising."

"Hallelujah! Thank you, Jesus!" Rev. Mellowin yelled out.

Rev. Taylor's voice became firmer. "Can you imagine seeing crippled bodies dancing? Severed limbs rejoicing? And I say, here we are in America, minds in the right state, hand bone connected to the arm bone, and arm bone connected to the shoulder bone, and thigh bone connected to the knee bone, and leg bone connected to the waist bone."

"Amen!"

"We're all put together, and when trouble comes, we break down and turn from God." His voice had a hardness, filled with emotion and agitation. He continued, and it seemed his words pushed up from his stomach and hit his cheeks before they bellowed out."We got legs," he bellowed, standing up, "and we won't stand for God!"

"What you say!" Rev. Ed yelled out.

"We got hands, and we won't clap for God! We got voices, and we won't sing for God! The children and people of Sierra Leone had the real thing. Many of us got the fake thing. The front thing. Because we stop believing when broken. We get discouraged too quickly. We get thrown off too easily. We need to go back and get a lesson from the lowly! The broken-hearted! The damaged worshippers! The exiled prisoners! The runaway slaves! The beaten foreigners! The outcast lecturers! And the unflinching, old-time preachers!"

"Yes!"

"Jesus was broken at Gethsemane, but he kept on believing. Praise God!"

14

Where Is the Sacrifice?

Genesis 22:7

The righteous must be faithful
The righteous must be strong
We're living in a time
Where the government is wrong
We're living in a time
Where the lust controls our songs
We can not just be patient
We can not just ignore
Our lives are much to precious
Our children deserve more

After the rendition from Rev. Taylor and the confession from Bishop Samuel, everyone seemed to be drunk from the intoxicating spirit that had been served. After ten minutes of high praise, Rev. Ed seemed to collect his thoughts and bring back order.

"I want to deal with the issue of faith and sacrifice," he said sternly. "Faith is what we believe, and sacrifice is what we give. It is not mentioned so much as it was experienced by Abraham, when he had to take his son, Isaac, to the altar to be sacrificed. And because of this, I would say that faith and sacrifice combined is the essence of the Christian experience, because it truly speaks to the life of Jesus Christ, who walked by faith and gave by sacrifice. That is Gethsemane, when you can believe to the point of giving all you have, and all you have is yourself."

"I like that," Rev. Mellowin interjected.

"Now, for Abraham this experience must have been painful and frightening in two ways. One: this was his only son with Sarah, and a son born to him in his old age. God told Abraham that he would be the father of many nations, and the fear of God's withdrawing his promise may have been upon Abraham. Two: Sarah, his wife, was a no-nonsense type of woman. She laughed at God when he told her that she would have a child in her old age. She possibly would have killed Abraham if she'd known he was going to sacrifice her son. He must have snuck out the back door early in the morning."

"You're right about that—I know women!" Rev. Taylor interrupted. "I can hear it: 'I carried that child for nine months, varicose veins, and stomach all over the place after delivery, pain during pregnancy, and now you're going to do *what*? Because *who* said *what*? I will sacrifice you first, you touch my boy.' Ha, ha!" Laughter rang out, just at the time when it was needed.

"But Abraham followed by faith," Rev. Ed continued, "trusted in the Lord and went with his son up to the mountain and prepared the place for him to be sacrificed. Isaac said, 'The fire and wood are here, but where is the lamb for the burnt offering?' Isaac felt something was wrong. Abraham, with faith, answered Isaac and said, 'God himself will provide the lamb for the burnt offering, my son.'

"But my point in all of this is: where is the lamb for the burnt offering? Where is the sacrifice for our people? Who is going to pay the price for freedom? Who will lay at the altar of the nation and speak fervently and unflinchingly for justice, for the hungry, for jobs, for peace and calm? Who is willing to risk what they love for the love of God? Where is the sacrifice, Dr. Smith?"

Dr. Smith quickly turned her head when she was called. "Well, I absolutely agree with you, and I could not have referenced it better myself. I remember the early Christians being willing to put their lives on the line for Jesus, justice, peace, and people. Shadrach, Meshach, and Abednego. Stephen and Barnabas. Peter and Paul. Where are the sacrificers like them? During the early days of Christianity, Christians were thoroughly disgraced, but the grace of God was sufficient. In a book on Christian martyrs, dc Talk called them 'Jesus Freaks.'"

"Jesus what?" Rev. Taylor asked, squinting and visibly disturbed.

"Jesus Freaks, as in those who were considered crazy for Christ," Rev. Charles jumped in.

"It figures you would read a book like that, you freak!" Rev. Mellowin couldn't resist.

"Please continue, Dr. Smith," Rev. Ed quickly suggested.

"The book records the story of Ptolemaeus and Lucius. In AD 150, the guards brought Ptolemaeus before Urbicus, who was the city justice in Rome. Ptolemaeus had been accused of being a Christian by a man whose wife was trying to divorce him. He had earlier reported that his wife had become a Christian, and when he tried to force her to continue in the wild and decadent life they had been living together before her conversion, she served him a bill of divorce. She was afraid he would hurt her if she stayed with him. However, his accusation came to nothing because Emperor Pius granted her protection from a trial until she put her household affairs in order.

"So since he could not see his wife tortured and killed, he would see her teacher, Ptolemaeus, suffer. Urbicus looked at Ptolemaeus, an old man, and asked him if he was a Christian. Ptolemaeus, whose reputation was of being a man who loved truth above all else, answered simply by saying yes. Immediately, the guards were summoned to take him and execute him. Another man stepped forward from those present at the trial. His name was Lucius. Lucius inquired of the charges against the old man. 'This man is not a criminal,' Lucius stated. 'He is not an adulterer or a fornicator, nor is he a murderer, thief, or robber. He has broken no civil laws either. All he has said is that he is a Christian. Such a sentence of death for such an honorable thing will not bring honor to yourself, Prefect Urbicus, nor to Emperor Pius, nor to the emperor's son, the philosopher, nor to the sacred senate,' said Lucius. Urbicus then looked at Lucius and asked him if he was also a Christian. Lucius, understanding the truth, said yes. Urbicus then said 'Good. The old man will not die alone.' Lucius was then taken to die also. Urbicus expected Lucius to try to flee, but Lucius simply bowed his head in respect and said, 'I am grateful for the opportunity to live with the Father and king of heaven.' As Lucius made his proclamation, another servant in the court stepped forward and declared that he was a Christian also, and that he would like to share in their punishment—but, more importantly, in their reward."

Everyone was in awe, as Dr. Smith told the story with great eloquence and flow. "There were other martyrs who sacrificed their lives as well: Timothy in Ephesus in AD 98, and John Mark, who wrote the book of Mark, in Alexandria, Egypt, in AD 64, and Justin Martyr, in Rome in AD 165, and of Ignatius in Antioch in AD 111. The list goes on, from kitchen cookers to long-distance walkers and farm workers. They sacrificed life and limb. But the question is, where is the sacrifice? Abraham is indeed one of the most obedient and faithful servants of God in the Bible. His task and responsibility was extraordinary and, some may say, incomprehensible. For how can a man be tested to sacrifice his own son, whom he loves? God was looking for faithfulness and needed to provide for us through Abraham the unthinkable and greatest form of sacrifice. For the Bible says that some time later, God tested Abraham. He said, 'Take your son, your only son, whom you love, and go to the region of Moriah and sacrifice him there as a burnt offering.' God tested Abraham with his son, whom he loved. We must remember the test is not for God. God does not need the test for himself, for God already knows what the outcome will be. God knows if we're going to pass or fail."

"That's right." Came from Lady Johnson.

"And no examination is simple; no test is uncomplicated. Isaac was the exam, Abraham was the test-taker, and God was the teacher. Abraham wasn't taking Isaac, his son, to the table; Abraham was taking an exam of his faith. The question was whether he would pass or fail. What made the test difficult was Isaac. The answer to the exam was not Isaac; the answer was Abraham's faith. Isaac asked the question but Abraham didn't have to answer to Isaac, because Isaac wasn't grading Abraham. God was grading Abraham. Abraham had to answer to God through faithfulness."

"That's good. I like that," Bishop Samuel seemed amazed by her sequence.

"In order to determine whether or not one has sufficient faith, a test is given in circumstances of conflict and crisis, not idle moments. Abraham's faith was determined not during his good times but rather during his dilemma. It is similar to the story of Jesus and the disciples on the ship, spoken of in John 8. In the story, a storm arose. The disciples became frightened and ran to Jesus and yelled, 'Master, Master, we're going to drown.' Jesus then rebuked the wind and the raging waters until the storm subsided and all was calm. Then he asked the disciples this pivotal question: 'Where is your faith?' When Jesus poses the question of 'where,' it is not about location but rather about ratings."

"I like this even more," Bishop Samuel applauded her.

She paused, said thank you, and continued. "The ratings give us an indication of exactly how we're faring with our faith in connection with our crisis. If you were to rate your faith from one to ten, where would it be? Where is your faith?" Dr. Smith challenged us. She seemed to be looking into our souls. "And would your faith be sufficient or insufficient to deal with your issues? Jesus asked, 'Where is your faith?' Where is it when sickness arises? Where is it when emptiness and brokenness capture your heart and pockets? Where is it when death occurs? How would you rate your handling of the problem in connection with your faith? It's review time; it's inventory time; it's examination time."

Dr. Smith caused all of us to think, and then she delved deeper into the examination. "Let's do some calculating to get our rating. I want everyone in this room to think about his or her issues. I'll give you time—some of us came in here with them, others have so many they don't know where to begin. I've been there, done that."

I began to think about my issues. Everyone seemed to be doing the same.

"Now take your circumstances and add them up," Dr. Smith continued. "One by one, as many as you can remember. Allow the most pressing problem to lead the way. Now, add the consequences to them. What is the worst that can happen as a result of your issues? For instance, will the sickness result in blindness or death? Will the marriage end in divorce or death? Will the single life end in no children, no love, nobody? Are you all with me?"

"Yeah, I got you," said Rev. Mellowin.

Lady Johnson began to moan, as if her problems mixed with consequences were heart-wrenching. So did Rev. Mellowin, who seemed saddened by her outcome. The others were silent. Even Rev. Ed seemed to be really thinking about consequences. After a few minutes, Dr. Smith continued her experiment.

"Now take your circumstances plus your consequences, add them up, and then subtract the sum from your faith. Your faith is what you believe about Jesus: Is he a miracle worker, a comforter, a healer, a lawyer, a friend in the times of trouble? Faith is the substance of things hoped for, the evidence of things not seen. Faith is how he walks with you and how he talks with you. It is the scripture: 'God promised to never leave nor forsake me.' 'I have never seen the righteous forsaken nor their seeds beg bread.' 'Weeping may endure for a night, but joy comes in the morning.'"

"Amen. This is good," Rev. Ed said, allowing himself to be the student and not the teacher.

"Now after you have said all of that about faith, you should feel a power, a sense of relief. You should feel confident and strengthened. If, after you've added and subtracted, you find that your circumstances and consequences are still greater than your faith, then you have a low faith rating."

"Good God!" Lady Johnson yelled out.

"Your low faith rating is when your circumstances continue to outweigh your faith. In other words, when you add it all up, you cannot see the problem dissipating. There is no subtraction occurring: problems are either getting worse or remaining the same. You cannot feel God taking away the pain. You cannot see God calming the storm in your life. The problem with the disciples was that their ratings were low. Their faith was low in comparison to the circumstances. They could not see themselves living through the storm. This is evident from their communication. They said to Jesus, 'We're going to drown.' The conversation was in the direction of their ratings—down."

"This is brilliant," said Rev. Ed.

"They were going to drown, according to their faith. Because when your faith is down, your talk is down. Your life is down, and your outlook is bleak. When they added their circumstance with the consequences and compared it with their faith, they came to the worst conclusion. The disciples were walking around with a 5 percent faith and a 10 percent problem."

"That is really good. Where did you get that?" asked Rev. Ed.

"When I had no faith," Dr. Smith answered sincerely. "When I allowed fear to rule my life. When I sat home too afraid to step out of the house for fear my husband would leave me and my children would go astray. I suffered from paranoia for many years. And fear is counterproductive to faith. It is its worst nightmare. The test I am asking you to take, I took myself. I've been there where my consequences outweighed my faith so much that I was afraid to live the next day. I've always been one to see the worst in a situation. And seeing the worst makes one less likely to believe they can overcome it. The worst was my conclusion. I've not only seen the worst but I've experienced the worst, which added to my fears. I have few friends because I'm afraid to trust anyone. The last good friend I had swindled me out of all my money. She had a gambling problem and somehow managed to get over fifty thousand dollars from me. The last husband I had beat me physically into submission. I was to afraid to leave him and afraid he would leave me. I've always been too afraid to say what's on my mind, because I feared I might hurt someone or someone might hurt me. And this fear has been throughout my whole life. I used to add everything up and found that my fear outweighed my faith." She spoke with passion, but her reminiscing made her voice deeper than a hole in the ground.

"And a lot of it came from my early sickness. I was always ailing with something, but the doctors told me a lot of it was in my head. I always had this fear that I was going to die, so each day I lived my life with caution and more fear. However, one of the last times I went to the hospital, God spoke to me and asked me that question that I just asked you all: 'Where is your faith?' And that's when I began to test my faith."

"Amen," Rev. Minor whispered.

"And when I tested my faith, that's when I began to sacrifice, to cut some things off. I stepped away from my husband, like Abraham, not knowing where I was going.

"Amen! Don't ever stay with a man that beats you. You should have never went for that." Rev. Mellowin called out loudly. Dr. Smith seemingly ignoring her just went on.

"But in the middle of the night, I packed my bags and my children and left, and God was good. He led us to a shelter where we were able to stay, and I was able to get on my feet. I always had read everything I could get my hands on, so when it was time, I stepped out on faith and went to school, and I earned my degrees, from a bachelor's to a doctorate."

"That's faith," Rev. Ed backed her up.

"Yes, it is," Dr. Smith said. "I wasn't afraid to let my children go away to college. Faith helped me to overcome my fear. Because you can do so much for others and then find no one is sacrificing for you."

"You're right about that," Lady Johnson confirmed.

"I was doing so much for friends and so much for family that I couldn't find any room for me. So I suffered in my fear but I gained in my faith. It is true as the word says: if you have the faith the size of a mustard seed, you can say to this mountain, 'Be moved,' and it will move. I thank God I've moved that mountain of fear that dragged me down for so long. And because of faith I now see beyond the worst and into the glory of God."

"Amen."

"Jesus at Gethsemane saw beyond the accusations and the ridicule, beyond the trials and the betrayal, beyond the abandonment and denial, beyond his broken body and his bleeding side. He looked past all of that and saw into his glory. When we see glory, our ratings go up, and it's easier to sacrifice."

"That is very well thought out," Rev. Ed noted.

"But I'm not finished yet," Dr. Smith insisted. "I want to clarify what I mean by sacrifice. Sacrifice is more than just giving. Giving is optional—it doesn't hurt—but sacrifice hurts. It reminds me of the chicken and the pig. The chicken says, 'Let's get ready for breakfast. I love breakfast. It's my favorite time of the day. That's when the farmer uses me most.' But the pig says, 'That may be your favorite time, but understand all you have to do is drop an egg. I have to give up a whole leg.' All the chicken had to do was donate—the pig had to sacrifice."

"I've always liked that one," said Rev. Taylor, looking amused. "When you sacrifice, you have to give up something that it hurts you to give," Dr. Smith explained. "Within the biblical context, it's the same thing. You have to be willing to give up something, cut something off, something that pains you to lose. Many of us are like the rich young man in the Bible. When the rich young man asked Jesus, 'What good thing must I do to get eternal life?' Jesus said, 'If you want to get to heaven, obey the Commandments. Do not murder, do not commit adultery, honor your mother and your father, and love your neighbor as yourself.'

"The rich young man responded with confidence. 'All these I have kept. What do I still lack?' And Jesus hit him where it hurts. Jesus said, 'Go and sell your riches and give to the poor, and you will have treasure in heaven.' The rich young man walked away with his head down because he was not willing to sacrifice and separate himself from that which he loved more than God. It's easy to give up those things that are simple for us. Adultery, murder, and stealing meant nothing to the rich young man. But when Jesus got to the areas that meant something, it became difficult to sacrifice. It would hurt too much. If someone tells you to give up smoking, and you don't smoke, it doesn't mean anything to you. But if someone tells you to give up your job, you would have a hard time accepting such sacrifice."

Rev. Charles immediately took over the floor. "Anybody here ever think God will tell them to stop paying taxes because your tax money is aiding and benefiting anti-religious doctrine, such as war?" Everyone stared at him as if the question were rhetorical. He quickly went on, "Many reject the war but at the same time contribute consciously to it, knowing of the wrong. Henry David Thoreau, in his most revolutionary wisdom, perfects this discussion in his essay, 'Civil Disobedience.' He wrote, 'Those who, while they disapprove of the character and measures of a government, yield to it their allegiance and support are undoubtedly its most conscientious supporters, and so frequently the most serious obstacles to reform.'"

"That is radical," Rev. Bryant stated.

"No! That is sacrificial!" Rev. Charles shot back. "At the time, Thoreau objected to the treatment of slaves and the Mexican War. Here's what he wrote about slavery: 'I cannot for an instant recognize that political organization as *my* government which is the *slave's* government also.'"

"Now that's not only sacrifice but for a black person that would be suicide to say something like that." Bishop Samuel stated.

"Thoreau was one of the great revolutionary thinkers," Rev. Ed pointed out.

"Yes. And he was one of the great revolutionary sacrificers," Rev. Charles added. Just when he was about to pull the pin out of his next grenade, Rev. Mellowin jumped in. Rev. Charles was stuck with his mouth open and hands in the air.

"Well, when I think of sacrifice," said Rev. Mellowin, "the question becomes, who will go? That is the question proposed by God and accepted by Isaiah. Isaiah is more in line with Paul, when he says in the book of Romans, 'To offer your bodies as living sacrifices, holy and pleasing to God —this is your spiritual act of worship.' Like Paul, we are to present ourselves and not anyone else. Jesus is looking for all of us to present ourselves for the cause of justice and mercy." She had set the hook and was reeling us in. Her talk was quicker and sassier than when she had assaulted Rev. Charles, yet she had a good touch of logical brilliance. "I want to talk about the personal sacrifice that we must offer as a people for a people. When God made man, he made sure that all man's needs were provided for. There was food and a job for Adam. God told Adam to take care of the land and gave him the vegetation for his own delight. Today, brothers in the hood can't find a decent job to feed themselves or their families. Sisters, like myself, complain they can't find a good man because many of our brothers are locked inside jails. And jail is not only locking our men away from society and family, but jail also has locked our men into automatic and unwilling vasectomy."

"You talk, sister," said Lady Johnson, now in her corner.

Rev. Ed turned to Rev. Mellowin and asked her to expand upon her last point. Without hesitation she took off faster than a speeding bullet.

"They have locked men into an unproductive environment. The more black men in jail, the fewer children they produce. Understand the detrimental and unreplenishing effects of such isolation. And that's one danger. Look at the other. Man is with man, locked up for years. And men with men get used to being with brothers, not only for friendship but companionship and pleasure. Now the system is creating a whole lot of down-low brothers because brothers get used to being with brothers and eating with brothers and sleeping with brothers and touching on brothers. And now the most intelligent, strong, and handsome brothers are loving each other instead of their beautiful black sisters, like myself."

"What you say, sister?" Lady Johnson shouted out, as did Dr. Smith and others, all laughing.

Rev. Mellowin paused and touched her face, as if to reveal her beauty. With little a smile, she ran another red light: "They have been forced into a condition of homosexuality."

"You're right." Rev. Franklyn of all people squeaked out.

"But let me not get away from our subject of sacrifice." Rev. Mellowin continued. "We need a personal sacrifice along with a political sacrifice. That is the only way we're going to save our brothers and sisters and family members from doom and destruction. That is where the Bible says, 'To offer your bodies as living sacrifices, holy and pleasing to God—this is your spiritual act of worship.' So you ask where is the sacrifice? The sacrifice is us. We must put ourselves on the altar of justice and the stage of righteousness. But more important, in the homes of brokenness."

"I like that; speak on," Rev. Ed encouraged her again.

"Our homes are broken, our brothers are abandoning us, and our lives are ruined. The question becomes, who will present themselves to fix that which is broken? That is Jesus at Gethsemane; he was presenting himself on the cross as a sacrifice to fix our broken relationship with God. Yes, we must confront the political, but the verse is calling for us to confront personal issues that linger in our lives. What are we willing to cut off, to sacrifice, in order to make our families stronger, our brothers responsible, and our sisters happy?"

"That's a biased assertion and ridiculous assumption!" Rev. Charles lashed out. "How come the sisters must be happy and the brothers responsible? We're all in this together. Everyone has to be more responsible to make everyone happy."

"Yes," said Rev. Mellowin, looking him straight in the face, "but if the brothers were responsible, it would not only make the sisters happy but make them happy too, because they would be doing what's right by themselves and their families. The reason we're in the mess we're in is that many times, a brother is not willing to give up his penis to be with one woman!"

The hit was below the belt; she knew this was Rev. Charles' weak spot. Rev. Ed's jaw dropped as he sat in stunned silence.

"The Bible says in Matthew 5, verse 29, 'If your right eye causes you to stumble, gouge it out and throw it away,'" Rev. Mellowin quoted. "That's sacrifice. Brothers are allowing their eyes and their penises to cause them to sin. It is not only a sin; it is a sin-sickness because every woman, every leg, every breast, every ass a man sees, he wants. That's sick! Whether he's married or not. Preacher or politician. So in order to save him from going to hell, some of our brothers need to cut their stuff off—some literally and some spiritually. If you can do the spiritual, it will take care of the physical, but if you can't do the spiritual, you must allow us to do the physical."

"Stop! You're hurting us!" Rev. Bryant shouted.

But she just kept on cutting. "Some of our men need to sacrifice it! You ask where is the sacrifice? Well, it's the area that causes one to sin, and for many men, that's their penis, their eyes, their hands. They need to sacrifice to save themselves and their family. The same verse in Matthew also says, 'It is better for you to lose one part of your body than for your whole body to be thrown into hell.'"

"You go, girl!" Rev. Johnson screamed out.

Rev. Mellowin didn't need any encouragement. "Brothers are losing their whole body for a piece of vagina—for lack of a better word. Some may complain at an early age of being impotent, but God may be saving our brothers from killing themselves. They're going to overdose on sex. That Viagra is doing more harm than good for some men. Some men need to just cut it off. Some men need for it to be dysfunctional, because it's killing them.

"This is Jesus as Gethsemane, willing to cut off his body so that we do not die of sin. The spiritual outweighed the physical. He overcame the temptation of the body at Gethsemane and the spirit prevailed. Brothers can overcome the body by allowing the spirit to cut off the body's desire for constant sex and temptation. The spirit must prevail if we want to see real sacrifice."

Rev. Ed then jumped in before Rev. Charles could say anything. Everyone was again applauding and laughing at Rev. Mellowin's abuse of Rev. Charles. Just when he was trying to make a comeback, she put him back in the hole. Rev. Charles looked furious, and his mouth was open like he was about to cough.

"Before we go any further into the fire, let me cool it off by doing something I should have done earlier, that is to formally introduce Rev. Michelle Mellowin, who has already introduced herself." Rev. Ed said. "Rev. Michelle Mellowin is the assistant pastor of arts and drama at Greater Love Church in Los Angeles, California. She is a graduate of Stanford University in California and Fuller Theological Seminary. Prior to her calling, she was a drama major and has been in many plays. Her calling came not in a dramatic way but in a challenging way. She has said that being torn between the world and God had a twisted impact on her soul and that the unethical activities of her life left her more lonely than happy. Although she accepted the ministry at an early age, she was not living the ministry but still was in pursuit of Hollywood and Broadway. But the Lord called her and spoke to her during a performance. In the midst of it, before hundreds of people, she broke down and accepted Jesus Christ into her life. She got rebaptized and has been living for him sincerely, consciously struggling, ever since. Let us welcome Rev. Michelle

Mellowin." We all applauded her, except Rev. Charles, who simply shook his head up and down.

Rev. Mellowin then seemed to turn back into the ghetto-fabulous person she was. In a sassy and smart way, she quickly waved her hands and said, "That's all I have to say." She then reached into her purse, pulled out lip gloss, and started applying it. She then leaned back, crossed her legs, grabbed her drink, and began to sip—loudly.

15

I'm Going to Get My Brother

Genesis 14: 11–16

And I almost lost faith when you took my man
Monty, Paso, and Jay's brother Dan
And I fear that what I'm saying won't be heard until I'm gone
But it's all good 'cause I really didn't expect to live long
So if it takes for me to suffer for my brother to see the light?
Give me pain till I die! But please Lord, treat him right.

—"Prayer" by DMX

That was very good, Rev. Mellowin. You really captured the conflict of men and women here at the conference," said Rev. Ed.

Lady Johnson opened her mouth to speak but the voice of Rev. Charles was heard instead. Rev. Charles, visibly upset, couldn't be shut down on this one. The male condition was his specialty, and even if he had his problems, he was going to speak.

"How are you going to allow her to be the voice of the brothers' condition? She ain't lived in our shoes! She ain't walked in our paths! How is she going to talk for us, when she is many times responsible for what we're going through?" His voice was loud, like a bomb, his finger pointed like a rocket, and his legs stood like missiles. He was determined to blow up something regardless of what anyone said.

"I was wrong with my sinful actions, but 99 percent of the time when I came home, I heard nothing but complaints from my wife. Everything I was doing was wrong, never right. I heard how she felt bad, and her needs were not being fulfilled. And it may have been true, but men have needs, too, that they can't talk to anybody about. Black men are hurting more than anyone. Why is it that when it comes to black men, everybody wants to go to sleep, including black churches? I'm tired of having our men ignored."

Rev. Mellowin jumped in. "I don't think anybody is sleeping on black men; I think black men are sleeping on themselves. They're on the corners; they're players and married; they're leaving their children. They're spreading HIV and AIDS to our black women, and they're running off with white women!"

"What are you talking about?" Rev. Charles shot back. "You're falling into the same stereotypes of our black men as the motherfucking general public!"

"Wooo, easy!" Rev. Ed's entrance was swift and certain.

But Rev. Mellowin shouted even louder, stood even taller, and jabbed her finger at Rev. Charles. "I have not! I've experienced and witnessed this for myself. Black men need help." Rev. Mellowin's eyes did not waver from their fixed gaze on Rev. Charles, even as she stood up to get in his face.

"Yes, they need help getting up, not being put down," Rev. Charles came back. "Especially by their black sisters. You have your own distorted perception, but black men are hurting, then harming, then dying. We need a campaign in the church just for our black men."

"I agree," Rev. Mellowin said. "And it should have been done yesterday, and when you do it, make sure you add a session on what it means to be faithful to the black woman."

"I'll add a session on what it means for the black woman to uplift the black man." They were all in each other's face.

Rev. Ed stood up forcefully between them. He lifted his hands to both of their faces. "Wait a minute!" As he shouted, security burst through the door. Everyone immediately became quiet. They asked Rev. Ed if everything was okay, and Rev. Ed assured them, with the little breath he had left, that everything was fine. They then closed the door slowly. He then asked Rev. Charles to elaborate on his passion. And he asked Rev. Mellowin to listen to his perspective.

She hesitated, then sat in her corner, waiting for the bell to signal the next round.

Rev. Charles' frustration kept him from articulating clearly. He stuttered and stumbled for a while, breathing heavily before he was able to collect himself. "What will it take to minister to the brothers? This is a question that is hard to answer. We have to find the right dose."

"What do you mean?" Rev. Ed asked softly, as if counseling him.

"I mean it seems as though no one knows how much spiritual medication is needed to sustain black men and heal them from their sickness and save them from their wickedness. We have found the dose for many of our black woman, and they eat it and get strong from it—spiritually, economically, legally, politically, and educationally. Black women are ahead of the game. And one cannot doubt that their spirituality and connection with the church has a lot to do with their advancement." His voice had calmed considerably, and he sat down slowly.

Rev. Mellowin, seeing the threat against her was over, listened rather than argued.

"Once women decide to accept Jesus, they use it as a strength to raise their children, go to school, find a job, work overtime, and do without a man, if necessary."

"Amen," Rev. Mellowin said.

Rev. Charles continued. "We read the story of Mary; she was the first to carry the word, which was the Son of God, and the word became flesh inside her, and it changed her life. Before the word she was poor in pocket and in spirit. Her self-esteem was low. When she discovered she was carrying the Son of God, she became hopeful and proud. She was no longer ashamed but empowered. She went away jumping and Skip-to-My-Lou-ing, and singing the words, 'From now on all generations will call me blessed.' She felt more blessed than rulers and kings."

All the women in the room looked at him and thanked him for such a profound revelation and connection.

"That's Gethsemane—when the spirit can empower the body, free it of its misery and poverty, and make it feel blessed. We have found the dose it takes for women to excel in family and society. And it works. However, I don't think we have found a similar or sufficient dosage for our brothers. Not only in amount but mixture. What is the compilation and combination of substances in the word needed for brothers to be saved in soul and in society? What is the combination we can bring from the word to give to the brothers in the world and free them and empower them out of their misery?

"When Mary got the word she tried to give it to Joseph, but he wouldn't take it. He thought she was actually fooling around on him. And it hurt him, and he was going to secretly divorce her. But think how hurt he was. How disgusted he felt. How broken he became. Many of our brothers are hurting badly over relationships in which women have done them wrong. Too many of us are too proud and ashamed to admit it. Myself included."

Another sudden admission; everyone just listened because he wasn't attacking—he was being attacked by his own mind. "So we walk around in silence and with a false appearance of sternness and strength. Outside, we're laughing and leading. Inside, we're hurting and bleeding, Rev. Minor, like you said earlier. And that's real suffering. That's Gethsemane; Jesus in pain and having no one to understand or stand with him. Sleepers in the body over watchers of the soul. It wasn't until God himself spoke to Joseph about the situation, told him that Mary was truly faithful and that he should forgive her and help her, that Joseph was transformed and receptive. God realized Joseph needed a different dose of Jesus than did Mary. Joseph's pain was different. His pride and ego were different. God has to come to the brothers directly, or he should use real, godly people to get to the brothers. Because although sisters are ahead of the game, brothers are tired of the games. Games won't do."

It was true. Even Rev. Mellowin seemed absorbed by his words and sympathetic to his thinking.

"Black men are like the pharaoh; they are not going for the games and tricks in church. They're looking for realness. Men are used to playing games, so the church can't come with any games. Black men know game when they see and hear it. That's why the pharaoh wouldn't bow down to Moses—the pharaoh figured it was just all games. Whatever power Moses threw at the pharaoh, he threw back at Moses. The pharaoh was letting Moses know he couldn't be swayed easily. The pharaoh had his own tricks, as well as stubbornness, to combat Moses. Moses had to come hard or go home. God hit the pharaoh hard to let him know he wasn't playing games and that he was serious about delivering his people out of bondage."

"Amen," said Rev. Ed, seeming highly impressed.

"Preachers have to hit hard to let brothers know they're serious about delivering them from their condition. Because many of our brothers' hearts are hard, just like the pharaoh's. And I do believe that God has hardened the black man's heart—and for that matter, every man's heart—so it takes a lot more to convince us of the gospel and to deliver us from the garbage. God has hardened our hearts, not because he dislikes us but because he can show his power through us."

"Good talk, young man," said Rev. Taylor.

"The tougher the man, the harder he bows to God. The more others will praise God when he does bow. Because people will see the power of God through the transformation of the truly wicked and rebellious. And once people see the conversion, they'll know only God could have changed his heart."

"Amen. I hope I can find the man God touches," Rev. Mellowin said with a laugh.

"Like Paul. They're tough," Rev. Charles continued. "They're prideful. They're controlling. They're hard-hearted like the pharaoh, but God is able."

"Amen."

"I found Jesus when my leg was blown off, and then found him some more when my life was ruined by my stupid, lustful submission." He looked at Rev. Mellowin as if to agree with her condemnation of him. "We find Jesus when we're in serious trouble. We find Jesus when we lose our children, our freedom, and the women we love. Somehow, when men find themselves lost, we have to find the dose to bring them to Jesus."

Just then Bishop Samuel jumped in. "We all have to make a concerted effort to go and get our brothers. I'm going to get my brother." Bishop Samuel got a wave of permission to continue from Rev. Charles, who seemed to have rested his case.

"I am reminded of the story of Abram, who eventually becomes Abraham," said Bishop Samuel. "Although the Bible says that the blood relationship between Abram and Lot was that of uncle and nephew, their true relationship was one of friendship; they were brothers. Abram even referred to Lot as his brother in Genesis 13, verse 8. Genesis also tells of some dispute that arose and caused dissention in the two camps. Abram's possessions had grown, and his wealth and his livestock had multiplied upon leaving Egypt. Lot had similar fortune and prosperity. This double abundance caused disruption in a land with limited space. Quarreling arose between the herdsmen from both camps. Overcrowded conditions led to arguments, then to bad attitudes and bad vibes. But Abram, being older and wiser, stepped up to Lot and said, 'Let's not have any quarrelling and dissention amongst us, between my herdsmen and yours, for we are brothers. We are brothers.' Abram understood that as brothers, they would have their disagreements, but they didn't have to disgrace one another. They could agree to disagree and maintain their peace."

"Yes, I like that," Rev. Ed spoke up, looking happy that calm had been restored.

"And I believe all brothers should look at how we respond to one another, and understand that our relationships should not be to hurt one another but to heal and help one another. And when we can't get along, we should separate with brotherly kindness. Abram went in his direction, and Lot went in his direction. Abram's direction was guided by God. Abram followed God's instructions and went to a place that was safe for his family and secure for his possessions. And although we get on our black men and say that they are not doing well, Rev. Mellowin," Bishop Samuel paused and looked her directly in the face. "we must applaud those who go in the right direction in life. I don't care how bad some of our brothers are; there are some brothers that are law-abiding, loyal to their women, hard-working, family-committed, and God-fearing. There are many men who go to church or mosque for their religious instruction and take their families with them. There are many men serving our communities well. Working every day. Studying late and waking up early to take their children to school. I know, because I've done my wrong but I've done my good also. I know men who are strong and committed in my church. They are moving in the right direction. When a man is moving with God, his whole family is blessed. His wife is blessed. His community is blessed. Believe it or not, there are many who are doing the right thing." He looked at Rev. Mellowin again. She just steered without saying a word.

"This is not to ignore the brothers who move in the wrong direction," Bishop Samuel continued in a more urgent voice. "Lot went in the wrong direction and ended up in the wrong place. The Bible says Lot pitched his tent near Sodom. The people of Sodom were wicked and were sinning greatly against the Lord. But still Lot decided to go in that direction. Not out of ignorance, but out of rebelliousness and disobedience. This is where a lot of our brothers get messed up. A lot of them knowingly go in the wrong direction."

"I like your play on words," Rev. Ed called out.

"A lot of our brothers know that dropping out of school can lead to a dim future. A lot of our brothers know that smoking and drinking excessively is dangerous. They know that going to jail is destructive. A lot know that selling drugs is destroying our community. They know that womanizing and baby-making without taking care of the child is damaging to the family. But still a lot of them move in the wrong direction."

"Yes!" Rev. Mellowin and the other women shouted, apparently not able to stop themselves. Bishop Samuel was an equal-opportunity assessor. He continued in his urgent voice. "Lot planted himself near wickedness, although he came out of righteousness, which means he knew better but chose to do the opposite. A lot of our brothers come out of good homes— including gangsta rappers and whoremongers and crack sellers— but they choose to do and promote just the opposite of what they were taught. Which goes to show that you can be an educated parent with two degrees, get down on your knees and pray every hour, go to church every other day, and work for the community and family, and still your child could go in the wrong direction."

"Amen. I know that's the truth," Dr. Smith spoke out.

"The prodigal son had a good father—a God-fearing man—a home with riches and comfort and nurturing and support. But the son decided he was going to take his riches and fulfill his wicked desires."

"Good connection," Rev. Ed continuing to support Bishop Samuel thesis.

"And you don't have to be a dropout to move in the wrong direction; you can be in college and move in the wrong direction. A mother asked me to pray for her because she said her son got to Harvard and got hooked on crack while he was there."

"What?" someone asked, shocked.

"Yes," said Dr. Smith "I've heard it before."

"But not only hooked on drugs," said the bishop, "but on a bad perspective and wrong-thinking. A lot of our children go to majority-white colleges and go in the wrong direction in terms of conscious understanding. They don't want to be black and proud anymore. All of a sudden, they get brainwashed and decide to go in the direction of those who persecute them. And that's why you have some brothers not marrying sisters when they get educated. They start thinking differently. Their color and persuasion hasn't changed, but their content and perspective have."

"That's true."

"That's real."

"Our brothers are moving away from the workforce into no force, not even Air Force. No one wants to give brothers a job. But at the same time, it used to be a time that when brothers couldn't get a job from the man, they created their own jobs."

The women started clapping their hands in approval after that remark.

Bishop Samuel, chewing his gum, waited for the hands claps to cease before he spoke on. "Brothers would take a piece of wood and make a table and sell it to somebody, just to make a dollar. Brothers went down to the well, pulled up some water, put it in the freezer, and made some ice and sold it to somebody."

"Amen," Rev. Taylor came in. "I had to do it when I was younger. Best money I ever made."

"Now we're just sitting there." Bishop Samuel suddenly seemed to lose his cool and become more agitated. "Waiting on someone to do for us what we can do ourselves. Jesus told the crippled man at the water to pick up his mat and walk. He had sat there for thirty-eight years, waiting for someone to pull him into the water at the appointed time. But Jesus told him, 'You are able. I am your strength and your redeemer. Pick up your mat and walk!'" Bishop Samuel was giving it like it was. "The dose our brothers need is the directness of Jesus, Rev. Charles. Give it to them straight. Like you said, don't play games with them or with words. Pick up your mat and walk. Straight talk. Stop pitying yourself. Stop making excuses for your hurt. It's time to make that change in your life. We baby our brothers too much—especially mothers. We ought to give them more confidence and more tolerance at an early age. Let them know that if the man ain't hiring, then you hire the man."

"Yeah," Rev. Bryant jumped in, and then took over and decided to give his own assessment. "We might get on rappers, but one thing about the rappers, they know how to hustle. When the industry wouldn't talk to 50 Cent, he took his tapes to the streets and sold them himself. The industry came later. Wu-Tang Clan and DMX did the same thing. That's because one thing we know how to do as a people is sell something, like you said, Bishop."

"Amen."

"When I was in college and couldn't find a job, I took some old portraits of famed black-history personalities and sold them on the streets. Sympathetic white folks ran to purchase them. Made them happy and made me money."

"All right now." Dr. Smith again supporting Rev. Bryant.

"But wait, I got another one, better than that rap stuff," Rev. Taylor said determinedly. Rev. Ed looked at him and gave him the floor. "Brothers," said Rev. Taylor, "seem to be going in the wrong direction in their appearance and presentation. I may be getting old or maybe it's just me, but there used to be a time when brothers appreciated looking like a man. A little rough and rugged, and dirt didn't bother them. But now you have too many brothers who are more concerned with their looks than are the sisters."

"Yes!" Just then every woman jumped up and praised him for his observation. Maybe they had thought it, but never said it. Lady Johnson and Rev. Minor couldn't contain their laughter. Dr. Smith looked stunned, but appreciative of the remark. Rev. Mellowin just looked up and said, "Thank you, Jesus."

"It's not just me," Rev. Taylor continued. "When a man is taking pride in straightening his hair and putting it in a ponytail, shaking the hair out of his face, I wonder about our society. And these are men who claim they love women and are heterosexual. What has our society done to our men? And some of them are these so-called rappers you talk about."

"Oh God, talk, please," Lady Johnson and Rev. Mellowin yelled out.

"Brothers can't even take out the garbage for fear their nails are going to get dirty or break. Can you picture that? A nigga scared to break his nails?" Everyone looked stunned but amused at his directness. He paused, knowing the effect it had on us, but then went right back to his brutishness. "When a man has more appointments on his schedule for manicures and pedicures than does his girlfriend or wife, there is a problem. Brothers standing in the mirror, fighting their girls over the mirror just to pick their eyebrows. Niggas are in the bathtub, taking bubble baths and sipping vanilla lattes. What kind of shit is that?"

"Aaaaay ..." Rev. Ed jumped in to calm his verbiage and tone. Rev. Taylor was getting out of hand. This was being recorded and videotaped and certain language had to be suppressed.

Rev. Taylor quickly apologized. "Just cut that part out of the tape, but if I slip again, leave it in because it was meant to be." Everyone looked at him, still in awe. Rev. Taylor continued. "And we must admit that sisters are partially responsible for the bad direction that these men are going in." The sisters looked up as Rev. Taylor eased into his conversion. "Mothers are left with the sons and are contributing to their 'metrosexual' and even homosexual approach to life. When a mother takes her son to the nail salon and to the beauty shop and dress store, a son has to sit there and watch that, and what he's watching he's absorbing. He's not only learning how to appreciate a woman, he's learning how to be a woman."

"Oh, that's unfair," Lady Johnson said. However, Dr. Smith confirmed, saying, "Let it stand; it's true."

Rev. Taylor didn't hesitate to make his case. "Yes, boys are absorbing all that hair weaving and nail polishing and dress fitting. That's why it's important for a boy to have a man present. If you don't like the father, leave him with the grandfather, uncle, brother, somebody strong. Even if you don't like your baby's daddy, if he's doing right by the child, leave him with him.

Women shouldn't allow their anger at the baby's daddy to dismiss his worth as a father, because boys need a man in their lives."

"Amen," Dr. Smith said, supporting Rev. Taylor again.

"And sisters are not only confusing their boys, they are confusing their daughters. Mothers have to do so much alone because of an absent father that their daughters can grow up believing they don't need a brother because momma can do it all. And now they get another woman rather than a man."

"Ooh."

"And the sisters' handshakes are harder than the brothers' handshakes," Rev. Taylor said with seriousness, yet for a laugh. "I shook this sister's hand the other day, and she almost broke my fingers. I said, 'Damn, girl, what are you eating?' Everyone around us died laughing."

"But we all have to go and get our brother!" Rev. Charles came in with a loud shout, as if to take back the discussion he had started. He pulled out a Bible and began to read from the text that Bishop Samuel had started about Abram and Lot. "The Bible says that a man came to Abram and said, 'Your brother Lot has been taken.' Abram, upon hearing, gathered up his soldiers and went to get his brother from the arms of the enemy. Abram rescued Lot and his family and all his possessions.' Those who move in the right direction are responsible for going to get those who move in the wrong direction. I am going to get my brother!" Rev. Charles was now yelling. "That's Gethsemane—Jesus going to get us from our mess and madness in sin to bring us to salvation. I'm going to get my brother and give him the truth. No games. No lies. No tricks. Just the God-to-honest truth." Rev. Charles stood up like the soldier he was and shouted again, "I'm going to get my brother!"

Bishop Samuel followed his lead. He stood at attention and shouted, "I'm going to get my brother!" Rev. Taylor did the same, then one by one, everyone stood up in the lounge, even Rev. Mellowin and Rev. Ed. We all stood up and shouted, "I'm going to get my brother!"

16

Spirit and Truth

Luke 4:18–19

I wonder why
These demons keep chasin me
I try to run
They keep on racing me
I try to hide
They keep up pace with me
I try to eat
They keep on tasting me
I try to sleep
They keep on waking me
I wonder why
Jesus keep saving me

Lady Johnson waved her hands but was too slow to get in front of Rev. Bryant. He spoke up with strain in his eyes and passion in his voice. "I just don't know if the God of Abraham, Isaac, and Jacob is with us no matter who we are—black man, white man, American, Christian, Muslim."

"Excuse me?" Rev. Ed, surprised, turned toward him.

Rev. Bryant continued, "I mean, really, check it, we've come far but it is absolutely disheartening to see where we are. Progress is seen in economic advancement, freedom from institutional slavery, and in constitutional amendments that have been passed to restore our humanity. We have gained civil rights to enhance our liberty, and there's better political representation from our elected officials. Barack winning the presidency—it is a great step for America. But it seems as though God is aloof and disinterested."

"You watch your mouth, boy. How can you speak like that after all the Lord has done for you?" Rev. Taylor jumped at him, scolding. He seemed to take Rev. Bryant's comments personally, and he quickly was all over him. "Your faith is weak, your mind is tampered, and you don't know if you want to be a preacher or a thug. You seem to be troubled. Your situation at your church sounds more like a break in your own ego rather than God's not intervening. When our ego desires satisfaction, it seems like God is not there. You should have followed and prayed to the Lord, rather than your own pride. If you young people would get more involved with civil rights than rap, we would have more gains in this country. But you young people don't want to do nothing but shake your butts all day. Even in the church. Why don't you fight for rights and make this land listen to you? There was a time when the young folks in college would band together and fight for political power and civil rights—the Student Nonviolent Coordinating Committee and others. Now all you kids want to do is rap, act, and dribble a ball up and down the court. How pathetic. If it weren't for the NAACP and SCLC, you wouldn't even be where you are today! Why not continue the struggle to get your rights fully restored? Stupid!" Spit showered out of his mouth at that last word as he turned his head in discuss. Rev. Taylor was candid when it came to speaking his mind. He wasn't afraid of anyone, no matter how rough and tough they looked or where they came from. He had a particular dislike, it seemed, for rappers and thugs.

I looked at Rev. Bryant. His face had the squint of a corner thug ready to rob, kill and destroy. He didn't look like the type to be punked by nobody. But he respected his elders and allowed Rev. Taylor to bellow on, but his face had a meanness to it as he bit his bottom lip, like a fighter before a punch.

Rev Ed jumped in before anyone got hurt. "Wait … wait a minute. This is an interesting discussion, and it's not the first time it's been raised. Let's allow him to make his point on that subject: Is God with us?"

Rev. Bryant punched his fists together—his normal style—then took a deep breath.

"Be careful, son, this is not rap. You have to develop your truth," interrupted Rev. Taylor before Rev. Bryant could utter a word. "And I know it's hard for you to speak the King's English, but please keep it reasonably standard. I wasn't that impressed the last time." Everyone was quiet. Rev. Charles moved away from Rev. Taylor, perhaps just in case Rev. Bryant decided he was going to hit him rather than debate him.

Biting his lip, Rev. Bryant managed to rise to the occasion. "Iaight, old man. I respect what you had to say, but let me get mine now that you've had more than your share."

"Who you calling 'old man,' young boy?" ferociously responded Rev. Taylor, slowly moving out of his seat towards him.

Again Rev. Ed quickly and forcefully calmed the storm. He told Rev. Bryant to continue. Rev. Taylor looked angry but stayed silent and sat back down.

"What Jesus does in the beginning of his ministry is define his theology by first recognizing his spirituality," said Rev. Bryant. "He goes into the temple, pulls out the scroll of Isaiah and begins to read the part where it says, 'The spirit of the Lord is on me.' What validates Jesus' ministry with authority and power is the spirit of God. The reason I say God is not with us is not because of God; it is because of us. We have not defined our ministry with him. How can God be with us if we don't have his spirit in us?"

"The boy is really onto something," Bishop Samuel smoothly breezed in, directing his comment to the scary gaze of Rev. Taylor.

"Jesus defined his ministry based upon the spirit," Rev. Bryant kept on. "What compelled Jesus toward justice and convicted him toward salvation was the spirit of the Lord. What renewed him at Gethsemane and gave him strength to face his enemy was the spirit of the Lord. When you have the spirit of the Lord, it gives you authority and direction, regardless of the assaults and injustices in life." Rev. Bryant's language and argument had changed. He had dropped most of his slang and used standard English, as requested, but still, his voice had a roughness, and his face was hard. He spoke on, impressing everyone with his "bilingual" ability. "I am going to be so bold as to say that the reason our people are not advancing is because we've taken the spirit out of the struggle. The reason why civil rights has gone wrong and not gone on is because we've taken the spirit out of it. The movement stopped in the sixties because it ran out of *gaspirit*." His made-up word caught everyone's attention. "That's why the civil rights movement can't keep up with the times and is struggling to stay alive: we stopped fueling it with the spirit of the Lord."

"No, we stopped funding it and joining it," Rev. Taylor threw out.

"And we stopped funding it and joining it because it lost its spirit to appeal to us and keep us interested and active," Rev. Bryant retorted. "And everything that is being done for civil rights today is being pushed by intellectuals and corporations. Most people today study civil rights and fund civil rights rather than fight for civil rights. We have turned civil rights into a memorial to remember, capitalizing and confirming its death. As stated earlier by Rev. Minor, when the spirit is gone, death comes. When Rev. Martin Luther King, Jr., died, the spirit left him and wandered with nowhere to reside.

"It's like when your car runs out of gas on the highway, and you have to push it to a gas station or call a tow truck. That's what we're doing to the civil rights movement; we're pushing it from behind or allowing corporations to pull it from the front because it has no gas to move on its own."

"Woo, I never thought about it like that, that's a good argument." Said Rev. Charles.

"That's why it's a struggle." Rev. Bryant continued "The struggle is our trying to keep it alive rather than keep it recognized. We're struggling to resuscitate it. But it's on its last breath. A lot of the civil rights organizations are basically self-serving. They're good for America's conscience, and they're good for the individual's résumé. But they're no good for the times. Not because of the purpose but because of the power. The purpose of the organization is necessary but the power of the spirit is absent! Therefore the purpose has no power to make it relevant!"

"Ooh." Rev. Charles shot out again.

"When you don't have spiritual power which transfers into political power, then you're the living dead, used without being useful. Many of our civil rights organizations are politically driven and corporately sponsored. Our politicians are lawfully directed. Our academicians are scholarly and bound for tenure. Our attorneys are monetarily and judicially motivated, and our businesses are strictly profit-focused. And many of our preachers and pastors are philosophers and deal-makers, rather than prophetic voices and sacrificial leaders."

"Nice breakdown."Rev. Ed admiringly said.

"To be prophetic," Rev. Bryant suggested, "one needs the spirit of God. Moses was a prophetic leader because he had the spirit of the Lord in him. When King's home was bombed in 1956, during the Montgomery bus boycott, he was angered and, I'm sure, revengeful. But King found the spirit to rise above his human anger and urge peace and love in the tradition of lectures from Howard Thurman and Gandhi. Juan Williams, in his book *This Far by Faith*, records that King said, 'This is a spiritual movement and we intend to keep these things in the forefront'"

"You must be a King reader," Rev. Ed said.

"Yeah. So I love civil rights, but I love the spirit in it even more," Rev. Bryant stated firmly. "The way I see it, there are four types of prophets."

"Break it down," said Rev. Ed, smiling.

"There are the false prophets that Jesus warned against. The false prophets are those who spread wrong information. Their misinformation leads people in the wrong direction. They spread it because they love to be heard and love to be seen but they know not what they speak. Then there are the for-prophets."

"I like that. Explain that," Bishop Samuel urged.

"Well, the for-prophets are those who are dirty in their dealings. They cut deals, and tell people what they want to hear, based on the amount of money they've been paid. In 2 Chronicles 18, Ahab had for-prophets when he went to fight against Ramoth Gilead. They said what he wanted them to say. They were on his payroll. All four hundred of them."

"That's good. Go on," Rev. Ed suggested, as if he were taking notes.

"Then there are the not-for-prophets."

"That's really good." Everyone laughed.

Rev. Bryant continued, "The not-for-prophets are those who compromise on information. They sway with the wind. They're like some politicians—whichever way the wind is blowing, that's where they're going. And the sad thing is many of them don't get paid; they're in it just to be a part of the power. Just to be noticed. Just for the attention. A lot of preachers are like this; they sway whichever way just for attention. They want a seat at the king's table to make themselves look important. They're not prophets—they're puppets."

"Somebody's not going to like you after this gets out," said Lady Johnson.

"You think I care? They already don't like me. One more won't hurt. Then there is the true prophet—that's Jesus. The true prophet does not do things for friendship, attention, admiration, or money. No! The true prophet does everything for salvation. That is Jesus at Gethsemane; he did it for our salvation. He didn't do it so people would like him; he did it because he loves us. The spirit moved him to speak and give himself up for us."

"That was a very good analysis. I'm going to use that," Rev. Franklyn said in his high-pitched voice.

Rev. Bryant simply nodded his head and went on urgently, "But we have taken the spirit out of the movement. Out of the struggle. Out of the organization. Out of the politics. Out of the preaching. And now we find ourselves just as hateful and oppressive and corrupt as others. This is what Howard Thurman warned against. It is a shame when you see our own people cutting each other's throats and keeping each other down." He looked at Rev. Taylor as he spoke. Rev. Taylor simply looked away. Rev. Bryant continued. "This is what I was talking about, our hurting each other. We didn't lose black organizations because of politics; the spirit left the movement and now politics stands to win. And don't get me wrong—it may be necessary for some things to die. But it's the twenty-first century, yet some of us are still stuck with 1960s rhetoric and action. Why? Because when the spirit was taken out, the movement stopped. We can't rely upon marches and picketing and sit-ins and speeches to solve all the problems of today. Pushing for civil rights is still necessary, but the practices of yesterday are dead. If we had kept God's spirit in the movement, we would have kept up with the styles and times and methods needed to impart civil rights, economic parity, and political clout for our day and time, which would have resulted in further advancement for our people."

No one said a word. Rev. Charles was his biggest fan, standing and supporting him like a body guard does a super star. He wanted to hear him speak and any interruptions at this point would have to go through Rev. Charles who put on his military demeanor.

"Today our civil rights should be based on theological prosperity, a way to get rights and get rich. Like Barack said, no one in America should be poor. And I don't mean gain the whole world and lose our souls. But the biggest threat to America is when you mess with their money. And the biggest basis for the spirit is total transformation. Check this." He rubbed his nose with his thumb, then pointed his finger and bent forward toward the face of Rev. Ed. "Before Dr. King died, he was on a mission to bring awareness to the government of our people's desolate and inhumane condition of poverty. He died with an economic push in mind. The spirit was leading him to move our people out of poverty and into economic equality, which would have resulted in opportunity and prosperity. Check it. When God led the children of Israel out of Egypt, he was taking them to a land flowing with milk and honey. The land was to show the total transformation of their condition, from slavery to freedom and from freedom to empowerment. That would be total transformation. Liberation is when the Israelites sang of their freedom out of Egypt land. God used Moses to bring the people out. But the goal was not only to get free but also to reach prosperity. Liberty is out of condition without a true placement. You can be free and have no home to live in; you're just not under your landlord's roof." "I like that!" Called out Rev. Charles still standing by him as he spoke.

Rev. Bryant was interrupted for a moment then went on. "You can be free and have no clothes on your back. The Israelites were free when they wandered in the wilderness. But you are not prosperous or grounded until you are in the place of your transformed condition. That is the limitedness of liberation theology. It supports rebellion and freedom to come out of oppression, but it never gets to a landing to get in a placement. And the placement should be a total transformation from oppression, which would then be prosperous."

"Amen. I never saw it that way." Bishop Samuel stated to the murmur and claps of those present except Rev. Taylor.

"In verse eight of the first chapter of the book of Joshua, it says, 'Then you will be prosperous and successful.' We're looking for prosperity, not just liberation, because prosperity is the opposite of oppression. Liberation is freedom from oppression, but prosperity is the place of our landing. The promised land."

"Good God. He's hurting someone," Rev. Charles came in. It was true that Rev. Bryant was hurting Rev. Taylor with his series of thoughts, rather than a series of punches.

"Once we begin to receive economic clout, we can battle with the wickedness in high places," Rev. Bryant said, "whether it be corporate or presidential. Too many of our politicians and civil rights organizations are poor in pocket and therefore have to rely on unions and sponsors to fund their elections. This takes away from the voice of the people. He who pays the piper calls the tune."

"Right," Dr. Smith clapped her hands and stated.

"But when you don't have to rely on other people's riches to make decisions and win elections, you are more independent and spirit-driven. You don't have to serve two masters, because the one master is giving you all you need. We can fund our own elections. We can build our own schools. We can start our own businesses. And have our own purse. As I stated and say again even stronger," he looked into the eyes of Rev. Taylor "the biggest threat to America is to mess with its pocketbook."

"Sure, you're right," Bishop Samuel called out.

"Jesus never taught that money was bad; it was the love of riches that was destructive. The problem with prosperity preachers is that some of them are political cowards. They are afraid to use their prosperity to challenge national indignity. This must change if we are to live up to our calling as agents of change. Christ was not afraid of government authority.

"Jesus initiates the spiritual, which is the motor that gives power to the movement. After Jesus says, 'The spirit of the Lord is on me,' he then said, 'because he has anointed me to preach good news to the poor. He has sent me to proclaim freedom for the prisoners and recovery of sight for the blind, to release the oppressed.' Jesus' ministry through the spirit takes on a new life. The spirit is the power, and the theology is the truth. When you have the spirit and the truth, you become a theological worshipper and a prognosticating practitioner. Spirit ushers one into action to uplift the truth."

"We're listening," said Rev. Taylor, who seemed to be loosening up.

"However, the problem today is that there is a dichotomy—a severance, a division—between the spirit and truth. Few, if any, are compelled by the spirit and ushered into action by the truth. Martin Luther King, Jr., said it best: 'One of the great tragedies of life is that people seldom bridge the gulf between practice and profession, between doing and saying.' A persistent schizophrenia leaves so many of us tragically divided against ourselves. On the one hand, we proudly profess certain sublime and noble principles, but on the other hand, we sadly practice the very antithesis of those principles. How often are our lives characterized by a high blood pressure of creeds and an anemia of deeds? This strange dichotomy, this agonizing gulf between the *ought* and the *is*, represents the tragic theme of man's earthly pilgrimage."

"You've really been doing your homework."

"Yeah," said Rev. Bryant, who was keeping up with the big boys with his knowledge and logic. He then dove right back into his theory. "What King was saying is that we live with a duality of dynamics, separating what we preach from what we practice, which then leaves us ineffective and inactive and open to suffering as a people and as a nation. The separation of spirit and truth has led to stagnation, confusion, inaction, and further division within our community and country."

Rev. Taylor seemed to be holding back on looking impressed with Rev. Bryant's profound comments. Everyone else encouraged his spirit with hearty amens.

"The doctrinal and theological separated from the practical and applicable makes God look fictional, rather than actual or factual."

"Break it down, brother!" shouted Dr. Smith.

Rev. Bryant had gone back to his hip-hop roots. He allowed his hands to sway with his words. Every word he said was with rhythm and followed by his hand performance "Henry David Thoreau once said, 'Action from principle, the perception and the performance of right, changes things and relations; it is essentially revolutionary and does not consist wholly with anything which was. It not only divides states and churches, it divides families; it divides the individual, separating the diabolical in him from the divine.'"

"Amazing," commended Rev. Ed.

"But what about your dichotomy, your diabolical versus your divine?" interrupted Rev. Taylor out of the blue. Disrupting the flow and rhythm of Rev. Bryant like he had a score to settle and a tie to break. "You don't know if you want to be a theologian or a thug!" he continued. "You don't know if you want to speak for Christ or rap for the world. You better pull yourself together, or you'll find yourself falling apart. It's smart fools like you that make God look bad."

Everything seemed to freeze in place and time. And I wished time had gone backward, so that Rev. Taylor had never made that last remark.

Rev. Bryant looked up with eyes as cold as ice, his movement freeing time and allowing it to continue. "Yeah! You're right!" He stood up like King Kong on the towers of a building. Banging his chest as he spoke. "Sometimes I don't know if I want to be a theologian or a thug. A reverend or a robber. And that may very well be my dichotomy, my Gethsemane. Spirit and body clashing, tearing each other apart, rather than coexisting. The body wants to be in the streets. The spirit wants to be in Christ. I struggle, I battle. Because sometimes it seems there is more anger, politics, and cold-bloodedness in the church than there is in the world."

"I hear you," Rev. Franklyn squeaked out.

"When I was in the streets I didn't have to care as much about what I felt or what others felt. I could do my dirt and leave without a trace. But when I came to Christ, it created this conscious compassion, which compelled me to care for everything and everybody. I have ridden around the hood where I used to hang out, and sometimes I just feel like jumping out the car and standing on the corner and saying 'Hey, guess who's baazaaack.'"

"No! Don't you do that, son!" Dr. Smith cried out, as if talking to her own child.

"The strain of trying to please so many people—church folks, my children, my wife, my community, my momma—makes me wanna holler, throw up both my hands and say fuck all this shit; I'm outta here!" His roar frightened everyone including me. As he roared I could feel his struggle. "I don't give a fuck what nobody thinks! I don't need this shit; I'm tired; give me a motherfucking break!" He stood up even taller to release his anger and everything else that was trapped inside him. The sound of his fury and the wave of his body made a storm look steady. He went on cussing, then crying for the next two to three minutes. Everyone just looked at him, feeling his pain but afraid to touch him because he kept swinging his fists, as if he was hitting something created by the fury of his imagination.

Rev. Ed and I finally got up the nerve to hold him as he cried. And cry he did, like a baby. Then the grand motherliness of Dr. Smith moved us over and held him tight.

Finally, as he spoke again lightly, he slowly loosened her grip. "But the spirit in me has been stronger than the streets in me," he said, "As I've maintained and will continue to maintain, my willingness is in the spirit to overcome the weakness of the body. The truth is like Ezekiel's; I can't stop serving him. Even if I wanted to stop caring, I can't. I would be drawn and compelled back to God. For he is my strong tower."

Rev. Bryant with a look of exhaustion fell back into the arms of Dr. Smith and wept aloud. Bishop Samuel started singing, and we all joined him:

"I don't feel no ways tired. I come too far from where I started from. Nobody told me the road would be easy. I don't believe he brought me this far to leave me."

17

A Spirit-Driven Life

Luke 23:44–46

You can't hold God's people back that long
The chain of Shatan wasn't made that strong
Trying to pretend like your word is your bond
But until you do right, all you do is go wrong

—"Just Lost One" by Lauryn Hill

Rev. Ed looked impressed by Rev. Bryant and at the same time sorry for Rev. Bryant. So did I, to be so young and have to struggle so much was a weight upon the soul. Rev. Bryant's information, mixed with confession, contained some of the most original feelings and eloquently poetic language of the conference. Everyone seemed to be amazed by Rev. Bryant and wanting to comfort him. Even Rev. Taylor had eased up, but his stomach still growled for human consumption.

"Excuse me," Bishop Samuel spoke up, "but that was some brilliant stuff. I need a preacher for the fourth Sunday."

"Me, too," said Rev. Charles.

Everyone laughed, but Rev. Bryant simply leaned back in his chair, wiped his eyes, pulled out his Black Berry phone and said, "I'll see what I can do." Everyone again laughed.

Rev. Franklyn added his own thoughts then. "The nation has taken our spirit. The spirit contains dignity for humanity. We can't respect ourselves because dignity and integrity of our humanity has been taken."

Said Rev. Franklyn in his high pitched voice. Rev. Ed asked him to elaborate on what he had just said. Which was still a mystery to people like myself

"The last words Jesus uttered before he gave up the ghost were, 'Father, into your hands I commit my spirit.' Although Jesus was wrapped in the flesh and the word became flesh and dwelt amongst us, his operation was of the spirit. The verse in Luke that you so brilliantly captured, Rev. Bryant, as a defining theological mission was, in essence, a spiritually driven life. The spirit is what gave Jesus his purpose, and without the spirit we, as children of God, have no leadership in our mission, and our purpose can become easily misguided, misunderstood, and missed. One can have a purpose-driven life, but without the spirit leading, the purpose is more worldly than godly, and 'What good is it for a man to gain the whole world, yet forfeit his soul?'" Rev. Franklyn had caught our attention, and he knew it by the stares on our faces. Everyone wanted to see what he was going to do next.

"Jesus proclaimed in Luke 4:18, 'The spirit of the Lord is on me, because he has anointed me.' That gave Jesus a defined purpose; he knew what he'd come for, and he outlined it in accordance with the scroll of Isaiah. His purpose was to preach, proclaim, recover, heal, and deliver. However, as Jesus shows us, the spirit must precede the purpose. The purpose must not be in the driver's seat; the purpose must be in the passenger's seat. The purpose is dropped off and picked up by the spirit.

"We are often trying to gain without the spirit as our guide. That is Gethsemane, when the body seeks the purpose, absent of the spirit. The Bible says, 'But seek first his kingdom and his righteousness, and all these things will be given to you as well.' Purpose devoid of the spirit leads to selfish ambition. The reason mission and purpose get mixed up is because of the severance between the body and spirit. Once the dissection takes place, then although the spirit is willing, the body is weak."

He was a builder of systematic theology, and he constructed his argument with precision even though he had no formal education. As he spoke, he looked at the floor, as if searching for words to pick up for his next sentence. His voice was smooth, albeit annoying. "The separation is the conflict, struggle, and even war between the spirit and body. The body has its own purpose, absent of the spirit, to fulfill its earthly desires. This is where we are torn between what Thomas Aquinas describes as two cities in his writing, *City of God*. The one city is the secular, full of earthly and selfish desires. It reaps benefits for the body. But the City of God is full of love for God and others, seeking to fulfill the hopes and aspirations of the spirit. The Bible says, 'Do not store up for yourselves treasures on earth … but store up for yourselves treasures in heaven …. For where your treasure is, there your heart will be also.'"

Rev. Franklyn turned his gaze to Rev. Bryant. "Be careful with that prosperity preaching, Rev. Bryant, because it can lead to earthly riches rather than heavenly treasures." His words were cautionary rather than confrontational. Rev. Bryant just bowed his head, and Rev. Franklyn went back to his floor to pick up his argument. "Jesus' philosophical speech at Gethsemane made this duality clear. The disciples could not pray because their bodies were weak; therefore, the purpose could not be realized, although their spirits were willing. Jesus had encouraged them to pray so that they did not fall into temptation. One of the greatest examples of temptation is our personal greed: we no longer work for humanity or family or dignity; we work for personal prosperity. It is seen in the sociological result of our community—the haves and the have-nots.

"The spiritual mission that we are on is to teach our people history, preach our people empowerment, heal our people mentally, restore our people to dignity, and deliver our people from poverty."

"Good rhythm." Rev. Ed commended.

"Many times this becomes the problem with our churches. Many of our churches are purpose-driven primarily, instead of spirit-driven principally. The purpose is to get as many people into the church on a Sunday morning as possible. We are so into increasing the number of bodies that we forget about increasing the power of the Holy Spirit."

"You got it!" Bishop Samuel spoke out with his smooth baritone.

Rev. Franklyn looked up again, bowing to acknowledge the approval, then looked back down and went on. "You have a large crowd of spectators, rather than a large congregation of worshippers. Without the spirit of God, the people gather to socialize and politicize, not spiritualize, rather than putting spiritualizing above socializing and politicizing. In his book *Life Together*, Dietrich Bonhoeffer has a line that I like to recite and challenge. He wrote, 'Christian brotherhood is being threatened by its greatest danger, the danger of confusing Christian brotherhood with some wishful idea of religious fellowship, of confounding the natural desires of the devout heart for community with the spiritual reality.' And although I think he was extreme and severe in his claims of fellowship and brotherhood and its necessary social impact, I do believe that Christian fellowship is now built on socializing first, rather than spiritualizing foremost."

"Very good observation," Dr. Smith complimented.

"People come together for company, which can lead to corruption and conflict rather than communion and compassion."

"Well said," Rev. Ed complimented him again.

"The spiritual should lead the company, and the church should lead the community. Socializing without the spirit creates a social club rather than a house of God. And people come to befriend, rather than be found."

"I like that." Rev. Ed couldn't resist his constant commending along with the rest of us.

His voice had suddenly dropped to a deeper register, and he raised his gaze from the floor. Perhaps the repeated praise was giving him more confidence. He went on quickly, although his voice wavered between deep resonance and high-pitched squeak—heaven and earth. "When Jesus went to the synagogue and rolled out the scroll of Isaiah, he made it clear to the crowd of people that the spirit of the Lord was upon him. What Jesus' enemies were after was not his body but his spirit. They realized from his announcement and from his proclamation that it was a spiritual movement. The body of Jesus had little threat upon man—he wasn't a body builder like Sampson, his distant cousin. Jesus was spiritually strong and mighty. He lifted the sick. He stretched fish and broke bread. He knocked out demons and moved mountains. He walked on water and disturbed order. He put down death and body-slammed the grave. All with his spirit."

"I like that, preacher!" Bishop Samuel shouted out to give a backdrop to Rev. Franklyn's statement.

Rev. Franklyn went on, an even bigger smile on his face, as if almost happy he was able to recite everything without delay or pause. "If they would have killed his spirit, they would have ended his ministry and pulled the plug on his purpose," said Rev. Franklyn. "If men can kill your spirit, they don't need to hurt your limbs. If they can take and break your spirit, they won't have to beat your body. During slavery, when a slave tried to escape and was captured, the slave master would bring the captured slave back to the plantation. Then, before he was whipped, all the other slaves were brought out to watch the beating. The purpose was to execute the idea of escape, but more important, to slay the spirit of freedom. Once the slave master killed the spirit of freedom, the master didn't have to be present for the enslaved to act like slaves. The slave master could leave the back door open and the horses available and the enslaved would remain in place because the enslaved's ideas of escape had been battered, and their spirit of liberty had been broken. When your spirit is taken, it paralyzes you into a position of submission without question."

His passion and a rhythm of rage gave more volume and strength to his voice. "How many of us have had our spirits broken and live with submission rather than empowerment?" He looked at Dr. Smith and Bishop Samuel, then went on. "Just think of all those soldiers in Iraq—many of them spiritual but are forced to wrestle with supporting their nation of war, rather than defending their spirit of peace. Defending their spirits would leave them jailed and rebuked. Could that be Gethsemane, when your body is one place and your spirit is another? You are living divided."

"Very good comparison," Rev. Ed said.

"And before you insult me, Rev. Taylor," He looked down while speaking to Rev. Taylor. "yes, I was divided over my sexual preference at one time, but I am no longer divided; the spirit and the body are in the same space and moving in the same direction of heterosexuality." Before anyone could delve into it any further, he simply shut them down. "I don't believe homosexuality is of God, and I was caught in a trap of the flesh that almost killed my soul. My wife is my love, and my children are my heart. God has saved me from this body of death."

"I hope you got tested before you went back to your wife. You can't play games with that stuff," blurted out Rev. Mellowin, always ready for confrontation with a male.

"I've been tested by doctors but most of all I've been tested by God, and my faith has cleared me," Rev. Franklyn responded. Without a pause or a word from Rev. Taylor, who looked too shocked to speak, Rev. Franklyn, moved the subject off of him and onto his next point. I was surprised by his skill.

"Jesus had a strong spirit." His voice became even louder and stronger, possibly in a bid to erase his personal confession from our memories. "When they found that criticism did not work, they tried betrayal and trials. But that too did not shake his spirit. So they began to beat his body to get to his spirit. That did not work. They nailed his hands and feet to the cross to get to the spirit. But that did not work either. Before Jesus died, he let them know: You may beat my body, tear my skin, cut my flesh, pierce my side, but you didn't get my spirit. My father got my spirit! 'Father, into your hands I commit my spirit.'" He roared the words with a thunder I had not thought possible to come from him. Wind and rain seemed to follow. If he was trying to get our attention on his message and away from his mess, it was working. It was a burst of energy that lit me up.

"When we present ourselves at the altar, we are putting ourselves at risk for abuse and ridicule. Many politicians can think racism, but they can't say racism. Where is the sacrifice? Well, it's not in our lawyers." He paused. "It's not in our activists." He paused. "It's not even in our preachers." He paused, looked around and then back down, as if waiting for the guillotine to take his head off. And just as he seemed to expect, it came down hard as he said, "The sacrifice is in the rappers."

"The rappers?" everyone said at the same time with the same shock and amazement.

"What the hell are you talking about?" Rev. Taylor shouted at the top of his roaring voice. "Those artificial, lust-loving, demonic-talking, hedonistic, materialistic phonies. How the hell in the world can you say that?"

Dr. Smith and Lady Johnson appeared to be as disturbed as Rev. Taylor. Even young Rev. Mellowin and Rev. Bryant dropped their jaws at the suggestion. Then everyone began arguing against him all at once, pointing their fingers as if they were going to poke his eyes out for not seeing the truth. Rev. Charles and Rev. Ed were trying to calm everyone, while at the same time throwing insults at Rev. Franklyn. It was strange, but Bishop Samuel was quiet, as if he were waiting for the reasoning.

"Easy!" Rev. Ed shouted, visibly upset at the sudden disorderliness. He had to play referee rather than moderator. He stood up and clapped his hands, only to be looked upon with disdain, but at the same time got enough attention to chime in with a chastisement. "What is the fuss? Let him continue his thinking! There may be light at the end of this tunnel."

Rev. Franklyn picked up the little that was left of his head and began to speak. He stuttered through many of his words, unsure of his verbal footing. He then looked down and began to speak with reluctance. "The rapper is a good voice for the people."

Rev. Taylor dropped a bomb on him: "How can the rapper be good when none of us are good? You're not reading your word, son. Wasn't it Jesus who said, when he was speaking to the rich young man, that no one is good but God? So if none of us can be good, how in the hell can a rapper be good?"

I took a seat to the side, where I could get a good look at both of them. I didn't want to be in the middle of any verbal calamities that might leave casualties. This was a one-on-one. I had confidence that Rev. Taylor could not only take down Rev. Franklyn but make him bow and kiss his feet. It would be an unfair fight. Rev. Taylor was much more articulate, educated, seasoned, and confident, not to mention thunderous and comprehensively quick.

But Rev. Franklyn displayed a look of reluctant courage. He had made his bed and was willing to lie in it.

"We proclaim to be good," Rev Franklyn said.

"Do we proclaim or do we strive?" Rev. Taylor asked.

"We hope." Rev. Franklyn had gotten out of the web that Rev. Taylor was spinning for him.

But Rev. Taylor spun another one. "If we can never be, what are we hoping for?"

"We are hoping to do good," Rev. Franklyn responded.

"How is it that we cannot be good, but we can hope to do good?" Rev. Taylor hit him again.

"I don't know, but we can hope to do good." Rev. Franklyn had been cornered, but he tried to escape. His voice shaking, he said, "How is it that we can be good and not do good?"

"In telling the truth, we are doing good. But we are not good because we are not the truth. So to be good, one must be full of truth. Christ is the truth, and if you have Christ, you have the truth, but you are not the truth. We can strive and hope but we can never really be. We strive to be. To be is to exist. If we are to exist in Christ, we must strive for the truth."

"Hasn't our regeneration given us the truth?" Rev. Franklyn came back. It was a jab that landed in the air rather than on the head.

Rev. Taylor was ready for him. "Yes. We have received the truth but have not become the truth. The truth is what gives us our existence. But to say we have it and to say we are it is not the truth. If we are it, then who is Christ?"

"Woo!" It was as if everyone felt the punch that Rev. Taylor threw.

He rained on. "No one can be the truth except Christ. For he is the way, the truth, and the life. Therefore, since we cannot be the truth, it follows we cannot be good. For to be good is to be the truth, and only God is good and Christ is the truth. So as long as we are to be in existence, in this flesh, we are to possess the truth and do good, but we can never be the truth and be good. For we are because he is. Descartes, in recognizing God first, understood: 'I think, therefore I am.' But I could not think if God wasn't. What keeps us striving and doing is the truth that has been given through the spirit of regeneration. Paul strove to be good. He was not good. He strove to proclaim the truth, but he was not the truth. His struggles with sin showed his striving, not his perfection. Our acts will speak for our existence, but our existence will not show our perfection."

Everyone looked at Rev. Franklyn with pity, then looked at Rev. Taylor with piety. His logistical demeanor, philosophical tone, systematic comprehension, and sequential intellectualism were flawless. It almost made one ask out loud, What manner of man is this? Rev. Franklyn's face hung lower than usual. Everyone looked at him as if to ask, Why would you even go up against such a champion? It was like a pit bull against a Chihuahua. Rev. Franklyn was left for dead at the hands of Rev. Taylor.

Rev. Ed looked like he wanted to cut in like a medic in an ambulance to pick up the remains. But with a count that was nearing its end and after a silence that lasted too long, Rev. Franklyn looked up and spoke. "Why can't the rapper tell the truth and do good?" His abruptness caught everyone off guard, including Rev. Taylor, who had put his cigar to his mouth and claimed his prize.

Before Rev. Taylor could respond, Rev. Franklyn continued more aggressively. "Rappers can be the new prophetic voice, not necessarily because of their appearance but because of their audience. God can use rappers to be the voice of dissent upon America's injustice and insensitivity to a people. The media isn't listening to civil rights organizations or black politicians or so-called activists. The rapper has the media's mind. The media listens to them, and people listen to the media. When Hurricane Katrina hit New Orleans, the voice that was quoted was Kanye West's. He said 'George Bush doesn't care about black people.' Wasn't that the truth? Wasn't that good?

"The reason I say a rapper is because just like God used an ass to speak to Balaam, he can use a rapper to speak to the nation. God can put his spirit in anyone, for any amount of time, for any purpose. And God can use whom he pleases, whether rapper or so-called righteous. Many times, the righteous are not a voice sufficient for God. They've been talking, but few are listening. God needs someone who will shake up the nation and sacrifice his person, and what better person than the unlikely, the unusual. The preachers are the usual suspects—they're known for their criticism and questioning—but the rapper is an unusual suspect; any talk of justice or criticism of a nation from a rapper throws the nation off guard. Because rappers are seen as thugs and ignorant, money-basing, whoremongering, car-driving dummies.

"God used the unsaved nation of Babylon to destroy Judah. God can use the untruthful to bring truth and the no-good to bring good."

Everyone was stunned by his comeback. It was like he had gotten up before the countdown. And he got up punching, landing his punches where they could be felt. He looked up and aimed straight at the head. "One may ask the question then, can one be saved and not acknowledge Jesus?"

"No!" Rev. Taylor said emphatically. His roar was like a lion seeking to devour its prey. Other no's were voiced, but Rev. Taylor's trumped them all. He was visibly disturbed at the mere suggestion. "No man cometh to the Father except through the son," Rev. Taylor lashed out. "Learn your Bible, son!" It was obvious that the talking down to Rev. Franklyn was an attempt to bolster his own ripped ego.

Rev. Franklyn came back again suddenly, not giving Rev. Taylor enough time to theologize or politicize. His annoying voice gained an authoritative tone. He looked at Rev. Taylor as if he knew it was battle time. "There are many instances where Jesus is speaking and giving instructions toward salvation that are through him in principle and practice, rather than in name recognition. When you subscribe to the principles and practices, you have been moved toward believing and receiving Jesus—even if you don't mention Jesus' name."

"What kind of backward, unsupportive, twisted fanaticism are you promoting? In this case, higher education would have served you well." Rev. Taylor was doing his best to humiliate, but Rev. Franklyn, without pause or response to the insult, continued.

"Let me give you an example, Rev. Taylor. Jesus says, 'Blessed are the merciful, for they will be shown mercy. Blessed are the peacemakers, for they will be called sons of God. Blessed are the pure in heart, for they will see God.' What if you practice all these principles, but you don't say 'Jesus.' Are you not saved? According to the beatitudes, you are."

"I don't know about that," Rev. Taylor shot back as if stumped by the analysis. "Jesus was talking about coming through him!"

"No!" Rev. Franklyn thundered. "Jesus was talking about us in relation to him. When we relate to him are we not going through him? If you purport peace, are you not going through him? If you are pure in heart, are you not going through him? If you are merciful, are you not going through him? Yes! You are! Because Jesus is all of this."

Rev. Franklyn's words were seasoned with unusual reason. Bishop Samuel began to clap, and the rest of us joined him, showing we were no longer on the fence but had gravitated toward Rev. Franklyn's perspective—or at least to his good analysis. But I knew that once Rev. Taylor got his opportunity, he would bring us back to salvation in Jesus.

Rev. Franklyn set out to finish his assessment. "One of your favorite theologians, Dietrich Bonhoeffer, said it well in his work *Ethics*: He wrote: 'God calls the righteous blessed for those who are persecuted for a just cause. A cause that is true, good and humane.' Bonhoeffer goes on to say, Rev. Taylor, that Jesus cares for those who suffer for a just cause, even if it is not exactly for the confession of his name! He brings them under protection, takes responsibility for them and addresses them with his claim. Thus, a person persecuted for a just cause is led to Christ."

Perhaps without realizing it, Rev. Franklyn had hit Rev. Taylor with a knockdown punch. The hit caught him off guard. As if that wasn't enough, Rev. Franklyn kept hitting Rev. Taylor while he was down.

"Jesus also said, 'God is spirit, and his worshipers must worship in spirit and in truth.' As Rev. Bryant raised so brilliantly earlier, spirit and truth bring an act of worship. God is more concerned with action than name recognition. For it is *acts* of justice that make God good and Christ the truth." Rev. Franklyn paused abruptly and bowed his head, a normal mannerism for him, but perhaps this time in anticipation of Rev. Taylor's resurrection from the ground. The rest of us looked at Rev. Franklyn with newfound amazement. It was nothing but the spirit running through him that gave him access to speak the truth.

Some of us still appeared to be thinking about his remarks. Even though his head was bowed, I caught a good glimpse of his face. It was a bow of defiance rather than a bow of defeat. All present looked to Rev. Taylor for a response that would lead them back to the promise land. Even Rev. Ed looked hungry to see Rev. Taylor's comeback.

Rev. Ed knew that Rev. Taylor could convert any person to his favor. Rev. Taylor, however, sat back, seemingly unimpressed with his rival's position. As was his usual style, he started off slow. While looking at Rev. Franklyn, he smiled and said, "I appreciate your discourse. And to be truthful, I never saw it coming." My ears were open, and my heart was pumping hard in anticipation of Rev. Taylor's ax upon Rev. Franklyn's head.

Rev. Taylor extended his hand down toward the floor, where Rev. Franklyn was looking. It was a moment before I realized it was Rev. Taylor's way of giving his opponent the victory. All mouths were silent. Rev. Ed looked shocked. Bishop Samuel, Rev. Taylor's tag-team partner, was in no position to pick up where Rev. Taylor had left off. He could only pick up his friend from the floor. Still no one said a word, as if we were waiting upon Rev. Taylor for salvation rather than upon Jesus for revelation.

Rev. Franklyn grabbed Rev. Taylor's hand and shook it as he looked up and smiled. He was to take his prize home—that of defeating Rev. Taylor, the most highly respected preaching navigator of our time.

Rev. Franklyn had reigned in the discussion. It was as if he had knocked out the greatest prizefighter in the world, not with his artistic skill in conveying his message or years of experience in debating and articulating truth. Not because of his educational degrees or learned ability to deduce and reason. Not because of generational doctrine or systematic logic. Not even because of a towering voice, as his was more annoying than captivating. But simply because he had hit on a reasoning that defied any argument.

It reminded me of the prizefighter described by Ralph Ellison in his book *Invisible Man*. The prizefighter was boxing a yokel. The champ was swift and amazingly scientific. His body was one violent flow of rapid, rhythmic action. He hit the yokel a hundred times while the yokel held up his arms in stunned surprise. But suddenly, the yokel, rolling about in the gale of boxing gloves, struck one blow and knocked science, speed, and footwork as cold as a well-digger's posterior. The smart money hit the canvas; the long shot got the nod. The yokel had simply stepped inside of his opponent's sense of timing.

Rev. Franklyn had simply stepped inside his opponent's sense of timing and space as well and had defied any logical, educational, or biblical conclusion. Many times, Jesus never went with the flow but rather against the grain. Too many of us go along to get along, and we lose rather than win. I realized that if we were to truly spur change, we would have to propose and prepare for the unexpected, rather than the scientific. That's Gethsemane—unexpected. We wouldn't expect Jesus to go from agony to victory under the circumstances.

The room became somber, somewhat melancholy. It was dark and gloomy in tone. Rev. Taylor was still upright, without any sense of embarrassment, but his eyes held a twinkle of shame. His smile had the look of a dunce. But all in all, he looked strong. He simply looked at everyone and began to address us. It reminded me of a defeated candidate in an election, giving the concession speech. His voice was harder and stronger than usual. His words slurred and dragged longer than normal. His eyes squinted and his hands shook. It was a lot for an egotistical man like him to go down, yet he spoke with his usual confidence. "I did not come here to battle. I have come to learn. I only question to see if there is anything I don't know. I challenge to see if there is anything you do know. And I talk so you can know what I know. And I am at times aggressive in my position, overwhelming with my questions, and not too accepting of others' perspectives. I am a man of great ego and arrogance and at times need to be humbled. God will send the unexpected to humble you. And that is what Rev. Franklyn did. I am not ashamed; I am thankful. My arrogance has often taken me away from Jesus. I have focused on myself rather than on God. I have built up myself with arrogance and selfishness, and God has knocked me off my high horse. So I am not only receptive but humbly accepting. There is no need to debate. Please, I do not want any sympathy because of this rivalry. If anything, I will leave this conference better than when I came in because of this confrontation. I came here for help, and the spirit has moved, and I feel humbled and blessed.

"The spirit prevailed. The body lost. Leave it up to the body, we would still be debating because of arrogance. But the spirit is willing to accept the position given by Rev. Franklyn. It is well with my soul. And to tell you the truth, I feel good. I've won a lot in the flesh, but it feels good to lose to the spirit."

Rev. Taylor then leaned back and dropped his head to his chest. Everyone seemed to do the same. At that point, he gave us all something to think about. In his submission, he had won. It's better to lose in the body and win in the spirit. That's Gethsemane: to have the body lose so the spirit can win.

18

Finally, There's Relief

Matthew 11:28

I can – through Christ
I can reverse conditions
And fight off temptation
I can rework my past
For kingdom admission
I can climb up a mountain
With hurts and pains
I can watch the sunshine
And see a brighter day
Yes, I can - through Christ

There was calm in the room after Rev. Taylor's downfall. It was like finding out that Martin Luther King, Jr., had died—all one could do was take a moment of silence. Rev. Ed, looking exhausted, asked if we would like to take a break and continue on another day.

"No!" Lady Johnson yelled out with ferocity, breaking the silence and disturbing the calm. "I've had something to say since

Rev. Mellowin spoke about sacrifice and the family, which we mothers do all the time. I can't believe that we constantly blame the mothers for much of what's happening with our youth today. We have scars from carrying the children—scars on our stomachs, legs, and sometimes in our minds. And still it seems everyone's debasing the mother. Not the father, who made the child. Not other relatives, who are supposed to be the so-called village. The mother! Even you, Bishop Samuel, in your statements earlier referred to the mother who left the child unattended, as if that was intentional rather than accidental."

"I … I didn't mean …" Bishop Samuel stammered.

"Well, regardless of what you meant, it was a hit on the mothers!" Lady Johnson was visibly disturbed and seemed compelled to get her feelings out. She had been shut down and shut out during most of the session and was now busting down doors to be heard. This was her calling, to deal with hurting mothers all across the nation. Rev. Ed called upon her to elaborate. She responded with propensity and vigor.

"The ability to conceive life and bring forth creation is a wonder and a supremely awesome amazement that demands one's attention, appreciation, and respect!" Lady Johnson spoke with her eyes on all the men, especially Bishop Samuel. "Just as God brought forth creation out of the barrenness and darkness of the earth's womb, so has God blessed the mother with the womb of creation. We are postmasters for God's human creation. Special delivery."

"Amen," said Dr. Smith.

"When Mary discovered that she was expecting, the Bible says she and her cousin rejoiced, and Mary shouted, 'I am blessed!' But somehow, we have gotten to the place where happiness has been replaced by hostility. We have subjugated the greatest gift and gift-carrier on earth to the highest assault and shame. As a result, the bearer of creation is many times seen as carrying a burden rather than a blessing."

"Good words, sister." Dr. Smith had her back.

"Statistics will show it's not a good time for mothers, particularly in the African American community. Seventy percent of our children are born out of wedlock. Sixty-three percent live with only their mother. Mothers got it bad, and that ain't good." She looked upward as she spoke, as if speaking to us but talking to God. I could feel her annoyance and pain, and I suspected the others did too. As a result, no one dared to interrupt her.

"Despite the lack of support and assistance, the mother is still expected to perform the necessary responsibilities of raising the child. The public perception is that the mother is the primary caretaker of the child, and so the mother is left with the burden of teaching a child in the way he or she should go. If something dreadful happens to the child, like a boyfriend molests the girl or beats the son, the mother is accused of being stupid and irresponsible, Bishop Samuel." She looked at him and then cast her eyes upward again. "If the child gets hurt, children's services want to charge the mother. If a child can't read, somebody's questioning the mother. If a child's clothes are dirty, folks are faulting the mother. God forbid that a child dies—the mother is arraigned and convicted while she is grieving and hurting over the loss of her child!"

"Good God. You're right." Dr. Smith continued to support her.

"No one knows what it means to be compassionate. Being compassionate is what Jesus did when the woman in the Bible lost her son. The Bible says Jesus had compassion, and his compassion translated into virtuous actions. Jesus helped her and assisted her and wiped her tears away."

"Amen! Speak for the mothers, sister!" Dr. Smith yelled out.

"Compassion would declare war on poverty and deadbeat fathers. These are the infections that are killing the nation, Bishop." She looked at him again and then looked back up. "Mothers can't find help in the community. We touted at one time, 'It takes a village to raise a child.' We said it was an African proverb; Hillary Clinton took it and used it as the title of her book. However, the truth is, you can't trust folks in your own community with your child. We raised the issue earlier, but let me talk from a woman's perspective and experience. We have grown men in our communities who should be father figures to young people, but instead of being father figures, they're trying to be sugar daddies."

"Talk!" Rev. Mellowin yelled out.

"Instead of looking out for the children and protecting them, they're looking at the young girls to sex them. Thirty- and forty-year-old men looking at thirteen- and fourteen-year-old girls like they're grown women."

"She's touching on something now," Rev. Taylor interjected.

"We can't even trust the baby-sitter with our five-year-old son. And you would think that with all the family members that we have, there would be at least one we could trust with our child. But the biggest perpetrators are not always strangers but family members."

"Speak." Rev. Mellowin was continuing to offer her momentum.

"I read Donnie McClurkin's book *Eternal Victim, Eternal Victor*, and he spoke about how his uncle molested him for years. Oprah Winfrey had the same story. I have the same story. My uncle molested me from ages thirteen to fifteen, and the only reason it stopped was because he was shot by another man who accused him of having sex with his twelve-year-old daughter."

"We're sorry to hear that, sister." Rev. Minor, who had spoken of her own incident, clearly felt Lady Johnson's pain. Lady Johnson seemed surprised that her confession had leaked out. But when it was out there, she allowed the leak to pour. "It's okay. Like you, Rev. Minor, I'm healed and delivered now. But it's not me; it's all those who find themselves in this predicament that I'm talking about. Many children are beaten by family members and no-good men who come into the mother's life. My daughter was molested by my ex-companion when she was ten."

She started to cry as she spoke, and so did Rev. Minor, but Lady Johnson kept on speaking as her eyes touched the sky. She seemed like she was questioning God more than she was talking to us. "Sometimes I think if I had been Jesus at Gethsemane, I would not have died for humanity; I would have let humanity die." Her tone was harsh. "The stuff that we do to each other, even as Christians, doesn't warrant our receiving life more abundantly.

"And it is true: we as mothers have to be careful who we bring around our children. Our loneliness and desire for love and comfort should not blind us to imposters who put our children in danger. We can't allow our need for a man's touch to result in our children being touched by a man. Sisters have to learn to do the background check on the man they allow to come into their home. Every man in a tailored suit and shiny shoes ain't decent and honest. He could be a wolf in sheep's clothing."

"Amen." Rev. Mellowin continued her support.

"Sisters got to do the background check, the front yard check, the side yard check, the last relationship check, the baby momma check, the insurance check, the doctor check, the job check. Check the check before the man comes completely into the home."

"You better believe it, because they lie," Rev. Mellowin came in with her usual criticism of men.

"But we have so much to deal with as women," she continued with tears in her eyes. "There is no doubt we are the stronger sex." No male dared interrupt nor refute at this point. "We are strong, not only because of the work we do but because it takes strength to be faithful. It takes strength to be caring and compassionate. That's Gethsemane—the strength to move by the spirit and overcome the body. The spirit is faithful in its motion. Jesus went forward faithfully. Jesus went forward with agony but faithfully to God. Even while we, as mothers, are hurting and deceived and tricked and cheated on and lonely and ostracized and talked about—damn it!—we still have to be strong for our children. We still have to be faithful to our homes and to our husbands. Where are the men when all this shit happens? The weak motherfuckers!"

Silence covered the room. Her words were shocking. No one moved. She looked down, and covered her face with her hands with a heavy moan. She kept her face covered for a while, as if embarrassed by her cussing. Sighing, she slowly slid her hands down her face like she was pressing a pair of pants. Her eyes were bloodshot, and her face was red from the pounding she had given herself. The sophisticated-looking lady of heavenly beauty looked bullish and drawn. Her smeared black eyeliner gave her the look of a physically abused woman. Knowing her frustration had gotten the best of her decency, she quietly and quickly apologized for the slip into profanity.

Like the grandmother she was, Dr. Smith reached out and wrapped her arm around Lady Johnson's shoulder and held her. But Lady Johnson went on to finish her assessment as if to show that her emotions would not hinder her message. "Our children can suffer because of what we go through from the moment they're born. The position a woman is put into can affect the child's development. Hagar was put into a dishonorable position. Hagar was the third wheel. In Genesis 16, the Bible says Hagar was used to bear a child for Abraham and his wife, Sarah, because Sarah could not conceive. Sarah told Abraham to sleep with Hagar. When Hagar discovered that she was pregnant, the Bible says that she began to despise Sarah. There's a reason she hated Sarah: she had to have a child with a man who wasn't her man. Hagar was told to go into the room and lie down so he could use her body—like she was an oven that you put something in and take it out when it's cooked. Hagar felt used and abused because she had to enter into an unloving and unfaithful relationship.

"Many women find themselves being used in unloving and unfaithful relationships. Used for sex and good times. Used for the moment. Used for money. Used by someone who proclaims to love them. Used until things straighten out at home. Used!"

"I feel you, girl," Rev. Mellowin shouted out again. The look in her eyes said she had something to say on the subject.

Lady Johnson continued in a soft voice that was sharpened on the edges by her agony. "When Sarah found out that Hagar hated her, she got permission to throw her out of the house and onto the street while she was pregnant. Hagar fled and left everything behind, like mothers that have to flee today. The only thing she was carrying was her baby. Just like you, Dr. Smith. They are either thrown out of the house or feel the need to leave.

"Hagar had to be strong because she not only had to carry her baby, but she also had to carry her burdens. Mothers are born with two usable hands, men with one." She said it so quickly that most of the men didn't catch it, and even if they did, they had sense enough not to respond. "Our sisters have to balance the baby in one hand and the bottle to feed the baby in the other. In one hand is the baby; in the other hand are the bills to be paid. In one hand is the baby; in the other are the books for school—sisters still trying to get an education."

"You're talking good," Dr. Smith told her, still with her arm around Lady Johnson's shoulder.

"But I'm not done." Lady Johnson reached up to clutch Dr. Smith's arm. "And even in the church we have to deal with the baby in one hand and the judgment from church folks on the other hand—'Where is her man? 'Why isn't she married?'" With the utmost disdain, she mocked nosy church-goers. "They ask, 'Where is the baby's father?' or 'How come she's dressed like that?' Sometimes church folks don't have to say anything; they can judge the hell out of you with their eyes."

"That's true." Responded Rev. Charles who was then judged by the eyes of Rev. Mellowin as he spoke.

"Church folks got the biggest and most outspoken eyes. They look at you like you're from another planet. And not surprisingly, the biggest critics are the ones who were in the same situation when they came to the church. Like you said, Rev.

Charles—the ones who have received mercy are merciless. They've become holier than thou."

"It's true," he responded.

"The church's job is not to judge but rather to encourage," Lady Johnson said. "If churches want folks to do right by God, they shouldn't judge; they should encourage. Encourage folks to get married. Encourage them to abstain. Encourage them to read and apply the word of God. Encourage them to dress decently and appropriately in the house of God. When we judge, we put ourselves at risk of being judged by God, for the Bible says, 'For in the same way you judge others, you will be judged, and with the measure you use, it will be measured to you.'"

"Good connection," Rev. Ed said with a smile. She was a moving truck built for the toughest road. Even Bishop Samuel, who had run her over before, looked like he was moving off his path and into her lane. This was her vehicle, and she could ride it all day if she wanted to. And that's what she did; she rode on.

"We blame the mother because of her circumstances. We ponder her reasoning, her stupidity for having the child under such duress. We ask why would she have a child, knowing the man is no good, knowing there is no money and no family to assist. But if you look in the Bible, you'll see proof that there have never been any perfect opportunities to have children."

"Talk, sister," Dr. Smith said, still holding her.

"I'm talking." Lady Johnson looked at Dr. Smith as she responded. "Moses' mother shouldn't have had him because she knew of the government's decree to kill all boys. There was slavery going on when Moses was born. Those were not good times. If mothers had children only during safe and prosperous times, many of us would not have been born, because slavery was going on when our ancestors were born."

"You're right, sister," Dr. Smith said, holding and confirming her.

"Look at Jesus' mother, Mary. She was poor and unmarried when she had Jesus—so poor that she had to give birth to him in a manger. According to the circumstances, the savior should not have been born for me and you. But Jesus shows us that real change and recognizable transformation come out of undesirable conditions and bad circumstances. Mothers realize and believe that regardless of the circumstances, all children are a gift from God. Every child is a blessing to be appreciated, regardless of the state of affairs. And that," she said, making an abrupt U-turn with her truck, "is why I wonder how we got so into abortions." She looked at everyone for confirmation. "Nationwide, the makeup of abortion recipients is this: poor, mostly African American in proportion to the population, and in their early twenties. According to studies, African American women are more likely to terminate their pregnancies than are white women, even if they are making sufficient money to have the child. We kill children, even without the excuses of poverty, unstable relationships, and shameful decisions. And many in the black community believe that abortion is religiously wrong, but we still proceed to abort. I believe we can be pro-choice without being pro-abortion."

"Explain that," Rev. Ed requested.

"God in his divinity gave us free will—to choose good or bad, right or wrong. Since the beginning with Adam and Eve, we have had the choice to follow God's instructions or disobey God's will. Even today we have the choice to accept him or reject him. So the nation ought to give people the constitutional right to make that choice, to decide if they want to have an abortion. In the land of the free, a woman should have the freedom to make a decision that will affect her life. But politically and spiritually, we should not be pro-abortion. Pro-abortion is the actual termination of a child. Whether it is one week or three months—it's still a child."

"Amen." The amen came from Dr. Smith, who seemed to be the only one in agreement with her position.

Lady Johnson continued, not caring whether others agreed. She had shown she'd done her homework and was prepared to deliver her reasoning. "In other times in history, we have fought for the right of choice. When Rosa Parks sat on the bus, it wasn't about sitting in the front. It was about the choice to sit wherever she wanted to sit."

"That's a good connection," Rev. Ed came in, giving her more support.

"Abortion is the practice of termination. Choice is the decision that gives us an option. God is for the principle of choice, which he gave to all of us. But God is against the practice of abortion, which he took away from all of us through Jesus Christ. Jesus died so that our children would not have to. 'Let the little children come to me, and do not hinder them, for the kingdom of heaven belongs to such as these.' It is up to the nation to permit abortion; it is upon the individual to make the choice. For the nation to take away the choice is to deprive the people. For the woman to commit abortion is to deny the child. Both are wrong."

"You go, girl. I like that reasoning," Rev. Mellowin stepped up to say.

Lady Johnson went on. "I had one abortion in my life, and I've regretted it to this day. I was fifteen, and the reason I had it was that I didn't know if it was my uncle's or this twenty-five-year-old man's I was dealing with. So yes, I butchered it. But if I knew then what I know now, I would have had that baby, regardless of the circumstances." She put her dirty laundry out there. I wondered if she expected it would come clean. "We have gone overboard with our reasoning about abortion. We don't understand. God can bring a child to bring you a blessing that you need. Look at the Jacksons. Father Joe beat a note out of those kids."

"Easy now," said Rev. Ed. Everyone laughed.

"But it's true. You don't know how God is going to bless you when the child is born. If you dealt with a bad man, God may use that child to be the good man the world needs."

"Amen, and we need good men," Rev. Mellowin lashed out. Everyone looked at her as if she were going to continue with that thought. Even Lady Johnson paused to yield the floor so

Rev. Mellowin could go on. But Rev. Mellowin looked back toward Lady Johnson to continue. And she did.

"Mothers are strong because of Jesus. Philippians 4:13 says, 'I can do all this through him who gives me strength.' And that has been my verse in dealing with motherhood: 'I can— through Christ.' I can do the dishes and feed the children. I can pick up the garbage and pick up the children. I can go to church and go to work. I can go to school for me and after school for the kids. I can love myself, be tired, and make love to my husband."

"All right now!" Rev. Mellowin shouted out again.

Lady Johnson shouted back, "Like Chaka Khan or Whitney Houston, 'I'm every woman; it's all in me.' Like Alicia Keys, 'I am superwoman.' She sang the songs. Then went back to what seemed every women's problem.

"But who will do for us while we're doing for everyone else? Nobody but Jesus! That's why God sent Jesus in the way he did; through Mary, he spoke to all the heavily burdened mothers; to all the stressed out, lonely, abused, and mistreated mothers. Jesus knew that mothers would be shackled by heavy burdens, hurt by men, and set up by systems and sisters. Jesus knew we would need someone to hold us innocently and unmolested."

"I like what you're saying. I feel your talk," Dr. Smith came in.

"Someone with open and nonjudgmental arms. Yet strong and relieving, all at the same time. Someone with a shoulder you can cry on, but who respects your marriage. Someone who's holding you because he's honorable, not because he thinks you're beautiful and he wants a piece of you."

"You talk, girl!" Rev. Mellowin was her biggest cheerleader.

Lady Johnson's eyes now looked at everyone, rather than above everyone. "It's deceptive how beauty attracts lies and cheats and fools and hell. I've had hell until Jesus wrapped his arms around me and gave me hope. His arms were warmer than a hot tub."

"Yes, girl, we feel you."

"It's good to have arms to make you feel loved and needed and not have to worry about anybody wanting you just for your body and your beauty. Somewhere you can sleep without having someone wanting to sleep with you. Men want sex; mothers want rest."

"Talk, sister!" Rev. Mellowin standing to cheer her on.

"Somewhere you can rest and not have to be awakened by someone touching you or poking you."

"What you say."

"Someone you can talk to without someone talking to you for a date and a good time."

"Yes."

"Someone who looks at your heart and not at your legs, breasts, and behind."

"Yes, girl. You talk, talk it! You know what we go through," Rev. Mellowin continued calling out.

"That's why Jesus said, 'Come to me, all you who are weary and burdened, and I will give you rest.'" She stood up, breaking free from Dr. Smith's embrace. She opened up her arms and assumed the crucifixion position, tears in her eyes. "Mothers need rest. The arms of Jesus are summoning us to come unto him. He knows what we're going through because he's gone through it. His arms are where we find true compassion. True appreciation. True comfort and true concern for our condition."

"Yes!"

She lowered her arms and wrapped them around herself as she continued to weep and speak. "In his arms you get relief from husbands who don't understand. Relief from jobs that drain you dry. Relief from church folks that kill your spirit." Her voice was like lightning that repeatedly struck the earth's surface; each of us got hit by a sharp bolt. Each phrase was more powerful than the last. The lightning did not come without rain. Heavy rain that came from every eye. It built up and then, like a switched-on water fountain, it sprayed out. Big drops waiting to fall. And fall it did from her eyes to her feet. Everyone cried along with her.

But she kept talking until her lightning was spent and rain could fall no more.

"Finally, there's relief. I've had my share of problems with men! But I'm so glad that I met a man!"

"Preach!"

"I'm like the woman at the well who said, 'Come and see a man who told me all about myself.' He gave me water, and oh what a relief it was. I don't have to cry no more. Or feel ashamed or guilty about the past. The past is my problem, but I've found relief. I used to harp on my past. What I've done and what people have done to me. But I'm free because of Jesus.

"I've tried other men for relief. I have four children by three different men. I used my good looks to get my way. They bought me the world. They kissed my feet. They showed me off to their friends. They said they loved me to play me. They got me pregnant to dominate me. They beat me to keep me. They molested me to get me. They raped me to weaken me."

"Oh, God."

"I've done wrong to men. I said I loved them to fool them. I had children to trap them. I used sex to repay and get paid by them. But my heart was not happy. My body was so dirty. My soul was so lonely. And my mind was so empty. So many and so lonely. But then I met a man who opened up his arms and said, 'Come and get rest from all your mess.'"

"I love it!" Rev. Ed cried out.

Lady Johnson cried even more as she dropped to her seat. She held her stomach and rocked back and forth as if grasping the area of her pain. Dr. Smith reached over and grabbed her again, rocking and crying along with her. Her testimony was so powerful that it made everyone wail. Even Bishop Samuel shed a tear. Rev. Minor was on the floor in a fetal position, wailing with such a cry that the doves responded.

Lady Johnson spoke on as best she could. She spoke softer still holding herself and being held by Dr. Smith "And when you find relief in Jesus, everything else falls into place. I got a husband who loves me for me. I feel good about me for me.

I have children who had their problems but now they're serving the Lord. I've had family who hurt me, but now they're begging forgiveness. My body was sick, but now it's healing. Finally, there's relief. I feel good. Just like the woman at the well, I'm going to tell everybody about this man who gives relief." She paused suddenly, then screamed, "Thank you, Jesus, for relief!"

Her scream was so strong that it sent shivers through my body. The place looked like everyone had just come out of the water; drips of tears and puddles of pain lay on the floor. But so was joy and relief which seemed to wash the tears and pain away. Dr. Smith began to hum while holding Lady Johnson. Then she sang: "He's sweet, I know. Storm clouds may rise, strong winds may blow, but I found a savior, and he's sweet, I know."

19

Waiting to Exhale

John 11:21–22

So I try my best and pray to God
He'll send me someone real
To caress me and to guide me towards
A love my heart can feel

—"Real Love" by Mary J. Blige

Lady Johnson's spirit had released an awesome amount of power all over everyone—so much so that it destabilized the conference participants and left Rev. Ed in a state of confusion. Rev. Ed tried to gain control. He opened his mouth but said absolutely nothing. But then he tried again and whispered something that sounded like "God is good." Bishop Samuel responded, "All the time."

After that, it was clear that Rev. Ed didn't know how to proceed. But he was saved by a sudden outburst by Rev. Mellowin, who seemed to want to pick up where Lady Johnson left off. She had been weeping heavily, but found it in her to open the discussion back up in a sassy way and divert the tears.

"Well, I'm glad you found relief but I'm still waiting to exhale," said Rev. Mellowin. Her bluntness startled everyone.

Rev. Ed, in a quiet way, gave her permission to access the throne, and she stepped up to the seat with no problem.

"Yes, I'm still waiting for Jesus to bestow his relief upon my soul and produce a worthy mate who will secure his feelings for me and mine for him." Her voice was squeakier than when she gave her rendition in the last round, but not annoying, like Rev. Franklyn's. She had curves and rhythm in her talk that met at one intersection. To make sure she had an audience, she paused, then waited until everyone looked up.

"I am an early thirty-something woman and have not discovered, after much searching and wandering, debating and waiting, the human body with heavenly characteristics that God has for me."

"Oh, are we going to turn this into an emotional soap opera?" Rev. Charles predictably interrupted.

Rev. Mellowin responded swiftly. "No, we're going to turn it into a reality show to address the often hidden emotions and true feelings of young women in the ministry; thus, young professional women everywhere. Since we came here to talk, I'm going to speak truth not only for myself but for other sisters who are seeking and not finding, asking and not receiving, and knocking and no door or the wrong door is constantly opening." Her neck got into motion and began shifting like the gears of a car, only quicker because it had to keep up with her breathing. She looked threateningly into his eyes and then continued. "I am where Lady Johnson was years ago, as are many of my sisters, and I thank her for that testimony because it not only gave me courage to talk but hope to keep searching. But to be sure, whatever I say, it will not be a soap opera because I will back up my assessment with profound biblical truth and scriptural proof to show that my longing is neither shallow nor shameful."

"You talk, girl," Lady Johnson said while detaching herself from Dr. Smith and wiping her eyes with a handkerchief I had handed to her.

"There is a scriptural reference that connects with the impatience and the temperance as it pertains to women for Jesus. It was raised earlier but let me twist it for me—or should I say, for all those who find themselves in similar situations. Mary and Martha gave us the perfect scenario. Their story is replete with an expansive theological theme that speaks to the disappointed and disturbed soul. Their story captures the heart of what it means to wait and believe, even in death and despair. The longing that they felt was compounded by its duration. How long shall they wait before Jesus reveals himself?

"The story we refer to as Lazarus' story is a good one but a misleading one. Lazarus becomes the impetus and catalyst by which the story gets its foundation and begins its sequence. Lazarus gives introduction to the plot to begin the overall drama and suspense by which the story resonates. Lazarus gives a character witness for the basis of the story. And anyone who knows how to tell a good story knows that whether it is dramatic or tragic, suspenseful or comedic, it must have a healthy development of characters, thematics, settings, and plots."

She made everyone look up and listen, especially Dr. Smith, who enjoyed the arts. They looked up also because they had to keep up with her racing voice and vigorous hand movements. She spoke as if she was experiencing convulsions, rather than engaging in conversation.

"And any writer will confirm that if you put the characters in the right place, surround them with a potent theme, build up the plot, envision the setting and celebrate the conclusion, you have a good story, as well as a good sermon."

"I like that," Dr. Smith commended her.

"So although many people call this Lazarus' story—it's mostly men who do," she said, aiming the comment at Rev. Charles by looking at him, "it is really Mary and Martha's story. Because dead men don't tell stories."

"Ooh, that was a hit," Rev. Franklyn came in. But Rev. Mellowin just drove on.

"Mary and Martha are the ones who are taking care of their brother while he is sick. Mary and Martha send the messenger to Jesus to tell him to come because their brother is dying. Mary and Martha witness the death of their brother while waiting for Jesus to come. The waiting, the pacing, the breath holding, the hoping, the longing, the unsure expectation, and ultimate desecration and death because of Jesus' absence are all seen through Mary and Martha.

"Yes. Yes." Lady Johnson says while pulling herself together and straightening up some more.

"This is Jesus at Gethsemane. The waiting to give his life for mankind. The waiting causes the agony. The agony disturbs the peace. The more one waits, the greater the agony. I am waiting for Jesus." She switched gears so quickly yet so smoothly that I had no trouble keeping up. "And I can't sleep peacefully and breathe easily until he arrives. When I was in the dating world, it was easy to experiment and play with future possibilities for mates. But when I truly began to practice my faith and crystallize my Christological understanding, it became difficult to play the field and experiment with the world of men. And since I've been called, I call on Jesus to direct me in the path of righteousness for his name's sake. And disappointingly, he hasn't responded with a live being."

"Okay."

"I feel like Mary and Martha when they called Jesus, and he didn't come for their brother's sickness, his grave illness. When they called Jesus, they said, the one you love is sick. And they knew that nothing could move Jesus like love. If love can move him, then love is with him. All I'm saying is, come and show me some love. Someone to love and someone to love me."

"I like that," Rev. Bryant jumped in.

"I call on Jesus with real love, and I get no answer. When I say Jesus didn't come, it's that either he has not confirmed to me the one I'm with, or he has not revealed to me the one that's for me."

"That's kind of twisted logic," Rev. Charles came at her.

"No, that's logic twisted," she responded right back. "You can be with someone and not know whether he or she is for you, and you can be without someone and wonder when he or she is coming for you."

"She got you there, Doc," Rev. Taylor said to Rev. Charles. "The girl is quick."

"Jesus didn't come," Rev. Mellowin said, jumping back into her own discussion. "So when Jesus doesn't come, you don't know what to do but wait. Wait with the one you're with or wait without the one you're not with. But I've been waiting, sometimes with but most of the times without. Why I say that I'm waiting to exhale is because I'm holding my breath and trusting the Lord to bring someone my way."

"So, what's the problem?" Rev. Charles came at her again. "Give us something we can feed off of."

"The problem is, like Lazarus' problem, while waiting you can get sick and tired. You can actually die from waiting. Like Mary and Martha, while waiting you can become hopeless and sorrowful. Anyone knows if you hold your breath too long, you can expire."

"I see." Rev. Ed said.

"Sometimes I don't know if it's me missing it or not listening to what God has for me. Or if it's Jesus testing and intentionally procrastinating to examine my faith and endurance."

"Good analysis," Rev. Ed came in again.

"At times I know it's me because I can be superficial in terms of the type of person and personality I choose to be with. But the Bible says ask and you shall receive. So I may be looking for something Denzel-ish and missing the Wesleyan blessing that God is providing. And I'm not talking about John Wesley; I'm talking about Wesley Snipes."

"I like that." Lady Johnson whispered.

"And I've endured through late, lonely, and longing nights. Cold nights. Scared nights. Stormy nights. Weeping nights. My question is, when is my morning going to come so I can have my joy? And I must confess, sometimes I look up and say, Lord, my waiting is wearing out and my understanding is kicking in. Like Martha, I say, the one you love has called you and is sick and tired of waiting but is still waiting and dying to hear what you have to say. Lazarus died waiting for Jesus to come. I'm waiting, and I'm dying for Jesus to come."

"You sound desperate," Rev. Charles suggested.

"I'm not desperate for a person! I'm desperate for an answer!" She shifted back and ran him over in reverse. "If God says that's not the one, I'm fine with it. If God says there will be no one, I'll be okay. Although I hope and strongly pray he doesn't say that. But I want him to come and answer me before I die, sick and tired, like Lazarus."

I felt her pain; she drove it into us real hard. And then she parked it into our minds to make sure we understood just exactly where she was in life. And she kept driving until we got it.

"And allow me to be blunt. One of the reasons sisters like myself get sick and tired of waiting is because of a host of needs. One is emotional. We love to be comforted and uplifted and complimented."

"Then why you want to get married?" Rev. Taylor joked, and everyone laughed.

However, she didn't see the humor and just sped off. "Another reason is my family. Every time I go home alone, my mother and father want to know two things—well, three. When am I getting married? When will they get grandchildren? And what happened to an old boyfriend of mine?

"Yes, and the final reason sisters get sick and tired is because of lack of companionship. My parents have been married forty-four years and have a beautiful relationship. They are best friends; they share everything without thought. They are ideal companions."

"Oh, so none of your waiting has to do with your physical needs," Rev. Charles blurted out.

"Of course it does. But physical fulfillment comes best from what God has given. Other than that, it's just settling."

"That's right." Rev. Minor now feeling the need to confirm.

"And as you get older and the clock begins to tick, you wonder, is God going to give you someone to share your life with, for all the needs you have? Dr. Smith, when you did that faith rating earlier and you said to add up our problems with our consequences—well, I did mine. And my problem is not having a husband, and my consequences are fear of being reviled and exalted as beautiful and highly educated, articulate, and being praised around the world by strangers but going home and growing old alone."

"I understand, girl," Dr. Smith responded, moving towards her and holding her hand as she spoke.

"I love Jesus, but the one Jesus loves is sick of waiting." Her voice became soft, and she had shifted into a lower gear as if she were coming to a halt. But she was only stopping for gas. She drove off again. "I have gotten to the point where, although I'm not attracted to the opposite race, I have given consideration and even dated men of other persuasions. And I have been treated like a queen by them. But my revolt and their ultimate discouragement come from my strong connection and perspective of my people. They either think I'm racist or theologically disturbed and dogmatic. It's not in the color; it's in the character and content. It's not in the persuasion; it's in the perspective. And none of them seems to agree or accept my strong, uncompromising perspective. Aside from that, I really do desire and hope my brothers recognize this queen." She touched her face and slid her hand down her body to reveal her beauty, once again.

"So I've learned to wait because a more disturbing consequence is getting married and then getting divorced with children. I don't want that for me or for my child. The reason I've learned to wait is because my impatient, sinful actions blinded me and interrupted my path of righteousness in the past. The more I slip or give in to sin, the harder I fall, and the deeper the hole. Then I have to wait and dig myself out all over again."

"We've been there in one way or another," Lady Johnson said.

"I have dated educated fools. Christian pimps. Pastors with wives. I was young and impressionable and even though I knew it was wrong, I was fascinated by their propositions. So I must confess, Lady Johnson, I was like the woman you described. But I'm glad to say that no matter how desperate I get, I will never go down that path again. It weighs too much on my conscience, even if I get away with my wrongs and no one discovers my actions. My conscience is killing me to the point that my head aches." Her voice seemed to change from courageous to regretful, yet full of conviction. "This is not to suggest that I'm not sick and tired. It's to say I don't want the consequences of my actions and the absence of my blessings because of impatience. I've learned you can't wait and play at the same time. You have to wait and pray."

"That's right, sister." Dr. Smith was in her corner. Holding her hand and raising it and letting it down as she made a powerful point.

"When you wait and pray and watch for what God is doing, your faithfulness will produce a blessing. That's what Jesus asked the disciples to do at Gethsemane—watch and pray so that you do not fall into temptation. I see what God is doing for me; he's teaching me the virtues of patience. To be still and know that he is God.

"Mary and Martha waited, but Jesus didn't come. Lazarus died because Jesus didn't come. When Lazarus died, a part of Mary and Martha's faith died, because Jesus, the one they loved, didn't show up. When Jesus doesn't show up, I must admit a part of my faith dies. I get discouraged, especially when I see some of my sisters getting married, and they had not waited as long as I have been holding out."

"Oh, you're really experiencing life," Dr. Smith told her. Raising their hand again and suddenly letting it down.

"Look how much my faith almost died one time: A Christian sister who had been supposedly delivered from lesbianism—but evidently had not—came on to me. I rejected her advances with force and fierceness but don't you know, I thought about it. Just the thought scared the hell out of me. I don't want to turn this into a soap opera for lack of scholarly application but the death of faith can result in a disturbing mentality, a depressing reality, and sinful, unfaithful activity. I dread the death of faith, for its corpse is hellish."

"Nicely said. Woo!" Rev. Ed applauded.

"The absence of faith and the dependence on flesh can put one in a horrifying, deceptive position. It can really convert you into a monster." She yielded at the stop sign of her dreaded experience. Everyone seemed to sympathize with her; we'd all been there at one time or another, that place where our lives seemed to be at a standstill and faith seemed to be waning. She then took off again, making a U-turn back to Jesus.

"When Jesus finally came, Martha went out to meet him. With the disappointment of death on her breath, she said, 'If you had been here, my brother would not have died.' Then with the bit of faith she had left, she said, 'Even now, God will give you what you ask.' With that little bit of faith, Jesus was able to bring resurrection not only to Lazarus but to Mary and Martha. They were resurrected from their spiritual malaise and emotional malady. So I know I'll get up, even in the grave of despair and desperation, and as soon as I see Jesus, I'll say, 'Even now you can find me a man!'"

"Yes girl, you're right!" Lady Johnson, standing and affirming her, gave her more fuel for her ride.

"Thank you, but I haven't gotten to my connection yet. See, although I am saddened by my present predicament, I am not at all pessimistic about my future promise in Christ. Some may take this reluctance of Jesus at Gethsemane to suggest that he is less divine or too afraid to die for us. Well, let me straighten out the theological and epistemological and etymological interpretation with exegetical perfection and personal connection."

"You go girl." Lady Johnson still standing called out.

"I would submit to you the opposite of Jesus' so-called anguish, weakness, and reluctance at Gethsemane." She loosened her hands from Dr. Smith's and began to use them to make her point. "He remained divine but allowed his humanity to identify with our human suffering. He wanted us to see him like us. He wanted us to know that he knows what we're going through when we are in our most difficult challenges and life-threatening situations."

"You're going somewhere—finally," Rev. Charles hit her again.

She ignored him as if he didn't exist. "The Bible says he took a couple of disciples with him, and he went a little farther and fell on his face in prayer. Anguish puts you in a position of prayer. Jesus took it to the Lord in prayer. In order to identify with our humanity, Jesus, in his bended and wounded position, asked God to take this cup of suffering away from him. When we come to God in our impatient moments, we start telling God what to do: Lord, take this sickness away from me. Lord, take this loneliness away from me.

"Our way is to give God direction and make demands. That is why Jesus had to teach the disciples to pray. He told them, 'When you pray, say: "Father, hallowed be your name, your kingdom come. May your will be done on earth as it is in heaven."' Pause there." She stopped short, but then sped off. "'Thy will be done,' Jesus says. Because the truth of the matter is our will and our way may not be God's will and God's way. We may be going in the opposite direction. And going in the opposite direction of God is surely a head-on collision that we can't survive."

"I'm loving it all over again,' Rev. Ed chimed in.

"Jesus kept praying in anguish. He didn't stop praying because of anguish. He prayed some more to get answers for his anguish. The more you pray, the more self you lose and spirit you gain. Once 'self-flesh' reduces and spirit gains, you can breath easier.

"Jesus correlates his prayers and anguish with the sleeping of the disciples. Watch this awesome transition of the incarnation to spiritualization for our sanctification."

"We're watching. You better make it good. And slow it down so we can flow with you," Bishop Samuels blurted out.

"Okay, just watch, and don't fall asleep," she came back.

"The thing Jesus is praying about at Gethsemane is the same thing the disciples were doing in the flesh." She quieted down but kept the same speed. "Jesus is praying for God to take the cup away. Taking the cup away is Jesus praying humanity's way. The disciples become Jesus' human example by sleeping during his praying. At this point, both are in the flesh: Jesus and his praying and the disciples and their sleeping. Then Jesus says to the disciples, 'The spirit is willing, but the body is weak.' Jesus is not only speaking to them, but he is speaking to himself. Jesus then goes back to pray and begins the incarnate transition from flesh to spirit to show the disciples how they can overcome the flesh with the spirit. As he is speaking, he is releasing himself from praying his way to 'not my will, but yours be done.' With this, Jesus gives up his 'self-fleshness.' The coat of flesh comes off and the armor of spirit is drawn, and God's will is done. The disciples, however, are still sleeping. They did not follow Jesus' transition from flesh to spirit. Jesus became the human example in front of them to show how one can go from 'self-flesh' weakness to spiritual strength."

Everyone looked at her with wonder. We had been fooled by her initial sassiness, male anger and vanity, but now she was proving herself to be a real theological expert. She resumed, facing Rev. Charles and focusing all her energies on him.

"When you pray God's way, Rev. Charles, you can breathe easier. I can exhale because I'm not waiting on my will, I've submitted to Thy will. I am no longer hooked on the flesh but living by the spirit. I can breathe now."

To prove her point, she took a deep breath as if trying to consume all air left in the world. She stood up with a jovial expression on her face and choreographed movements to her body. "You may put me down. You may call me names. But I've learned to pray God's way. 'Not my will, but yours be done.' As the psalm says:

> The Lord is my shepherd, I shall not be in want.
> He makes me lie down in green pastures,
> he leads me beside quiet waters,
> he restores my soul. Hay!
> He guides me in paths of righteousness
> for his name's sake.
> Even though I walk
> through the valley of the shadow of death, Hay!
> I will fear no evil,
> for you—are—with—me; Hay!
> your rod and your staff,
> they comfort me. Hay!
> You prepare a table before me
> in the presence of my enemies.
> You anoint my head with oil;
> my cup overflows. Hay!
> Surely goodness and love will follow me
> all the days of my life,
> and I will dwell in the house of the LORD
> forever—and ever and ever, Hay! Hay! Hay!"

She shifted her neck, snapped her fingers, backed her body up to her seat, put herself in park, picked up her water, threw her hand up in the air, said "Hay!" and began to sip—loudly.

20

The Devil in the Desert

Matthew 4:1–10

A child is born with no state of mind
Blind to the ways of mankind
God is smiling on you but he's frownin' too
Cause only God knows what you go through
You grow in the ghetto, living second rate
And your eyes will sing a song of deep hate
The places you play and where you stay
Looks like one great big alley way

—"The Message" by Grandmaster Flash and the Furious Five

The mood became mellow after Rev. Mellowin spoke. Everyone seemed exhausted, either from the intellectual discussion or the emotional confession. I myself felt drained and drawn from all the outbursts. I was connected to them in spirit and in truth. Either I had heard their stories from others or experienced their trials for myself.

While the mood was somber, I managed to block everyone out of my head and reminisce on my own upbringing. I looked at Rev. Ed and began to speak to him, ignoring all others.

"I grew up in a rough community where evil triumphed over good. I went to school with gangsters. I saw the anger in their hearts and the blood in their eyes, those who would kill without remorse and take a mother's child's life and not think twice.

"They reminded me of Sanyika Shakur, a.k.a. Kody Scott, who wrote the book *Monster*. He was an LA gang member who executed ruthless, hate-hearted acts of criminality. He was a man with an inner bomb, a killer with little remorse—a malicious monster. But as he said, what he was part of was not his making. He had come into a murderous environment and was simply carrying out its wishes. In his book he wrote, 'I did not start this cycle, nor did I conspire to create conditions so that this type of self murder would take place. My participation came as second nature. To be in a gang in South Central when I joined—and it is still the case today—is the same as growing up in Grosse Pointe, Michigan, and going to college; everyone does it. Those who don't aren't part of the fraternity. And as is everything from a union to a tennis club, it's better to be in than out.'

"He was right, and even though I escaped my environment, I didn't escape without scratches. I, too, had my encounters with the monsters, which were no doubt devils. The friends I had as a youth encouraged my negative behavior. I did not follow for criminal activity but out of a need for companionship, and the need for companionship led to criminal activity. Saint Augustine told the story in his book *Confessions* about his own rambunctious and rebellious dealings during his youth. He talks about how he committed a crime by stealing a fruit with his friends. The fruit in itself meant nothing to him, which is why, after looking back, he despised his theft all the more. But his confession is not only about the theft but about the gang of influence by which he was encouraged. He admits that if he had been alone, he would not have committed the crime. He did not like the pear, nor did he desire it, for if he did, he would have partaken in the act alone and found more pleasure. But he confesses his desire was not in the fruit but in the friends.

"I feel the same way: I did not like crime nor do I like sin, but the need for friendship and companionship to take away loneliness can connect one with the devil. Like Rev. Mellowin said, you can connect with the wrong people when you're lonely.

"Jesus was tempted by the devil in the desert. The devil is the deceiver, and the desert is the environment where we reside. The devil made Jesus several offers in the desert. So if Jesus can be tempted by the devil, who are we that we can't be? And what are we supposed to do when we're down in the desert with the devil? What are we supposed to do when we grow up in a dirty, hellish environment? When everyone from your mother to your father is part of a gang or on drugs? When everyone in your neighborhood is killing and deceiving just to get by?

"I often hide on my biography the reality of how I made it through my family instability, went to the dean at the University of Pennsylvania, begged to get in, and graduated at the top of my class. Although true, my story is not a story of complete success; it is a story of constant escape, escape from the madness and the monsters. All my life I've been running from the devil in the desert.

"And I have to admit to the three ways that I—and possibly others—deal with the devil in the desert, ways that bring me either misery or victory.

"The first is simply to give in to the devil while in the desert. And at times, that's just what I did in my youth and beyond. To give in is to not fight against temptation. Many of the youth I knew simply submitted to the guns, drugs, and gangs without a fight. They didn't fall to temptation; they just went along with the environment. Like Kody Scott, that's all they knew. When you go along it is simply a perpetuation of the system that has already been created. There is no struggle with the devil.

"Alan Paton, in his classic South African novel, *Cry the Beloved Country*, has this great exchange between a father and his son. His son is in jail because of a crime he committed. And the father begs his son for a reason why the son did what he did. And Absalom, the son, says, 'The devil made me do it.' Then the father, in such a poetic and breathtaking way, says to the son, 'Oh, boy, can you not say you fought the devil, wrestled with the devil, struggled with him night and day, till the sweat poured from you and no strength was left? Can you not say you wept for your sins, vowed to make amends, and stood upright and stumbled and fell again? It would be some comfort for this tortured man, who asks you desperately, why did you not struggle against the devil?'

"And when I look back, I see that as I grew older, I could have fought harder against the devil. I could have said no or ran faster to get out of the desert. But instead of fighting temptation, I fell to temptation, sometimes without a thought. I've cheated on tests, even to graduate from high school. I stole money to get on the bus to Philadelphia. And I made myself cry while speaking to the dean at the University of Pennsylvania. I've plagiarized material for my books, I must admit.

"But fear, as I recall, had a lot to do with my doing what I did. I was afraid of failure and afraid of staying in the hellish environment of the desert. I was afraid of being mislead by friends to do wrong, yet I wanted friends. When you're in the desert, friends kill friends—either their body or their dreams. As Dr. Smith said earlier, you can't trust friends. So I found myself working with the devil instead of fighting the devil. And when I look back, I hate the fact that I did some of the things I did just to get by. I've tried to justify them for good but the truth is, I can't do wrong and celebrate right. The Bible says, 'Blessed is the man who does not walk in the counsel of the wicked or stand in the way of sinners or sit in the seat of mockers. But his delight is in the law of the Lord and on his law he meditates day and night.'

"I hate the fact that I was influenced by walking with the ungodly, and although I despised the sinful activity, I carried it with me to the university and my ministry. Certain people can mess you up for life. That's what I'm hearing from many of my colleagues who are here. They have been damaged by others and allow stuff like hate to do further damage to their lives. I can relate, when you don't or can't fight the devil and you look back, you hate what the devil has done to you and made you into. Like Rev. Minor, who is justified in her hate for the monster that raped her.

"But to some extent, the devil's domain has been planted in our lives at an early age. So the strongest ally we have against the devil is Christ. I found Christ while in college, and became a pastor a couple of years afterward, while in seminary. And Christ has helped me to struggle against the enemy for the greater part of my adult life. And that's the second thing one can do – is struggle against the devil. Although the struggle is not the antithesis of perpetuating the system, it is a higher step above going along with evil. The struggle is Gethsemane. Spirit versus flesh. Evil against excellence. The struggle can leave one confused and exhausted, because it is a psychological and spiritually righteous struggle. Paul has this struggle with sin in Romans 7:15. He says—and this is after he was saved—'I do not understand what I do. For what I want to do, I do not do, but what I hate I do.' He goes on to say, 'As it is, it is no longer I myself who do it, but it is sin living in me. For what I do is not the good I want to do; no, the evil I do not want to do—this I keep on doing.' Then he says. 'For in my inner being I delight in God's law; but I see another law at work … waging war against the law of my mind and making me a prisoner of the law of sin ....'

"This is a serious threat to mental stability. I have often felt this type of tug-of-war, as others have. Rev. Bryant relayed it best when he revealed his own dichotomy of not knowing if he wanted to be thug or theologian. It is psychological because it strangles the mind into confusion and submission. And it weighs upon the conscience. And the conscience weighs upon the soul, leaving one in absolute turmoil. And if the flesh wins the battle, there is great guilt, which can cause greater regret and a collapse of mental stability. If the spirit wins, there is grateful celebration but still a yearning toward temptation.

"But I feel that although the struggle is exhausting, it is a blessing. I am blessed when I feel this resistance taking place, this dichotomy in effect, because it means I am struggling not to do evil and seeking good. I am glad I have enough of a conscious to know right from wrong. Although this type of confusion can leave one worn, it does mean the battle is on and the spirit is fighting back, which is why I have been able to beat back issues with women in my life. Rev. Charles has the best example, but he was doing more falling than struggling. When you struggle, you have to win some battles with the devil. I've been able to struggle and win. And, believe me, it was a struggle. Different people have different temptations, and what's tempting for me may not be tempting for you. Not every man has women as his temptation; as Rev. Franklyn told us, his struggle was with men. But if that's not your temptation, like men have never been mine, it's not going to be a struggle. But your struggle is that which tempts you and can cause you to fall. Women have tempted me, but I've struggled with the devil and won on many occasions.

"My stubbornness and arrogance, like Rev. Taylor's, have often separated me from the woman I love. When you believe you know it all and the devil shuts your ears to everyone else and has you focus only on yourself, you find yourself by yourself. My will be done. But I've found that not only am I shut out from my wife but also from my children, and even a strong man can break down from such absence. Bishop Samuel's breakdown had to begin with sadness, and sadness prolonged can lead to depression. I've been saddened, but I've struggled hard not to fall into depression. I realized if I struggled against the cause of my sadness, which is arrogance, then I will be saved from the source of unhappiness, which is loneliness. My struggle has at times yielded wins, and at times yielded losses, but I've always battled to win.

"But how you beat temptation is to fight the devil. This is the real antithesis and antibiotic to perpetuating evil. The way many have escaped their deserts and killed their monsters is to fight the devil. To fight the devil is different from struggling or battling. Fighting means the enemy will fall, and I will not fall into temptation. To fight is to beat the enemy back from whence he came. The Bible says to resist the enemy, and he will flee. I've had to learn to fight the devil. And I realize that nothing good comes without a good fight.

"God promised Israel the promised land. But to get it, they had to fight with God for it. When I say fight *with* God, I mean fight alongside him, like soldiers teaming with the general to bring down the enemy. God is the general; we are the soldiers, and we fight with God to win the reward. God is the spirit; we are the flesh. That is Gethsemane. God's spirit in our flesh, fighting for the promise.

"God could have just handed the Israelites the land. Just as God could have just handed me the ministry and the university and taken away my dichotomy. But God said if you want it, you have to fight with me to get it. So God put his spirit in the Israelites' flesh, and their flesh had to carry out the will of his spirit. When the Israelites fought with God, they were able to break down Jericho's walls.

"And I've had to fight with God to get from desert to the promised land. From violent community to Ivy League university. From madness to ministry. When I allowed God's spirit to fall on me, I was able to knock down walls, overturn stones and build up courage to fight the devil and escape the desert. Yes, I've lied and I've stolen, but I've also fought with truth and integrity to overcome lies and dishonesty. The walls of poverty and instability were more often broken down by hard work and God's hand than with deception and devilish intentions. The desert could not hold me and the devil could not control me—I broke out.

"And yes, many times I've fought all night with myself. People couldn't see it because an inner battle leaves inner scars, which are easily concealed.

"Jacob found this out when he was alone and was wrestling with the angel; the angel was God. Jacob was fighting with the angel and against himself. Himself was his will, and his will was wicked. So within himself was a battle, and he enlisted the assistance of the angel to help him fight his battle. The Bible says Jacob wrestled with the angel. He wrestled *with* the angel, not *against* the angel. He and the angel fought hard all night against the flesh. The angel went so far as to knock his hip out, thinking he would let go, but Jacob held on to the angel, regardless of the hits, and kept on fighting until the win.

"And hits in the midst of a fight are what have caused me to give up and go back, rather than fight on. I've been hit with disappointment, hit with tragedy, hit with sickness. Similar to Job's experience, sometimes they came like a combination of punches, all at the same time. And the hits resulted in my falling to temptation, rather than fighting temptation. The bigger you are, the harder you fall—and the harder it is to get back up and fight again. But as I grew older and stronger, I realized, like Jacob, that regardless of how hard the hits and how many the punches, you can't stay down for too long. Like a Timex watch, you take a lickin' and keep on tickin'.

"It will take time before you see the blessings from your fighting. Jacob had to fight all night until the morning light before he was blessed. 'All night' for me has been days and sometimes years before I was able to reap what I sowed. They say patience is a virtue, but so is persistence when you're in a fight for your life. You never know what round you're going to win; you just keep fighting until you win. I've been persistent, determined, steadfast, unmovable, and always abounding in the will of the Lord.

"I've learned that no one becomes successful without getting hit. Nelson Mandela got hit with twenty-seven years in prison before he became president of South Africa. We, as a people, got hit with whips until we won our freedom. 50 Cent got hit with nine bullets to the leg before he walked away with a million-dollar record deal. My brother got hit with two failures on the bar exam before he passed it with flying colors. Getting hit will never stop me again.

"Why? Because like Jacob, I need my blessings. I need my family, ministry, and university. I need my sanity. I can't allow falling to temptation to leave me crazy. Every time I fall, I feel like the madness and the monsters have gotten a hold of my mind. And they're trying to keep me in the desert with the devil. But then, like Jesus, I feel when I'm in the desert, God comes and helps me to fight my way back to clarity and sanity.

"Jesus had already prepared himself for a fight. The Bible says he fasted forty days and forty nights. And preparation is necessary in any spiritual fight, whether it's prayer, fasting, meditation, or worship. So when the devil came at Jesus the first time, Jesus hit him with a right blow. Pow! 'Man does not live on bread alone but on every word that comes from the mouth of the Lord.' Then Jesus hit him with an uppercut and left hook. Pow! Pow! 'Do not test the Lord your God.' But it wasn't until that final combination blow that Jesus knocked the devil down. 'Worship the Lord'—Pow, bing, pow! 'Thy God'—pow, bing, boom! 'And serve him only'—pow, boom, boom, pow, kabam! Jesus knocked the devil out.

"I've learned to fast, pray, meditate, and worship daily to prepare myself for a fight against the devil. I've learned to block hits and hit first in a fight with the devil. Therefore, no weapons formed against me will prosper. One thing my father told me, which was the only lesson he taught me, is that when someone approaches you with a threatening look, don't allow that person to hit you first. Hit him first, and hit him until he's knocked down. And even though I've never been a fighter in the world, I am a fighter in the spirit. And I've learned to hit first, before getting hit by the enemy—hit with all the strength and power and, most of all, the spirit that God has given me.

"I come here with arms up to fight the devil. Lust. Boom! You're down. Hate. Bam! No more. Fear. Bam boom! Good-bye. Depression. Bing! Get out. Arrogance. Bing, boom! Never again. Loneliness. Bop! Don't need you. Homosexuality. Bop, bing.

Never knew you. Confusion and regret. Bop bam, bing, kapow! You're dead."

I could feel myself standing and swinging uncontrollably. The conference members tried to hold me, but for some reason I kept swinging hysterically. I kept swinging to get them off of me. Unlike Rev. Bryant, they could not contain me. I don't know what got into me, but I felt angry and empowered all at the same time. I just kept swinging and swinging and swinging until I could swing no more.

21

It Is Finished

John 19:30

Sometimes I don't like who I am,
when I look in da mirror my reflection is Uncle Sam (Uncle Sam)
And every night I have these weird dreams,
that a preacher trapped inside of me wake up and can't breathe I
     feel like its twenty of me,
goin' twenty different directions on a one way street Lord

—"Don't Let Me Die" by R. Kelly and Jay Z

I had finally gotten hold of myself. When I looked up from the couch in the lounge that I was laying on, everyone was gone except Rev. Ed. I didn't even want to ask him what happened to the others, because I figured they had gotten tired or afraid and left during my tirade. Rev. Ed looked at me. He had listened without interrupting while I spoke. I saw the two guards at the door. But then they left as soon as they saw me drop to my seat. Rev. Ed, although standing in fear, waved to them to close the door.

Rev. Ed looked at me, and I just looked aside without saying a word, mostly out of embarrassment. A big man like me, intellectual, with degrees, confessing and going crazy all at the same time.

Rev. Ed spoke softly to me. "I think a whole lot of people reap a grave misunderstanding upon Christianity, confusing its meaning with actions of excellence, rather than human weakness struggling toward perfection. The misunderstanding has resulted in a false perception and misguided interpretation as to what Christianity means and does to the individual who accepts it. As is the case, I'm sure, for all religions."

Rev. Ed spoke calmly and eloquently. All I could do was look aside and listen. "The gospel in its original meaning derived from the word godspell, meaning good tidings, or the Greek *euglena*, meaning good news. It is the good news of a savior. The gospel is directed in its theology to a particular people with a particular condition. It is for the desperate, the deprived, the desolate, and even the disconsolate.

"It is a gospel for the meek and those who mourn. Oh, Mary, don't you weep and tell Martha not to moan. The hated and insulted. The rejected and persecuted. The tempted and most of all - the sinner. The sinner is Christianity's greatest goal. To gather the sinner is to make Christ a winner. And in order to gather the sinner, the spirit must fall upon the flesh and bring the body under God's authority. The body is scattered, the spirit is contained. The spirit is fighting to contain the flesh and if the spirit is not nurtured regularly and matured constantly, you will have split personalities. That's Gethsemane—the flesh going in one direction and the spirit going in another, each with its own personality. The personality of the body seeks the world while the personality of the spirit seeks God's will. And if the strain becomes too burdensome for one's humanity it will produce multiple personalities that will regulate the mind toward insanity. The constant collision of body weakness and spiritual willingness is disturbingly dividing.

"Our hope is that the spirit will persist and the flesh will be dismissed. But our fear is that the body will succeed and the spirit will be defeated."

I tried to look at him but could not. Rev. Ed just kept pacifying me with kind words.

"The gospel pronounces its love upon humankind for its profound errors and simple mistakes to forgive and redeem. Wasn't it the great Henry Ward Beecher who declared that preaching the gospel is 'the art of moving men and women from a lower to a higher life'? Understanding that we who accept the gospel are all at a sinking and lower state, and we are seeking constantly solid and higher ground.

"Gethsemane, because of its dichotomy, can make one look like a big hypocrite. Many will see the outside faults but not the spirit's fight. The condemnation and judgment from others for allowing the body to sin and the spirit to slip will be harsh and swift. People don't know that you struggled; all they know is that you stumbled and fell. But as you stated, Rev. Parks, you should feel good, knowing you fought the devil, which should make you grateful but not satisfied."

He was calm and offered good counsel. He had listened to me, so I felt compelled to listen to him. I slowly worked myself up from lying down and sat up with my hand down while he spoke.

"When I come into the gospel I am admitting that weariness, sickness, sinfulness and foolishness are tied to my humanness!" Rev. Ed's voice shook me, as if he himself was confessing and wanted me to respond. "I am confessing that brokenness, weakness, desperateness, and loneliness are wrapped up in my 'somebodiness'! Even as pastor—and sometimes especially as pastor—I am connecting my brokenness to my humanness, like Jesus at Gethsemane, when he showed his agony as part of his humanity.

"Many would think that a pastor would be the epitome of sinlessness, with a high altitude of resistance. But even we in ministry must confess to areas of leniency. Impiety has led to indecency, and indiscreet tendency has resulted in debauchery. Jesus had his human imputation at Gethsemane. One would think that a man who had helped so many with their anguish would be above agony and ready for fateful delivery into the hands of his enemies. Instead, his humanity coupled with his agony struggled against his deity and destiny, as if agony had no remedy. For if it did, he would've been better prepared for death's certainty."

I slowly looked up at him. What he was saying was making a whole lot of sense and made me feel better. I still could not say a word.

"To be pastor, your conversion should have taken you to an elevation that is above the normal levels of sanctification. Sanctification is not perfection in our conversion; it is a maturation process in our salvation. We are maturing as pastors every day. We still have weaknesses, no matter who we are or what others make us to be. Jesus' human sanctification fell to a low level at Gethsemane. The agony outweighed his many moments in ministry, which means God can call you with blemishes!" Rev. Ed raised his voice as he looked at me, and from that yell I couldn't help but look at him. "Jesus had agony. Noah had drunkenness. Abraham had fear. He lied and said his wife was his sister. Isaac followed in his father's footsteps and genetically took on a lying spirit. Jacob had deceit. David was a man after God's own heart, but David had lust in his heart. Samson had Delilah. Esther had selfishness. Moses lacked faith. Jeremiah had reluctance. Peter had denial. Judas had betrayal. Paul had confusion. It is funny how God can bless you and curse you all at the same time!"

I lifted my head even higher at that last remark, which seemed to come out like lightning and strike me right in the temple. Rev. Ed paused, knowing I was absorbing the immensity of that remark. How God can bless you and curse you at the same time. How true. Rev. Ed looked at me with wide eyes and a concerned expression on his face, he saw he had my attention, and then continued.

"God can bless you with the ability to convey the truth and save souls in a unique and exceptional way and at the same time, curse you with a penalty that's hard to take away. God can bless you with power to raise the dead and at the same time, curse you with the feeling of the dead. Wasn't it Paul who had a pain in his side? God blessed him with grace but left him with the pain.

"And pastors can be as conflicting in their ministry and sanity as anyone else. Like Bishop Samuel, you can be blessed with wisdom and self-control and cursed with weeping and depression. Like Rev. Taylor, you can be blessed with revelation and vast understanding and be cursed with arrogance and self-righteousness. Like Rev. Bryant, you can be blessed with inquisitiveness and love for others and cursed with confusion. Like Lady Johnson, you can be blessed with beauty and brains and be cursed with regret and past transgressions. Like Rev. Mellowin, you can be blessed with articulateness and creativity and cursed with intemperance and vanity. Like Rev. Minor, you can be blessed with attentiveness and keen observation but cursed with vengeance and unforgivingness. Like Rev. Franklyn, you can be blessed with knowledge and great assessment but cursed with lack of confidence and struggle with sexual preference. Like Dr. Smith, you can be blessed with compassion and focus and cursed with fear. And like Rev. Charles, you can be blessed with strength and confidence and cursed with stubbornness and lust, lust, and lust."

He seemed to have analyzed everybody's Gethsemane. I sat there, too immersed in thought to respond. His words were analytical yet therapeutic. While he was picking me apart, I felt a realization coming over me, one that supported his theological premise of being blessed and cursed all at the same time. But still I just sat there, unable to speak but fully able to comprehend.

"However, the blemish that God gives us is not to subtract from our ministry; it's a battle to add to our sanctity. The challenge makes us stronger. The more we fight, the more we win. The more we win, the stronger we get. God will never give us anything we can't handle. Paul's thorn in his side was to make him stronger in spirit and faith. I believe that God gives us the roses of pastoral position and the insight of intellectualism so that we can fight the world's injustice and the thorns of our own existence. God gives us strength to feed the hungry and to fight our own agony and treachery. We have the strength to fight poverty and our own misery. We can fight unjust wars in the world and unjust wars in ourselves. We can fight the perils of the nation and the appearance of temptation, all at the same time. Yes! We can carry the cross on ourselves and the cross of the world. It is part of our calling. Jesus carried the cross of humanity and agony, and when he fell, he got back up.

"If we had nothing in our humanity to fight, then we would be perfect, rather than striving for perfection. Humanity, as long as it is alive, will always have something to fight for. And the fight is to gather the flesh under the spirit, and the spirit to control the flesh, so that both spirit and flesh are moving in the same direction. That is the gathering at Gethsemane, when both personalities become one, and the spirit's willingness subdues the body's weakness for God's gloriousness. When both spirit and flesh are gathered, God gets the glory.

"When we have gathered it all, then it is finished. The guilt, the shame, the past. It is finished. When Jesus said those words before he gave up the ghost on the cross, it was an understanding that all he had gone through was now coming to a completion. There comes a time when every wrong you've done must be forgiven. It is finished. You don't have to harp on it and allow others to bring you down because of it. You did wrong. You admit it, and you've suffered for it. But now you must say, 'It is finished.'"

Rev. Ed pressed his face closer to mine and forced me to look at him. He spoke with a big-bang explosion that contrasted sharply to his coolness throughout the conference. "Christ said, 'It is finished!' You must declare, it is finished! The depressed can say it is finished. The luster can say it is finished. The high-tempered can say it is finished. Jacob the thief said it is finished.

Paul said it is finished. I once was lost but now I'm found, blind but now I see. You must fight to the finish!"

He stood up, with what seemed like love in his eyes, and walked out of the room, allowing the door to slam behind him. My body shook, my mouth shut, and my eyes followed him out of the room.

22

Take This Cup Away From Me (Doxology)

Jude 1:24–25

The Gathering at Gethsemane
Please pray for me
The spirit is willing
The spirit is willing
But the body, the body is weak
I try to hold on
To my Jesus
But temptation is hard to defeat
But when I see Jesus
When I see Jesus
I'll gain the victory

Nurse Fields, it's good to see you."

"Rev. Ed—I mean, Dr. King, good to see you. You were in there for a long time. I hope you got through to him. How do you think it went?"

"I'm not sure. He is the most interesting case I've had. He did make it a lot easier for me by setting up the names on each table before I came in. Letting me know how many were going to be attending. The night before he, or she, called me and told me that two of them were going to be late, which from the conference was Rev. Mellowin, and the other never showed. The personalities were almost consistent with our interviews, absent one person.

"When I introduced myself, one of his immediate personalities came out: Rev. Taylor, who was quite abrasive yet amusing. The others quickly followed as I read their bios that I had gathered during the interviews. Bishop Samuel was very distinct yet distressed. Rev. Franklyn was smart yet reluctant. Rev. Bryant was tough yet conflicted. Rev. Minor was serene yet revengeful. Lady Johnson was beautiful yet regretful. Dr. Smith was comforting yet fearful. Rev. Charles was knowledgeable yet lustful, and Rev. Mellowin, who arose later, was creative yet desperate.

"He also made it easy because each time one of them spoke, their voices were very distinct, he was able to make quick shifts in his personalities."

"I heard a lot of outbursts in there. Was it hard to contain him, Dr. King?"

"Well, there were a couple of incidents when the guards burst in the door while one or more of his personalities erupted irately, but it was mostly calm. Most of the interruptions came as he spoke—the laughs, the amens, and other forms of confirmation or condemnation broke into his speech, but it was fascinating to see him handle so many voices and personalities all at the same time.

"In the beginning, he captivated me through the multiple persons with his vast knowledge—everything from the black community to forgiveness, abortion, the death penalty, sacrifice, and the war in Iraq was discussed with excellence and clear articulation, proving his biblical and intellectual might. His scholarly perspective and references on the issues are incomparable. I have never heard such brilliance.

"However, when I laid him down on the couch, he began to open up more about his conflicts and confessions. Rev. Minor led the way with her confession of rape and sodomy. Then others, like Bishop Samuel, Dr. Smith, Lady Johnson, Rev. Franklyn, and Rev. Mellowin, gave theirs freely. A lot of the personal issues he confronted, I determined, were absorbed from other people's issues. He actually became the very people he encountered, either in his ministry or university, and it intruded upon his personality, creating a ten-headed monster."

"Wow. That's interesting—and scary."

"I found that two of the personalities actually complemented each other. Rev. Taylor's arrogance seemed to offset Bishop Samuel's sadness. They were like a tag team that added some balance to their existence. But many of the personalities conflicted with each other. When I left the room, I observed Rev. Parks going at it with himself. When I came back in, I discovered that it was Lady Johnson and Bishop Samuel debating the war in Iraq, which is consistent with his last book, in which he stated he wasn't sure if he was for or against the war. Then Rev. Charles and Rev. Mellowin went at it like cats and dogs throughout the conference. Rev. Mellowin seemed to be the merciless condemner of Rev. Charles's lustful behavior. She was his guilt and penalty without sympathy. And Rev. Charles challenged Rev. Mellowin during her confession of desperation and loneliness, which led me to conclude that the reason that lust and loneliness were at odds was because each was being used to fulfill the other.

"Rev. Taylor, in his arrogance, challenged the dichotomy of everyone, including Rev. Bryant, for his theologian and thug confliction, and Rev. Franklyn, for his lack of education, until he himself was defeated and humbled by Rev. Franklyn's awesome biblical rendition. His arrogance proved to be a front to hide his ignorance on certain issues.

"When Rev. Parks tried to speak himself on the condemnation of the nation, he was interrupted by the confession of Rev. Charles and the onslaught of Rev. Mellowin. You could see his annoyance and his disturbance clearly from his demons. He twitched constantly from their interference. So much so that he abruptly ended his discussion. But even with the admitted regret, hate, and desperation he had suffered there was also comfort which came from Dr. Smith who although admitted fear used it to console the other personalities with hugs. When one of his personalities such as Lady Johnson spoke in pain, he often wrapped his arms around himself. An indication that Dr. Smith was present. It is true that the only hope one has against fear is being comforted and comforting others. "

"His appetite seems to be very good, Dr. King."

"Yes. He ate like he was eating for ten people—then again, he was."

"Do you feel good about the results, Dr. King?"

"I'm not sure. With so many personalities, it usually takes more time to remedy. He did begin to confide in me about his upbringing and confess some of his wrongs during his youth, which seemed to haunt him into his adulthood in the ministry and the university. His confessions were a shock. But it also showed he was getting comfortable with me. A lot of the struggles he faced with himself as an adult were due to the guilt and the shame of his past mistakes with family and friends.

"While he spoke to me there were no outbursts from the others, which I thought was a good sign of serenity. But then he began to go wild, swinging uncontrollably which summoned the guards to come in and him to pass out briefly from exhaustion. I'm not really sure what his outburst meant—whether it was his freeing himself from his body-snatchers, or if he was being further invaded by his own enemies. It's hard to tell.

"However, when I began to speak to him, after he calmed down and woke up, he had the look of exhaustion and ambivalence on his face, like he had actually been in a battle. He sat there like a fighter in his corner, looking down, and only when

I yelled did he look up. I don't know what he was thinking or if he was thinking at all. I don't know if he heard my words or if he purposely shut me out.

"I'm not sure how much this psycho-theological session produced. It's really hard to say, Nurse Fields. But it's so sad to see someone with so much promise, admiration, and intelligence suffering with so much spiritual and psychological warfare. We'll just have to hope and pray he makes it through."

"Okay, you better write your report, Dr. King. I was just about to take him this cup of medicine. The last time I gave it to him was this morning. He probably still thinks I'm his wife. Afterward, I'll get the guards to escort him back to his room."

"Very well, and thanks for all your assistance, Nurse Fields."

"No, thank you, Rev. Ed—I mean Dr. King. It's a pleasure working with you."

***

"Rev. Parks, I have a cup of juice for you."

"Thank you."

"Rev. Parks, are you okay? You look—different."

"I'm just fine. Glory to him who is able to keep us from falling. The Bible says, 'A man ought to examine himself before he eats of the bread and drinks of the cup. For anyone who eats and drinks without recognizing the body of the Lord eats and drinks judgment on himself.' I've examined myself; I've drunk of the Lord's cup. Therefore, I don't need your cup. The spirit whom we've been waiting for has arrived. And when the spirit comes, all others must run. I feel like everything is coming together. Like Rev. Ed said, at the gathering at Gethsemane— mind, spirit, and body in harmony. So, nurse, will you please take that cup away from me?"

"You called me 'nurse.'"

"Yes."
"Dr. King! He called me 'nurse'!"

BIBLIOGRAPHY

Adams, Charles Francis. *Familiar Letters of John Adams and His Wife Abigail Adams During the Revolution With a Memoir of Mrs. Adams.* Boston: Houghton, Mifflin and Company, 1875.

Alinsky, Saul D. *Rules for Radicals: A Pragmatic Primer for Realistic Radicals.* New York: Vintage Books, 1971.

Augustine, Saint. *Saint Augustine Confessions: A New Translation by Henry Chadwick.* New York: Oxford University Press Inc., 1991.

Augustine, Saint. *The City of God.* New York: The Modern Library, 1993.

Barnhill, Carla, ed. *A Year with Dietrich Bonhoeffer: Daily Meditations from his Letters, Writings, and Sermons.* New York: HarperSanFrancisco, 2005.

Bevington, David, ed. *Shakespeare: Four Tragedies.* New York: Bantam Books, 1988.

Bonhoeffer, Dietrich. *Life Together: A Discussion of Christian Fellowship.* New York: HarperSanFrancisco, 1954.

Broadus, John A. *On the Preparation and Delivery of Sermons: Fourth Edition.* New York: HarperSanFrancisco, 1979.

Chapman, Abraham, ed. *Black Voices: An Anthology of Afro American Literature.* New York: Mentor, 1968.

Cone, James H. *A Black Theology of Liberation: Twentieth Anniversary Edition.* New York: Orbis Books, 1986.

Dillenberger, John. *John Calvin: Selections from His Writings.* Montana: Scholars Press, 1975.

DMX. *E.A.R.L.: The Autobiography of DMX as told to Smokey D. Fontaine.* New York: HarperEntertainment, 2002.

Ellison, Ralph. *Invisible Man: Thirtieth Anniversary Edition.* New York: Vintage Books, 1947.

Foner, Philip S., Branham, Robert James, eds. *Lift Every Voice: African American Oratory 1787–1900.* Tuscaloosa: The University of Alabama Press, 1998.

Garvey, Amy J., ed. *The Philosophy and Opinions of Marcus Garvey.* London: Frank Cass and Company Limited, 1967.

Guthrie, Shirley C. Jr. *Christian Doctrine.* Atlanta: John Knox Press, 1968.

King, Martin Luther, Jr. *Strength to Love.* Minneapolis: Fortress Press, 1963.

King, Martin Luther, Jr. *Why We Can't Wait.* New York: Mentor, 1963.

Lass, Abraham H., Tasman L. Norma, eds. *21 Great Stories.* New York: Mentor, 1969.

McNeill, John T., ed. *On God and Political Duty: Calvin.* New York: The Dobbs-Merrill Co., 1950.

Paton, Allan. *Cry the Beloved Country.* New York: Macmillan Publishing Company, 1948.

Rose, Tricia. *Black Noise: Rap Music and Black Culture in Contemporary America.* Connecticut: Weslyan University Press, 1994.

Shakur, Sanyika. *Monster*: New York: Penguin Books, 1994.

Shange, Ntozake. *For Colored Girls Who Have Considered Suicide When the Rainbow Is Enuf.* New York: Macmillan Publishing Company Inc., 1975.

Talk, dc. *Jesus Freaks Vol.II: Stories of Revolutionaries Who Changed Their World: Fearing God, Not Man.* Minneapolis: Bethany House, 2002.

Thoreau, Henry David. *Walden and Civil Disobedience.* New York: Penguin Books, 1984.

Thurman, Howard. *Jesus and the Disinherited.* Boston: Beacon Press, 1996.

Williams, Juan., Dixie, Quinton. *This Far by Faith: Stories from the African American Religious Experience.* New York: Amistad, 2003.

SELECTED DISCOGRAPHY

Arrested Development, *Tennessee* (EMI Blackwood Music, 1992).

Boogie Down Productions, *Stop the Violence* (Jive/Zomba, 1991).

DMX, *Prayer* (Rush Associated Recordings, 1998).

Erik B. & Rakim, *Paid in Full* (Island Records, 1986).

Grandmaster Flash & the Furious Five, *The Message* (Sugar Hill Records, 1984).

Grandmaster Melle Mel & The Furious Five, *Beat Street Breakdown* (Hargreen Music, 1984).

Kanye West, *Never Let Me Down* (Roc-A-Fella Records, 2004).

Lauryn Hill, *Just Lost One* (RuffHouse Records, 1998).

Mary J. Blige, *Real Love* (MCA Records, 1992).

Nas, *One Mic* (Columbia, 2002).

R. Kelly, *U Saved Me* (Zomba Recording, 2004).

R. Kelly and Jay Z, *Don't Let Me* Die (Def Jam, 2004).

Steel Pulse, *True Democracy* (Elektra/Asylum Records, 1982).

Terrence Trent D'Arby, *If You All Get to Heaven* (Virgin Music, 1987).

About the Author

Edward A. Mulraine is Pastor of the Historic Unity Baptist Tabernacle in Mount Vernon, New York. He is a sought after preacher, teacher and revivalist as well as a former President of the NAACP Branch in New York City. Edward Mulraine has taught Homiletics at New York Theological Seminary from where he graduated with a Masters of Divinity. He also lectures on African American Religions and the Political Philosophy of Martin Luther King, jr. at Manhattanville College in Purchase, New York. In 2006 he started GodTalkNow.com, a website geared to Christian publications and discussions on political and cultural issues from a biblical perspective. The Gathering At Gethsemane is his first full publication.

You   can   email   Edward   Mulraine   at: edmulraine@thegatheringatgethsemane.com

To order bulk copies for educational use go to:
earainepublishing.com or thegatheringatgethsemane.com
or call us at 914-309-5216

Other productions by E.A. Raine publishing go to:
GodTalkNow.com for religious issues and videos

Bulk copies for educational, business or sales promotional use go
to: www.thegatheringatgethsemane.com